I wanted An r go
but she didn't feel u
through me when she n so
strong, and she's canc ound it startling and
frightening when she admitted to feeling less than
wonderful. But, as *Let There Be Hope* shows, cancer
changes one in sometimes indefinable ways. Maybe this
is one of those changes.

Mark and I visited some islands off the Maine
coast once, in our early days. I was so enthralled that he
bought me a house on one of them, a little strip of green
called, appropriately enough, Hope Island. It reminds
me of Bennett's Island, the fictitious utopia of Elisabeth
Ogilvie's books, except that Hope has all the mod cons.

I love to go there. It's a place I can be myself with
little regard to what anyone else thinks. I sit in my
bathrobe on the wraparound porch of the Victorian
horror that is my house and drink coffee with Lucas
Bishop, our neighbor. I read Jean's books without
worrying that someone will see the covers.

I've never taken anyone else—it was Mark's and
my private getaway—but I wouldn't mind if it was
Andie who was there. Or Jean and even Suzanne. Andie
and I could work on her book. Jean could cook and
keep house since she's so crazy about doing that, and
maybe even spin out one of her romances placed on an
island. And Suzanne could...do our hair or something.

We would all be together as we are that single
night every year when we drive to the lake and pretend
we're facing down our ghosts. I am a little afraid that
the day will come that we'll have to face them down for
real.

I wonder if they'd come.

The Girls
of Tonsil Lake

by

Liz Flaherty

The Girls of Tonsil Lake

Cover Art by *Tina Lynn Stout*

The Wild Rose Press, Inc.
PO Box 708
Adams Basin, NY 14410-0708
Visit us at www.thewildrosepress.com

Publishing History
First *Last Rose of Summer* Women's Fiction Rose Edition, 2014
Print ISBN 978-1-62830-249-3
Digital ISBN 978-1-62830-250-9

Published in the United States of America

Dedication

For Judith Palmer, Jenni Licata, and Tina Runge.
Although we haven't always traveled
publishing's bumpy road together,
it was a letter Jenni wrote that started the journey.
With thanks and affection to you all.

And for Muriel Jensen, who told me to never give up.
Bless you!

Part One

"The last thing I remember seeing was a cobweb above the lights that looked lethal. When I woke up, I felt as though I had been put in a stranger's body.

Therefore, at the age of fifty-one, I suddenly don't know who in the hell I am and have developed an unreasonable fear of spiders."

Andrea Hart Logan
Let There Be Hope
Gunderson Publishing, 2007

Liz Flaherty

4

Chapter One

Andie

When my friends Jean and Suzanne were visiting me in the hospital, Jean told me I should write everything down. "If it's on paper," she said, "it won't be on your mind so much."

Right away, Suzanne, who's never had an original thought in her life, ran out and bought me this fancy-dancey journal to write in along with a package of gel pens in all different ink colors. When I tried to get her to take them back, saying I'd do fine with a coil-bound notebook and a few fine-point black stick pens, she got this hurt look on her face. I had to hurry up and smooth her ruffled blonde feathers. There, that sounded literary, didn't it? Ruffled blonde feathers—hmm, I like that.

Anyway, my first entry read, "This hurts like a sonofabitch." When Jean read it the next day, she complimented my succinctness but suggested I try a little description, so the next entry was, "It hurts like a goddamned sonofabitch," written in putrid purple ink. She said I was catching on. Jean knows these things because she writes romance novels.

When I said maybe she should send my journal to her publishers, she told me that wouldn't work because they wouldn't let a writer say things like "goddamned sonofabitch" even if she was lying in a hospital bed with her one real boob sunk into her armpit while her new, fake one stood up proud on her chest like the left half of her was seventeen years old instead of fifty-goddamned-one.

That made Suzanne start staring at my chest with something like horror in her eyes. I reminded her that she was going to be fifty-one on her next birthday and if her tits weren't already falling into her armpits, they soon would be.

Jean told me I was being a bitch, because we all knew Suzanne was going to have hers stitched permanently into place.

We got to laughing so hard one of the nurses came in and said I was giving mastectomies a bad name. But that's how I've gotten through this whole thing. Laughing and writing stuff down in that journal Suzanne got me. I got so attached to those silly gel pens that I asked her to buy me some more when they all, except the brown one I didn't like, ran out of ink. It made her so happy, doing that for me, that I felt guilty because I'd never been as good a friend to her as she was to me. But I can't help it. She drives me forny nuts.

("Forny," in case you're wondering, is a word we Tonsil Lake girls coined when we were young and we wanted to say the f-bomb but couldn't make ourselves do it because deep down inside we knew we'd go to hell for it. Jean had read the Bible some and she knew what fornicate meant, so we created "forny." It's been real handy over the years.)

Suzanne's a beauty consultant. I mean, really, she is. She's been with this same makeup company for over twenty years, and she looks so good her picture's in their flyers that urge you to buy their stuff instead of what's at eye level in the drugstore.

Even though we laugh at the shallowness of her *career*, we accept the free makeup she's always giving us and feel like we're being punished if we have to use off-the-discount-shelf. The stuff she gives us never clumps up on your lashes unless you leave it untouched in your medicine cabinet for two years the way I do sometimes. Especially during chemotherapy, when I didn't have any eyelashes, clumpy or otherwise.

Suzanne's got a heart of gold, but she's like a southern belle caught in some kind of time warp. She's always thin, always cute, and always able to coerce a man into doing what she doesn't want to.

She even uses this breathy little southern accent sometimes, which just drives me over the edge because she grew up in a trailer down from me on Tonsil Lake. Other than the occasional "y'all" no one else on the lake has even a trace of a drawl.

And, yes, the lake's shaped just like a tonsil. Or at least some drunk's idea of a tonsil's shape, since most of us have no idea what one really looks like. But I'm digressing here.

By the time I finished chemo and radiation and had gotten a nipple put on my stand-up boob, I had filled that journal. I'd been declared cancer-free—at least for the moment—and my hair had grown back, sort of.

Only instead of being long and straight and the color of brown I'd kept it ever since I got up close and personal with do-it-yourself hair color while I was still in my thirties, it was as white as Christmas snow and so curly Suzanne took a curling iron to me to straighten it out some. She burned my neck, too, and I yelled like a banshee. She got smart right away, saying it looked like a hickey, probably the first one I'd had since high school, and I should be grateful.

Jean, who was cooking supper for me because the radiation made me so tired I couldn't see straight, laughed so hard she wet her pants. When I told her I was real glad to have entertained her so, she called *me* a bitch.

When I got to feeling enough better I set about getting my house cleaned the way I like to do it a time or two a year. I got to looking for that journal, thinking maybe I'd burn it before one of my kids got their hands on it and decided their mother was a fruitcake. Well, the damned thing wasn't to be found anywhere.

And that's when I learned that Jean had sent it off to Vin Stillson, a Tonsil Lake girl who had moved to New York after high school and made good. She's an editor in one of those snotty publishing houses—the kind that doesn't print books like Jean writes.

Vin comes back to Indiana once a year to see her mother at the nearby retirement community she lives in. Vin stays with one of us while she's here and at least once while she's around, we load into a car and drive the fifty miles to Tonsil Lake just to convince ourselves we don't mind going back.

Not much has changed—though we always go in the dark; we're only so brave. There is a little mom-and-pop tavern where the schoolhouse used to be, and we go in there and end up getting so drunk we have to call Jean's husband David to come and get us.

The first few times this happened, it took him an hour to get there. By that time, at least one of us would be to the puking stage and another—usually Suzanne—would be bawling. This made for a miserable ride home. Finally David went to giving us a few hours to get started and then would head on out toward the lake, bringing along someone to drive the other car home.

Vin's different from us. In the first place, once we finished going to elementary school at the lake and started riding into town on the high school bus, she started hanging out with kids who were a few rungs higher on the social ladder than Tonsil Lake kids were. This didn't take much, since Tonsil Lake was caught somewhere between the county dump and the rows of ramshackle cabins where the migrant workers stayed come tomato-picking time.

Later on, we all went to college because abject poverty looked good to financial aid offices. While the rest of us went to one of the state universities, Vin got a full scholarship to Bryn Mawr. After graduation, we settled into smallish Indiana towns and got married to guys we'd met while we were in school at Indiana University or Indiana State.

Vin settled into a New York brownstone. She married a guy old enough to be her father who was also richer than any of us, who mostly lived paycheck to paycheck, could begin to understand. She had a housekeeper before any of us even had houses.

Mark, her husband, died last spring. We all wanted to go to New York for the funeral, but she told us not to, so we made do with a planter. Jean sent it, so it was probably very tasteful.

Oh, damn, I'm digressing again. I never used to do that, but cancer and medication and having lopsided breasts all conspire to do weird things to you. The point I'm trying to get to in this new journal I've started—in a coil-bound notebook full of lined yellow paper—is that Vin wants to publish the old one.

Apparently her publishing house has no objection to the use of "goddamned sonofabitch." They want to make my illness into a hardcover book and pay me a nice little bundle of money for it. I think I'm going to let them.

Jean

Sometimes when David's gone to play golf, which he does at least once a day and sometimes twice, I sit and stare at my computer screen and think about getting divorced. I did not spend thirty years being married to his job just to turn around and be married to Fallen Tree Golf Course when he retired.

If I got a divorce, the first thing I'd do is turn one of the kids' bedrooms into an office. Our youngest daughter got married six weeks ago, for heaven's sake, so why is it necessary that their rooms remain intact?

"Megan might want this bed someday," said Carrie, leaning against the poster of her old canopy bed with her arms crossed under her breasts.

I caught myself staring at her, wondering how her thirty-six B-minus mother ever gave birth to two daughters who grew into thirty-four C-pluses. I also thought it was going to be at least a couple of years before my granddaughter Megan was ready for the tall white bed. She couldn't even climb into it yet, though she was making a mess of the counterpane by trying.

And then there was, "What if I need to come home?" Kelly stood in her underwear on the day of her wedding, her hand in a possessive grip on the footboard of her sleigh bed with her C-plus breasts spilling over the top of her strapless bra. "Do you want me sleeping on the couch? Or maybe on a cot in the basement?"

My son was different. "You want this room?" said

Josh, his David-blue eyes wide with incredulity. "Go ahead, but if you find a Reggie Jackson card in a plastic sleeve, it's mine. I lost it in there in 2003."

Well, no, I really didn't want *his* room, the tiniest in the house, so I turned it into a library, which David and I both love.

When Josh and his wife Laurie come to visit, they sleep in Kelly's sleigh bed. Laurie has thanked me for not bestowing Josh's old football trophies and rock star posters on her when we cleaned out his room, although she wouldn't have minded the Reggie Jackson baseball card. She says if she ever kicks him out, it's perfectly all right with her if he sleeps in the basement.

I love Laurie. She wears a thirty-four A and never tries to make me feel guilty because my son is occasionally a jerk.

But, getting back to my divorce fantasy...David doesn't think we should change the girls' rooms against their wishes. So we don't. And I'm writing my eleventh book as I wrote my first, in the corner of the dining room. It makes me mad, you know, makes me feel as though I don't count. I don't tell David that, of course, and don't ask me to explain why not. I can't.

This journal, on the other hand, I'm writing in a book Suzanne bought me at the same time she bought Andie's first one. I write wherever I please, whenever I please. I must admit, it's liberating.

I'm glad Andie's speaking to me again. When she found out I'd sent the stories of her illness to Vin, it was a tossup over whether she was going to kill me or just maim me for life. She wouldn't talk to me for days. I thought it would be bitterly ironic if I lost her friendship to something like that so soon after I'd come so close to losing her altogether.

But then she bought me a package of rainbow-hued gel pens like hers and told me to mind my own blankety-blank business in the future. I almost sang with the relief of it, which would have horrified us both. Better than bursting into tears like Suzanne would have, but still not good.

When I told David about it, he laughed and hugged me, rocking back and forth with our bodies in full contact. "Andie loves you, you dope," he said, "and you love her. People don't split up over every fight. We'd never have made our first week's anniversary if they did, much less our thirtieth year."

That's not strictly true. We never have fought very much, just minor skirmishes over money and the kids and toilet seats. One reason we don't fight is that I hate confrontation. This has led to many, many hours of silent anguish on my part. However, the other reason we don't fight is that I still love David O'Toole as completely and mindlessly as I did the day I married him.

So divorce is probably out.

I have to admit that I was jealous when Vin's publisher made an offer for Andie's story. Her advance is more than mine was after ten books, and *Let There Be Hope* is going to be hardcover. Oprah would probably have wanted to bring her on the show, if she still had one, to talk about it. And there won't be a nubile young thing in a pushup bra on the dust jacket the way there always is on the covers of my paperbacks.

Vin called me first. "I'm glad for this," she said, "and I'm sorry. I wish I could buy your stuff, Jean."

"Don't be silly," I said. "I'm thrilled for you both."

But then I went over to Suzanne's and cried and drank a half bottle of white zinfandel, which I usually only do when we're all together and I know David's going to drive me home. Then I had to sober up a bit before Suzanne and I could go over to Andie's and act surprised about Vin's call to her.

"It's not fair," I said, laughing, when we got there. "You get this great contract and I can't even get an office in my house."

"Why not?" asked Suzanne.

"Because David says—"

Andie interrupted me. "Wait a minute. Don't make David the bad guy here. You could have an office if you really wanted one, just by saying so. You're still playing the 'let's please everyone' game, but you don't want to take responsibility for it."

I stiffened right up. What did Andie know about making a marriage work? She'd bailed on hers the first time the going got tough. She didn't know the first thing about compromise and damage control.

Suzanne was staring at us both with those worried brown eyes of hers, so Andie and I exchanged a scowling glance and let it go at that.

I made up my mind to talk to David that night about remodeling Carrie's room, but he'd brought home brochures about Hawaii, where neither of us have ever been, and we planned a trip all evening instead. We ended up in bed with the brochures spread all around us, laughing about the roach-laden hotel where we'd spent our wedding night.

Then we made love, and when I was falling asleep with my body spooned into his, he asked, "Was it all

11

worth it, Jeannie? Have the good times made up for all the bad ones?"

I was too drowsy to give much thought to the questions or to the intonation of his voice. I mumbled something, laid my arm over his around my waist, and went to sleep.

I woke at two in the morning, pain in my stomach forcing me into a jackknife position. It went away after a while, mostly, but I made up my mind to confine my wine drinking to a glass with dinner. At least until Vin came home.

Suzanne

Let's get this straight right off the bat, all right? I'm blonde. Not naturally, but blonde nonetheless. I started frosting my hair in freshman year, when everyone else seemed to fit in at the high school and I didn't, and it worked so well I've never looked back. This does not, regardless of what Andie, Jean, and Vin think, make me stupid. Nor does it make me a bimbo, shallow, or a sex maniac. Just between you and me, I will admit that sometimes I am every one of those things, but it doesn't have one thing to do with me being blonde.

I went to college to be a kindergarten teacher, attending Indiana State University at Terre Haute. For those of you born outside Indiana, this is pronounced Terra Hote, not Terra Hut or Terra Hoot.

Only a few semesters away from graduation, I got pregnant. The baby's father, who suddenly discovered he had a wife and kids, paid for the abortion. Andie and Jean drove over from Bloomington, where they were in school, to take me to the clinic. Jean tried to talk me out of the abortion, Andie yelled at both of us all the way across town, and I cried. But I went through with it.

It's something I try not to think about. I'm not always successful at that in the middle of dark and lonely nights, but uninterrupted nights of sleep are some of those things that reside in the rose gardens no one ever promised me.

There was no concentrating on classes after that, so I sold my books for a pittance, packed up, and left Terre Haute. I got off the bus a couple hours later in Lewis Point, a nice town about an hour south of Indianapolis, and that was where I stayed. I got a job over Christmas in a classy department store, and the most exclusive makeup supplier they had offered me a job as a sales rep.

It's been the saving of me, I guess, outlasting two marriages and sending both my kids to college. I love what I do, love making women look and feel better about themselves. I wish it was a job that earned respect from others, but I respect it—so maybe that's enough.

One of the big automotive companies has a plant in Lewis Point. Jean's new husband David got a job there as soon as he graduated. Jean did her last year by correspondence and at the university extension in town. They moved up steadily—buying a bigger house with each kid—ending up in Willow Wood Estates with the doctors, lawyers, and other people who wore ties to work and drove foreign cars to DAR meetings.

Andie moved here after she got divorced from Jake Logan about twenty years ago. She went to work as a hostess in a swanky restaurant to earn a nest egg so that she could settle in Indy. Eventually she bought the place and then opened three more. When business was booming and her kids were out of college, she sold the whole corporation.

She was having a good time, substitute teaching a couple days a week and taking trips whenever she felt like it. Then she got cancer and it was awful.

I've never been one to pray much, but I sure did then. I think we all did. She was so brave about it all, especially the physical disfigurement.

I don't know if I could handle that. Because truth be told, how I look is all I have. If I lost that, I wouldn't be anything. They say looks are only skin deep, but I've never known any men—outside of possibly David O'Toole—who really felt that way when they were doing the looking.

After she got sick, Andie spent a week in New York with Vin, which none of us had ever done. I think Jean and I were both jealous of that because Vin had never invited us to come and stay—just to call if we ever got to New York. Even when her husband died last year, she didn't want us to come at all. Not even Andie.

I've been to New York a few times for work, and Vin and I always have dinner at least once, and usually see a show, too, but she's never invited me to her place.

Andie said today that Vin asked her to come back to New York to work on her book, but she isn't sure she feels well enough for summer in the city. It scares me when Andie admits to not feeling well.

The others would tell you everything scares me, but that's not true. I just know enough to understand that most men don't want women who are braver than they are.

I said once that men didn't want women who were smarter than they were, either, and Vin and Jean got all pissy about it. But Andie said women had no choice but to be smarter, since they didn't have to think with penises. So now whenever a man says something about *thinking*, I get this picture in my head of a penis with a little cartoon balloon light bulb above it.

Jake Logan's been calling me from Chicago since Andie got sick. He calls for updates on her condition because he doesn't trust her to tell him the whole truth. He's such a nice guy. I wonder if Andie's ever forgiven him for whatever went wrong between them. She never talks about him. I wonder if he'll keep calling now that Andie's out of the woods. I wouldn't mind if he did.

Vin

I don't know what made Suzanne send me this journal, even though it's very nice and looks good lying on the coffee table. I've never been the journaling type—even entries in my calendar are terse and businesslike, with no smiley faces or exclamation points.

I must admit that I miss having a confidante. I told Mark everything about me up until the day he died, and now it's like no one really knows or cares who Vin Stillson is. His children certainly don't, and we never had any of our own.

Jean and Andie and Suzanne would have come when he died. Jean would probably have carried a casserole all the way on the plane. But I'm not a very good hostess at the best of times, and I couldn't very well just throw them into a hotel and tell them I'd see them when I had time. They sent a beautiful planter that still sits in the foyer, but to this day I wish I'd just let them come.

When Andie came alone, she didn't feel well at all, and she mostly just wanted to be away from Lewis

Point for a bit. I ordered the best takeout Manhattan has to offer and coerced her to eat.

Sometimes we sat together in front of the fire and talked a lot. But not about who we were. The closest we came to that was when she asked if I was afraid to be on my own and I said, "No, not really. Are you afraid of cancer?" She said, "Oh, hell, I'm forny terrified."

Then we both started laughing. We may have cried some, too, but we didn't mention tears to each other. It would have been a good time for Suzanne to be there—she likes crying, likes emoting on all levels. I just don't.

When Jean sent me Andie's journal—completely full of writing in a rainbow of colors—I thought, you know, what in the hell is she doing here? Jean's a fabulous writer, even if it is in a genre I can't buy at my publishing house, so I assumed she saw something in what Andie had written.

There was something there, all right. I typed it out myself on the computer in Mark's home office, sitting up late every night until it was finished, scarcely changing a word.

I was only sorry I couldn't show the emotion Andie's handwriting did. Sometimes she wrote in big, splashy red or turquoise; other days in somber black; sometimes in hopeless brown, the penmanship reduced to the spidery, wobbly writing of the very old.

At the end of entries on particularly bad days, she wrote, almost as a mantra, "Let there be hope." I slapped this on the title page and took it in to the senior editor of the division of Gunderson Publishing that does memoirs.

"Tell me what you think," I said, and walked out. I've never especially cared for Marian Nielson, and it grated on me that I was handing her a bestseller as a forny gift.

She had it back to me in twenty-four hours. "It's splendid," she said. "It'll make the *NYT* list in a heartbeat. However, I don't have five free minutes between now and the next decade. We're publishing the memoirs of the stars of the moment in every sport there is, not to mention actors and musicians. I'll buy it if you'll edit it. I've already talked to Gunderson and he says to clear your schedule and go for it if you think it's viable."

Speaking of forny gifts.

I wanted Andie to come to New York, but she didn't feel up to it. I felt a little shudder go through me when she said that. Andie's always been so strong, and she's cancer-free, so I found it startling and frightening when she admitted to feeling less than wonderful. But, as *Let There Be Hope* shows, cancer changes one in sometimes indefinable ways. Maybe this is one of those changes.

Mark and I visited some islands off the Maine coast once, in our early days. I was so enthralled that he bought me a house on one of them, a little strip of green called, appropriately enough, Hope Island. It reminds me of Bennett's Island, the fictitious utopia of Elisabeth Ogilvie's books, except that Hope has all the mod cons.

I love to go there. It's a place I can be myself with little regard to what anyone else thinks. I sit in my bathrobe on the wraparound porch of the Victorian horror that is my house and drink coffee with Lucas Bishop, our neighbor. I read Jean's books without worrying that someone will see the covers. I use expressions like "forny" and "well, shit."

I've never taken anyone else—it was Mark's and my private getaway—but I wouldn't mind if it was Andie who was there. Or Jean and even Suzanne. Andie and I could work on her book. Jean could cook and keep house since she's so crazy about doing that, and maybe even spin out one of her romances placed on an island. And Suzanne could...do our hair or something.

We would all be together as we are that single night every year when we drive to the lake and pretend we're facing down our ghosts. I am a little afraid that the day will come that we'll have to face them down for real.

Well, shit. I wonder if they'd come.

Chapter Two

Andie

Vin has asked me to spend a month with her on an island off the coast of Maine. It sounds like a setting straight out of one of Jean's books. All we need is a gorgeous heroine and a guy who doesn't want to fall in love. Vin says it's nice there, and quiet, and not nearly as hot and humid as it gets here.

At first I thought maybe I was dying and no one wanted to tell me. Vin's never been one to invite company before—just that week last fall when I was sick as a goddamned horse and she was still reeling from Mark's death. I don't remember if she invited me then or if I just went to prove I was still alive and could do things like book flights and wear real clothes instead of the sweats I wear around the house. I puked all the way to New York, but I never told anyone that.

Vin reminded me we need to work on that book, and I put dying out of my mind again. I feel stupid saying "my book," since I never meant for it to be one, so I just call it *that book* without even any capital letters. I think the title she gave it sounds way too...oh, poor little me, I guess, but she swears it's good.

I was just starting to like the idea of a month on her island when she told me she invited Jean and Suzanne, too. "What were you thinking?" I bellowed into the phone—it's good to have my bellow back. "Jean would be fine. She'll cook for us rather than entrust her palate to anything we might conjure up. But Suzanne? She'll be holding us down for makeovers every morning and giving us pedicures after our showers. *Pedicures*, for Christ's sake."

Vin was laughing, which was good to hear—she doesn't laugh near enough. "Oh, stop being such a bitch, Andie. They won't come anyway, except maybe for a weekend."

I have undoubtedly been called a bitch more in the past month than I have in all my life before. At least to my face. I've never been much for name-calling, since we heard more than our share of it growing up on Tonsil Lake. But it's different when it's Jean or Vin doing it. It's like they're saying "we're there for you" in tongues or something.

My daughter Miranda, who's a schoolteacher married to another schoolteacher, was over here this morning before her kids got up. "Mom," she said, "why didn't you ever get married again?" She looked down at her hands and her face got red. "Was it because us kids were terrible to every guy you ever dated?"

I was surprised at her perception and bothered by her guilt. "I made my own choices," I said.

But I spent the rest of the morning thinking of Paul Lindquist. We had met at the all-night pharmacy when Miranda had an ear infection and Paul's wife was dying. We talked as we waited—me in my flannel pajamas and my older-than-God car coat and him in butt-hugging jeans and a faded blue shirt that pulled tight over his shoulders when he moved.

I remembered there had been a little three-corner tear in the sleeve of that shirt I'd wanted to mend. That should have told me something right there, since I've never purposefully mended a goddamned thing.

Though he'd lived in Lewis Point most of his life, I had never seen him before. But after that night I saw him every time I turned around. He coached young Jake's Little League team, drove in Miranda's carpool, and, that Labor Day weekend, held out his firefighter's boot to collect money for the muscular dystrophy telethon. I put in a ten-dollar bill I couldn't afford.

When his wife died, I sent a card. And every time I saw him after that, my heart would do weird things and I'd get so damned horny it felt like a hot flash.

A year later, when he asked me for a date, I said no.

Because I knew I would love Paul Lindquist, and I wasn't going to do that again. Ever.

And I never did.

But every couple of weeks while I was sick, he sent me a card—never anything sentimental or familiar, just funny or mildly obscene. The first ones, he'd signed "Take care, Paul Lindquist," but by the time the cards slowed to a stop, he was scrawling, "Best, Paul," across the bottom. I'd missed those cards when I got better.

All this retrospection makes me restless. I called Jean to invite her to lunch, and she said no, sounding frazzled.

"I have to send this book in by Monday and I've still got fifty pages to write. I always make my deadlines, and I don't want that to change because every other forny thing in my life has."

"Okay, go back to work. I won't bother you."

I hung up quickly, but then I got to thinking about all the time Jean had spent with me over the past year. I was probably the reason she only had three days to write fifty pages. Oh, Christ, more guilt. I don't like guilt in the first place, and Miranda had already given me my dose for the day. Even though it was hers instead of mine, I'd felt it.

At noon, I went through a drive-through and got two burgers, two orders of fries, and two vanilla shakes and drove out to Jean's house in Willow Wood Estates.

She was in her dining room at her computer, wearing a nightshirt. She hadn't put on her makeup or combed her hair and she looked like shit. It was like seeing the American flag lying on the ground, incongruous and probably illegal. Jean was always neat. She didn't wear a lot of makeup, but she wore it right, and her soft brown hair was always in this smooth curve with the sides tucked behind her ears.

One of the things I love about her is that she's always the same. She doesn't look as young as Suzanne or as elegant as Vin, though she could still pass for an attractive forty-five. But today she looked every minute of her fifty-one—even her gray roots were showing. I'd never seen this before. Root concealment is like a religion with her and Suzanne.

"Shut it down," I said. I thought about bellowing it, since I'd rediscovered my bellow, but Jean looked too fragile to be yelled at.

I thought for a minute she was going to cry, but she didn't. She stuck her chin out and got up. "I'm sorry for the mess."

There wasn't a thing out of place in her house— there never was—and no dust mote had dared to land on any of the shining surfaces. The only mess was her. God, I hated that.

When we were sitting at the bar in the kitchen sucking down sloppy, artery-clogging cheeseburgers and fries, I said, "Call your editor. Ask for an extension," just like I knew what I was talking about.

"You don't understand. My editor's about twelve years old. She inherited me. She'd much rather develop her own stable of writers than nurse along an over-the-hill veteran."

"Then tell her to forny off. Ask for a new editor, one that is at least of legal drinking age."

"I can't do that."

As soon as we'd finished eating, she threw me out. "I have to work."

"All right, but tell David I need someone to take me out to supper. He's a good guy. He'll volunteer."

For a minute there, she smiled, so I did, too. But I wasn't happy when I went away. Not happy at all.

Jean

When I sold my first book, I got flowers from David, and also from every one of the other Tonsil Lake girls. My kids hung a banner from the roof over the front porch proclaiming their mother to be a published author. I spent an entire afternoon on the phone with other members of my writers' group saying, "Yes, it's really true. Can you believe it?"

Then I made the beds, dusted the living room, did three loads of laundry, and cooked a dinner that included all the major food groups. David was surprised.

"I thought we'd go out," he said, coming up behind me in the kitchen and sticking his hands in the back pockets of my jeans. "You know, celebrate your success."

I looked back over my shoulder at him, the carving knife stopping halfway through the roast. "You didn't say."

"I'm sorry." He nuzzled my neck. "I thought you'd know."

When I sold the second book, David sent me flowers, the Tonsil Lake girls sent me enough locally made and sinfully delicious chocolates to give me a week-long sugar high, and the kids wanted to know what I would buy them when I got my advance check.

I had just stepped out of the shower when David came into the bathroom, taking off his tie. He leered at me, then said, "What's for supper? I'm beat."

"I thought we'd go out," I said, wrapping my towel around myself because the only other alternative would have been smothering him with it.

He looked nonplused. "Oh. Well, we can, I guess."

"Never mind." I gave him my best June Cleaver smile. "We'll have BLTs and we'll eat in the living room. The kids are spending the night at Suzanne's."

"Oh, well." He leered again, and pulled the towel away. "Just a little preview," he said, tipping my face up to kiss me.

But he was asleep in front of the television by the time the dishes were done. I covered him with a quilt and went to bed alone.

And I thought, *If my advances were bigger, I just might get a divorce.*

When the third book sold, Vin was in town, so we all went out to Tonsil Lake and got drunk. Andie stood on a table and told all six of the other tavern customers that I had just sold my third book and it was going to be a bestseller.

Vin held up her glass and said solemnly, "And to the republic, for which it stands."

Suzanne cried.

I told David about the sale when he came to pick us up. He didn't say much, but stopped in the middle of the parking lot and put his arms around me and held me for a long time. "I'm proud of you," he said, "but it really doesn't have a damned thing to do with how many books you sell."

I would have liked to know what he was proud of me for, but Andie chose that moment to say, "Oh, shit," and throw up all over her shoes. They were new Birkenstocks, too, and she bitched all the way home. Then we all got to laughing and David said he'd better not find any wet spots on the seats of his new car, which made us laugh all the harder.

But now I'm finishing my eleventh book, and no one seems to think it's a big deal anymore at all. I have two days left to write twenty-some pages, so I'm not in too bad a shape. But my stomach hurts again and I'm tired. I'm so tired.

Andie saved my life when she brought over lunch today. Then David brought home Chinese and set it all out for supper. He even cut some flowers and put them in a vase in the middle of the table, which made me want to cry. Or maybe it was the combination of grease-laden cheeseburger and Chinese that twisted my stomach into knots that made me want to cry.

Vin called and asked me to spend a month in Maine. I don't know what she was thinking of. I can't leave David or the house for that long.

And I'm Carrie's backup babysitter, too. She's even pickier about her kids than I used to be. I thought she and her husband were going to break up when she wanted to go back to work and neither his mother nor I could watch the children fulltime. Tim told Carrie they could put them in daycare or she could stay home; the choice was hers. She was angry with him for forcing her to make that choice, and even angrier with me because I wouldn't take the children.

It's funny that I've always liked being needed, but at the same time I envy Vin and Andie and Suzanne because they're not. That sounded ugly, didn't it? I don't mean it that way, I really don't. I would just like the chance to be myself for a while.

Whoever that is.

Suzanne

My regional director's secretary called me last week and asked me to come to division headquarters in Chicago. I was surprised, even though I knew it was time for my annual evaluation. Amanda—my director—usually comes to Lewis Point for it. We have dinner and drinks, then she tells me what kind of year I've had and what kind of raise I'm getting. She also gives me my mid-year bonus check. I've always done very well, and there haven't been many complaints from either side of the evaluation table.

Even though Amanda's secretary didn't give anything away, I was certain I was in line for a promotion. Sales have increased in this area to the point that division has talked about adding a new regional director. Though I'm really not crazy about tooting my own horn, I know the sales increase is largely due to my efforts and my presence in the stores.

I bought a new suit to wear to the meeting with Amanda and had my hair colored a week early because it wouldn't do to go to headquarters with mouse-brown roots showing. I got a manicure and pedicure while I was at it, even though I usually do my own. I was packing when Vin called.

"Hey," she said, sounding friendlier than usual, "why don't you come to Maine for a month? Andie and I will be there, and we want to talk Jean into it, too. Do you have any vacation time saved up?"

I have plenty of vacation time, but I couldn't think about a month in the back of the beyond right then, so I probably got a little pissy with Vin. She turned cool in the blink of an eye, which usually gets me flustered, but not this time.

"Look," I said, "I'm getting ready for a very important business trip. I'll be back tomorrow night and I'll give you a call then. Just have Attila the Housekeeper put me through to you, okay?"

I heard a strangled sound from the other end of the phone that if it hadn't been Vin I would have thought was a laugh. Then she said, "Fine. Take care," and hung up.

I caught a puddle-jumper flight out of Lewis Point's little airport and spent the night in Chicago so I'd be fresh for the ten-o'clock meeting. I dialed Jake Logan's number when I got to my hotel room that evening. I hate eating on my own.

He wasn't in, so I left a message on his machine, thinking if he didn't call back in time, I'd just order room service. I had a paperback that Jean had recommended in my suitcase. I love to read, which always surprises everyone. It's like, "Duh, you mean Suzanne can read?"

Instead of calling back, Jake knocked on my door a

half hour later. He swept me into a bear hug that lifted me right off my feet. "Suzy-Q, it's been too long."

He put me down and held me away, looking me over with a sparkling blue gaze that was like a caress. As God is my witness, if he'd said the word or even swept those long eyelashes down in a suggestive manner, like Jean writes about in her books, I'd have gotten naked right then.

Although I'd seen him to wave to, I hadn't spent time with him since his and Andie's son young Jake, Jean's daughter Kelly, and my daughter Sarah had graduated from college four years ago. We'd had a big party to celebrate and Jake—along with both my ex-husbands—had come. I had kept my distance from my exes, but Andie and Jake were like old friends, laughing and drinking toasts and standing with their arms around each other. They'd looked almost as married as Jean and David did, and I remembered feeling jealous. Which wasn't very nice of me, I guess, but I just felt so alone, and I've never learned to like that.

I'd thought then that Jake was just about the handsomest man I'd ever seen this side of a movie screen and I still thought so. "But you've gotten so thin," I said. "Why is it men eat everything that's not nailed down and lose weight while women gain just by walking through a kitchen?"

He laughed and hugged me again. "Are you going to let me buy you dinner?"

"I could be convinced." I gave him a Mae West look and a little flip of hip.

"Be still my heart." He grinned at me. "Get your purse. If you're nice, I might even take you dancing."

He didn't take me dancing, but we did go to the

Comedy Shop and laugh ourselves silly before he delivered me to the door of my room before midnight.

"Oh, Jake." I put my arms around him. "How could Andie have let you go?"

A shadow seemed to fall over his eyes, dimming the ever-present twinkle. He was silent for an instant, his face a mask, but he recovered so quickly I thought I'd imagined it. "What, and deny the rest of the world the pleasure of my scintillating company by keeping me?"

"There is that," I said, and raised my face.

He took the hint, kissing me there in the hallway of the eleventh floor of the hotel. I couldn't really afford to stay here, but had given myself the night as a reward for the upcoming promotion. It was a first-date kind of kiss, and I broke it with every intention of going back for more, but he stepped away slightly, covering my mouth with two fingers.

"You need your rest for your big meeting tomorrow," he said, "and I need to be going." He kissed my cheek. "Good luck, Suzy-Q. I'll call you."

I thought about the evening as I undressed and showered. We'd talked about Andie's illness, about what all of our children were doing these days, about the pitiful state of gas prices in the Midwest. He'd asked about my job and I'd told him more than he probably wanted to know, but he hadn't talked about himself, something I found unusual and endearing in a man.

The lighting in hotel bathrooms is uniformly cruel to any woman over twenty-two. I kept my back to the mirror as I dried off, slathered on body lotion, and dropped a silky gown over my head, but I had to face it to take off my makeup.

The plastic surgeon did a good job with my eyes—I never have that vaguely surprised look I've seen on other women—and the partial facelift I had five years ago is holding up well. But as I looked at myself that night, I saw the hint of a double chin when I turned my head, and there were faint lines around my mouth and below my eyes that it took two coats of concealer and a healthy application of makeup base to hide.

I applied moisturizer, then applied it again just for good measure.

"You're damned near fifty-one," I told my reflection. "You can't fight gravity forever." I grinned at myself. "Well, maybe you can fight it, but you can't win."

I remembered Jean's joke about me having my breasts sewn into place and looked down at my chest, wondering if I should go ahead and invest in another surgical procedure.

Andie used to say, "I'll do something about them when they smack me in the knees when I walk, especially since my fallen ass will be smacking the backs of them at the same time." We'd always laugh, but it wasn't so funny anymore. I couldn't go braless in public anymore, because my nipples were exhibiting a definite downward trend, but I wasn't sure I wanted the expense or the pain of more cosmetic enhancement.

One of the things I tell the ladies who use my makeup is that the best things they can do for their skin have nothing to do with what they put on it. They need to drink lots of water and they need to get plenty of sleep. I tell them I may have to get up in the night to pee a lot, but I look good while I'm doing it.

It was hard to follow those rules that night. The water in the hotel room tasted terrible even with ice, and I wasn't about to pay the price of taking a bottle out of the little refrigerator.

Then I couldn't get to sleep when I finally lay down. Instead, I hugged the extra pillow to my stomach and planned how I would run my own region when I got my promotion.

I overslept in the morning, but still arrived for my appointment by ten. Amanda and I exchanged hugs, compliments on hair color, and air kisses, before taking seats in the conversation area over by the floor-to-ceiling windows in her office. She buzzed her secretary with a request that we not be disturbed. I felt a little shiver of trepidation.

Amanda opened a folder on her lap and took out a slip of paper. "First things first," she said, beaming. "You had a spectacular Christmas and spring season. The company is grateful for your hard work and creativity."

The bonus check was the biggest I'd ever had, nearly twice as much, as a matter of fact, as I'd ever received before. It nearly took my breath away.

Maybe I would get my breasts done.

"Now," said Amanda briskly, laying the folder on the table between our chairs, "let's get down to business. We need to discuss your future with the company."

Vin

I woke in the middle of the night, which isn't like me at all. Mark used to say I must be eternally innocent, because I'd sleep through an earthquake and wake at my regular time wanting to know what the fuss was about.

Menopause seems to have robbed me of that innocence in a way even his death had not. I slept around the clock in the days after losing Mark, but nowadays night sweats were attacking me at unexpected times.

I stripped off my soaking wet nightgown and took a shower, which served to leave me wide awake at four-thirty in the morning with nothing to do. I could have worked on Andie's book, I guess, but I really wanted to wait till we were together in Maine.

I brewed a pot of coffee and sat at the kitchen counter with a cup in front of me. I wished suddenly and desperately for someone to talk to. Another sign of menopause, I suppose, since I'd never been the type to exchange confidences over coffee. But then, I'd always had Mark.

Tears threatened, and I shook my head even though there was no one to see. "I know," I said aloud, looking up—because if there's a heaven, Mark is there. "I promised I wouldn't do the bereaved widow thing." But I am bereaved, goddamn it.

The Andie-like thought made me smile, but I still wanted to talk, and no one I knew got up at this time of the morning. Except one.

Jean answered on the first ring, sounding cautious.

"Were you up?" I blurted. "If you weren't, I'm sorry."

"Oh, Vin. No, I was up." Now she just sounded exhausted. "I've been up since three, trying to finish this dratted book."

I made what I hoped was an appropriate response, and when Jean spoke again a few seconds later, it was as though she'd just been awakened from some kind of dream state.

"Vin?" she said. "Are you okay?" It was her normal voice, laced with the concern and compassion-if-you-need-it that were an inherent part of her personality.

"Yeah, I'm fine," I said. "No, I'm not. This menopause thing is for the forny birds."

"Ah." She laughed softly. "Don't be brave. Go to your gynecologist and tell him or her to give you anything, you don't care what it is, just to survive."

I tried to imagine Jean rushing off to her gynecologist and couldn't. "What do you take?"

There was a second of hesitation, but when she spoke, her voice sounded normal. "Me? Nothing. It hasn't been so bad for me, but I thought we were going to have to shoot Andie to put us all out of our misery."

"What about Suzanne?" I was pretty sure if Suzanne woke up with night sweats, she'd have to go into rehab.

"She had a hysterectomy when she was forty, remember? It threw her into instant menopause, but hormone therapy's worked great for her."

Silence hummed between us, then Jean said, her voice as coaxing as if she were talking to a child, "Come on, Vinnie. What's wrong?"

The soft sympathy in her voice was the last straw. Before I could even draw a deep breath, I was sobbing and speaking in a rush of hiccups. "I don't know, Jean. It's like there's no reason for living anymore. I never envied you guys having kids before, but now I do. I don't have anything without Mark."

"Oh, honey, I'm so sorry."

"I rattle around this brownstone all by myself except for Attila—"

"Who?"

As abruptly as the spate of tears had started, it ended, the sobs segueing clumsily into giggles as uncontrollable as the sobs had been. "It's what Suzanne calls my housekeeper. Archie's just the slightest bit...er...militant about screening my phone calls."

Jean laughed, and I was glad I'd called her just because the sound of her laughter is enough to brighten anyone's day. "Oh, Jeannie," I said, "please come to Maine with us. We'd have such fun."

"Oh, phooey, you all just want me to cook because you're afraid you'll poison yourselves."

She was still laughing, but it struck me that maybe that's what she really thought. It also struck me that she was right.

We'd counted on her to rescue us from our cooking limitations of canned soup and frozen entrees. We'd been counting on her to rescue us for forty years.

"Nope," I said stoutly. "I'm taking along that cookbook series we published a couple of years ago and we'll all learn to use it."

"Oh, good heavens." There was another little silence. "Maybe for a few days. A long weekend," said Jean. "David's got a golf trip coming up. I know he'd like not worrying about me being home alone. And, believe me, after I send in this book, I'm ready for a break."

It irritated me that she always put David's and her children's needs before her own, but the thought crossed my mind that if Mark were only here, I'd put his needs before anyone else's forever and ever.

"You think about it," I said. "We'd love it if you came."

Silence again, then, "Okay," she promised. "I'll think about it, but not till I get this book done and to my editor. I'll call you Sunday."

I got to the office early and stayed late, making large inroads into clearing my desk in preparation for devoting a month to Andie's book.

Back at the brownstone, I ate the dinner Archie had left in the oven for me, took a shower, and went to bed. Although I consider myself a morning person, I don't believe morning starts at four-thirty a.m. I was exhausted.

The clock beside the bed read eleven-seventeen when the phone rang. I'd been dreaming, I think, because when I picked up the receiver, I fully expected to hear Mark on the other end.

But it wasn't him, would never be him again. Instead, it was Suzanne, speaking in an almost unrecognizable voice, one that made me sit up and say sharply, "Suzanne? Are you okay?" God, how often we said that to each other, we girls of Tonsil Lake. *Are you okay? Are you all right?*

"I'm fine."

That's what we always said, even when the damned sky was falling. "Are you okay?" they asked after Mark died, and I said I was fine even though I knew I'd never be fine again.

And Suzanne wasn't fine now. "Talk to me," I ordered.

"I really don't have anything to say."

I could hear her swallowing, her glass clinking against the telephone. "Suzanne, what are you doing?"

"I just"—her voice faded away, then came back strong—"just wanted to say goodbye to someone."

Chapter Three

Andie

I felt pretty proud of myself this morning. In the first place, I got dressed. Not in sweats but in a pair of khaki shorts and an aqua tee shirt Miranda bought me for my birthday. I'm a size smaller since my illness and not too many clothes fit well, but these did.

I washed my hair and ran a pick through it while it was still wet so that it lay in waves instead of kinking up. I was getting used to the white, and I kind of looked forward to not having it colored every five weeks.

I even put on makeup, something Jean and I do well only because Suzanne's drummed it into us when she gives us our free samples. All of her practice on us is the reason, we tell her, that she does the best makeovers in the Midwest.

I gave myself a critical look in the mirror. As long as I was wearing a bra, you couldn't really tell that my boobs didn't match. The discovery made me ridiculously happy, and I turned away from my reflection quickly. There was coffee in the kitchen calling my name.

Jake called, as he's done every few days since I got sick, and we talked while I drank my first cup. He said he'd seen Suzanne the night before.

"It was fun," he said. "You should come up here for a weekend sometime, Andie. It would be good for you. Things don't have to interfere."

"Maybe sometime." I frowned. "But, Jake, have you told Suzanne?"

The smile left his voice, and I was sorry I'd asked. "No," he said, "but I will. Nothing's going to happen there. Trust me, okay?"

We'd just hung up and I'd poured my second cup when there was a knock at the back door. Expecting Miranda, I hollered, "Come on in," and set about making a fresh pot.

My children are as addicted to coffee as I am. Only young Jake says my coffee is too good for him. He's a cop and considers himself a specialist in sludge.

But it wasn't Miranda at the door; it was Paul Lindquist. He was holding a green Mason jar with a ribbon tied around its neck and eight tulips inside it. He had on long denim shorts and a polo shirt in a peculiar faded green that turned his eyes the exact same color.

He looked, as my kids would say and frequently do, fine. Very fine. Tongue sticking to the roof of my mouth fine.

I was really glad I'd gotten dressed and put on my makeup and that he couldn't tell by looking at me that my breasts didn't match.

He thrust the flowers at me and pulled something out of his pocket, holding them up in front of me. When he spoke, it was all in a rush as though he'd practiced it on the way to my house.

"I've got two tickets to the Indianapolis Indians game this afternoon. I'd like you to go with me and have dinner afterward. If we leave right now, we can have lunch before the game. You look really beautiful with those flowers up around your face."

I'm not going to go into the subject of breast cancer, because I covered it all in that book, but I'll say right here and now that if you've only got one thing to say to one of its victims, "You look really beautiful," is an excellent choice.

I said, "Do I need to change?"

He shook his head, smiling. All of a sudden I could feel myself blushing like a kid on her first date. God, he had great teeth. "Do you want some coffee before we go?" I moved to the table to push aside the salt and pepper shakers and the sugar bowl and set the flowers in the middle of it.

"No, thanks, but we can take some along."

I poured the coffee into two commuter cups the convenience store out on the highway had given away, and snagged my purse off the back of one of the ladder-back chairs. "Okay," I said, cursing my wobbly voice. "I guess I'm ready."

He took the cups from me and set them on the counter, lifted my purse from my shoulder and put it beside them, and said, "There's something I need to do first, that I've been wanting to do for more years than either of us wants to think about."

Without further ado, (I've always wanted to use that phrase) he took me in his arms, leaned me back against the counter, and kissed me till I was breathless. It didn't take long, I might add. He gave me time to get my wind back and then kissed me again.

My tongue wasn't sticking to the roof of my mouth anymore. Along about the middle of the second kiss, it became otherwise engaged.

Jake and I have been divorced for over twenty years, and, no, I have not been celibate all that time.

Not that it's anyone's business. But I have been very careful about things. I never had anyone spend the night at my house while my kids still lived here, I've never had unprotected sex, and I've never entered into a relationship that had the remotest possibility of having strings attached.

However, after two kisses and one bouquet of flowers, I was ready to ask Paul Lindquist to have sex with me on the kitchen table—after I set the tulips aside—and then move in with me. Jesus, Mary, and Joseph, I'd been spending too much time with Suzanne, who falls in love at the drop of a zipper.

"Ready?" Paul asked, releasing me slowly and taking both the commuter cups in one hand.

I nodded, though I wasn't at all sure my knees would hold me up if I stopped leaning against the counter. "Where's my purse?" I asked.

He looked around, and I saw that his eyes weren't as clear as they had been. "Uh..."

I wondered if his knees were weak, too.

"Oh." It was on the counter behind me, one corner of it digging into my ribs, so I pushed off and slung it over my shoulder once more. "Let's go."

The trip to Indianapolis had never gone so fast. We spent the time driving and, while we ate lunch at a diner complete with waitresses in pink uniforms, catching up on each other's lives. We didn't even have our kids out of high school yet when he drove into the parking lot at Victory Field.

After the game, we ate dinner at Rosie Peabody's, the restaurant I used to own, which got us up to the year of Miranda's college graduation and her wedding and the birth of Paul's first grandchild. We kissed in the parking lot, and while we were waiting on a red light going out of town, and when he stopped at a filling station so I could go to the bathroom.

As we neared Lewis Point, we both grew quiet, though he held my hand on the console between the seats. *What would I do,* I wondered, *if he wanted to make love?* I'm not ready for that, unless we can do it in the dark with my bra and tee shirt still on.

There was no doubt I wanted him; the wanting had grown with each kiss. But wanting and having are sometimes two different things.

There was no hurry, I told myself, but I knew this day had been seventeen years in coming, ever since that night we'd met in the pharmacy. That's not much of a hurry.

He took my keys from my hand and unlocked the door and pushed it open, but didn't offer to go inside. I looked up at him, and he framed my face with his hands.

"I had a great time," he said.

"Me, too."

Just as I was stiffening my knees for another kiss, the phone inside the house began to ring. Paul followed me in, closing the door behind him as I picked up the cordless across the room.

"Andie?" Vin's voice sounded tense. "You need to go to Suzanne's right away. Something's wrong."

Jean

I remember the first time I typed "The End" at the bottom of the last page of a manuscript. I laid my head down on that old electric typewriter David had brought me home from the office and cried.

Fifteen years later, I typed "The End," laid my

41

head down on the dining room table, and cried.

"Oh, Jeannie." David scooted me out of my chair and sat in it himself, pulling me onto his lap and tucking my head into his shoulder. "Sometimes I wonder if it's worth how much of yourself you invest in your writing."

I lifted my head to take advantage of the tissue he was offering. "Oh, I don't know," I said. "I invest a lot of myself in you, too, and you're worth it. Most of the time."

He pushed my hair back from my face and kissed my eyelids. "Am I?" he murmured.

"Oh, yes." I snuggled into his arms, thinking I'd just like to stay there and go to sleep, but some kind of internal alarm went off. "Oh, my God. Oh, no. Oh, no. Oh, no."

"Whoa." He raised his eyebrows. "I swear, I'm innocent."

"Do you know what day this is?" I said, panicked. "It's Birthday Saturday and I forgot all about it." I looked over at the grandfather clock in the corner. "All of our children and grandchildren will be here within the hour. They will expect dinner and a birthday cake and ice cream." Except for November and December, we did this one Saturday every month, because our extended family included birthdays in all ten of them.

"Well, that's fine." He pushed me off his lap and got to his feet. "If that's the case, you'd better hit the shower. I'll hit the grocery store."

"What?" I stared at him. "I don't have time to cook a full meal now."

"You're not going to. I'm going there for the cake and ice cream." He grinned, his eyes crinkling in a way that had been known to make me want to sit up and beg—not that I ever did, but I wanted to. "I'll swing by Kentucky Fried Chicken for the dinner."

"But we can't—"

He interrupted me with a quick, hard kiss. "We can and we will. Now, go take your shower. It would never do to greet your children in your nightshirt."

I don't know how we did it, but by the time the kids began to arrive, I was waiting at the door in my favorite sundress and David was putting the finishing touches on the dining room table.

The girls looked a little askance at the meal, but Josh and my sons-in-law dug right in. Toby, Carrie's son, said it was the best dinner Grammy had ever cooked and got a big laugh.

We were eating cake and ice cream when I mentioned Vin's invitation to come to Maine. Everyone except Toby and his little sister Megan stopped eating and looked at me.

"I'm not going," I said into the silence, "unless it's for a weekend while Dad's playing golf in Georgia."

"Well," said Carrie, "I should hope not. I don't know what Vin was thinking of, asking you such a silly thing."

"No kidding," said Kelly, pushing her cake away from her ice cream with her fork. "As if you'd even consider it."

The chicken breast I'd eaten for dinner starting jumping around in my stomach, and for a ludicrous moment I wondered if it had been dead when I swallowed it.

"What do you mean, girls?" asked David, frowning. "Why shouldn't she consider it?"

"Good heavens, Dad, she can't leave you for a month. The house would fall down," said Carrie. "And who would watch the kids while Tim and I go to Florida, or Kelly and Brian's dog when they go to the Bahamas? And what about your own vacation? Aren't you and Mom going away this year?"

"Yes," I said, "we're going to Hawaii in October." Some little demon made me add, "I hope that's all right with you, Carrie."

"You know, Josh and I could watch the kids," said Laurie quietly, "if Mom wanted to go to Maine. And the dog, too."

"The kids have never stayed overnight with anyone but Mom and Tim's mom," said Carrie, just enough impatience in her voice to make it undeniably rude.

"That's awfully nice of you, Laurie," said Tim unexpectedly, ignoring the glare Carrie turned on him. "Would you mind, though? They can be a handful."

"It would be fun," said Josh, "for Laurie, anyway. I, of course, will have to keep Dad company on the golf course."

"Mom's already said she's not going," said Carrie, giving her head a toss that threatened to dislodge the clips holding her hair back from her face.

I leaned over to rescue Toby's cake from going off the edge of the table.

"I think you should go, Jeannie." David's voice brought the table once more to silence. Toby's cake hit the floor with a tiny muffled thump.

The look David sent around to our children was not a loving one. "She finished another book today, not that any of you asked, and she deserves a break." He smiled down the length of the table at me. "I think I'll plan to spend a couple of weekends in Maine next month, see if I can pick up some woman to spend the rest of my life with."

He got to his feet and started gathering dishes. "Now, if you'd all like to help me clear this mess up before you go home, your mother's going to bed. You can all go in and tell her goodnight before you leave."

"Oh, no." I found my voice, though it sounded weak to my own ears. "I can do it, and Josh and Laurie are staying here."

"No, we're not." Laurie swept my plate from in front of me. "We're staying at the Lewis Point Inn, and I'm going to have my way with Josh. I'll tell you all about it, Mom, and you can put it in a book."

"Ah, loose women." Josh wrapped her in a hug and winked at me over her shoulder. "You gotta love 'em."

"Come on, Tim. We're leaving." Her face flushed and angry, Carrie got to her feet.

"Carrie." I stretched a hand toward her.

"We'll leave when we're done helping your father clean up," Tim said pleasantly, facing down his wife and my eldest child in a way I'd come to admire. "I'm washing. I don't know where anything goes." When he walked past my chair, he bent to kiss my cheek. "Congratulations on your new book, Jeannie."

"I'll dry." Josh sounded resigned. "It's what I do at home. And if I put things in the wrong places, I'll just blame Dad." He kissed me, too, as he walked past. "Love you, Mom."

Kelly, Brian, and Laurie all hugged and kissed me on their way into the kitchen. Kelly whispered, "Sorry, Mama. I promise to grow up someday."

Carrie wouldn't look at me. With a sigh, I snagged

the grandchildren for a couple of sticky hugs and rose from my chair, feeling every minute of the fifty-one years I'd turned this month. I stood for a moment, wondering if there was something I could say to ease the straight line of my daughter's back. I met David's eyes across the room, begging him silently to do something.

He said, "Goodnight, Mrs. O'Toole. I love you."

I went to bed.

It felt as though I'd just gone to sleep when I opened my eyes to see David, fully dressed, leaning over me. "Honey, get up. We have to go to Suzanne's."

"What's wrong?"

"I don't know."

Suzanne

"I'd like that," I told Amanda. "I've been thinking a lot about my future with the company. Making plans, writing down ideas. You know."

Suddenly it seemed as though she was having trouble meeting my eyes. "Good heavens," she said, jumping to her feet, "I forgot. I bought you this."

"This" was a bottle of rosé from a winery in southern Indiana. I don't know one wine from another, but it's a fact that I like sampling the local ones, so I appreciated the effort Amanda or her secretary must have expended to get it for me.

"Thank you," I said, touched.

"I hope you enjoy it." She sat down again, took the folder from the glass-topped coffee table and put it in her lap. Then she put it back on the table.

"Damn it, I hate this," she muttered, "and there's no good way to say it. Suzanne, corporate is asking you to step down."

I thought I'd heard her wrong. You know how sometimes you expect something to be said, and when it's not, you think you heard it anyway? Well, that's where I was. I opened my mouth and closed it again. I must have looked like a forny guppy.

"Step down." I repeated what I thought she'd said. "Amanda, are you saying I'm fired?"

"Oh, God, no." She closed her eyes, and I noticed she'd had them done since I saw her last. She had that surprised look. "They'd like for you to take on more administrative duties, perhaps relocate to Chicago if that's possible."

"Step down." I said it again. "What exactly do they want, Amanda?"

"Damn it," she said again. "I want a drink. You?"

Without waiting for me to answer, she went to the credenza across the room and splashed whiskey into two squatty glasses, added water and ice, and came back. Her hands were shaking and the ice rattled against the glass. It reminded me of a scene from a television daytime drama.

"It's a young woman's game, Suzanne, and as lovely as you are, you ain't young anymore. They want you out of the public eye." She met my gaze over the rim of her glass. The scars at the corners of her eyes stood out in stark relief.

"But I thought the reason I was on the brochures and spent so much time in the public eye was to cater to the baby boomers who can afford our cosmetics—to show them fifty isn't all that bad." I know everyone thinks I'm stupid, and in this case they would be right. I didn't know what in the hell was going on.

"Yes," she said, "and you've been great.

47

Outstanding, as a matter of fact. But, the truth is, they want thirty-year-olds to show that fifty isn't bad."

This I could understand. I'd been in this business when I was thirty, too. But I thought we'd come a long way, baby, since then. "What about the new regional director position?" I asked. "I'd be great at that, too."

"Yes, you would," she agreed, and tossed back her drink so fast it made *my* eyes water. "But you don't have a degree, do you?"

"No. I came within a couple of semesters. What does that have to do with it?"

"It's company policy. Everyone in the position of regional director on up must have at least a bachelor's. Doesn't matter what it's in, as long as it's a degree."

"So what is the position I'd have if I 'stepped down' the way they want?" I sipped my drink.

"It would be created. Probably something like an administrative assistant." Amanda sounded miserable, which made me feel a little better, but not much.

My daughter had been an administrative assistant in college. It had been, in her experience, like being a waitress but not getting any tips. I know this isn't always the case, but it wasn't a chance I wanted to take.

"Would I remain at my current level of pay?"

"No."

Well, there went the tips. It was my turn to toss back the whiskey. My eyes didn't water; I didn't even blink. Amanda brought the bottles of liquor and water over and poured us both refills. She forgot about ice. I didn't care.

"They want me to quit," I said flatly.

"Yes, they do. The bastards." Evidently the liquor had loosened her tongue. I was pretty sure she wasn't supposed to refer to our corporate heads as bastards, no matter how accurate the term.

"Any incentive?" That had helped David make the decision to retire from the automobile plant, I knew. With the incentives and what they'd invested over the years added to his retirement, he and Jean lived very comfortably. Of course, David had been a vice-president. That hadn't hurt, either.

"Yes." She picked up the folder again and opened it. "This is what I'm authorized to offer."

I looked at the papers, but the print was small and I couldn't read the numbers. Besides, I wasn't ready to consider that. "Do you have to know right now?" I asked.

"No, but soon."

"How soon?" My voice was crisp, professional-sounding. Vin would have been impressed.

"The end of June," she said reluctantly.

"I see," I said coolly. "Seems fair. I give them twenty-eight years. They give me thirty days."

I swallowed the rest of the drink without tasting it and got to my feet, although two glasses of whisky at ten-thirty in the morning made me uncertain exactly where they were. "May I keep this?" I gestured with the folder, or I meant to. I lifted the wine bottle instead. "I mean this." I did it right that time.

"Of course."

I offered my hand to Amanda. I didn't feel up to any hugging or air-kissing. "I'll be in touch," I said, and left without a backward glance.

I tried to call Jake from the lobby of the office building, but he wasn't home. I left a message on his machine thanking him for the evening. Then I got my overnight case from the storage locker in the corridor, stuffed the wine and the folder into it, and walked outside.

When I got out of the taxi at the airport, I still had two hours before my plane left. I carried my overnight bag into a bar and ordered scotch. Straight up.

By the time the commuter plane landed in Lewis Point, I'd imbibed more liquor than all four of the Tonsil Lake girls usually do when Vin comes home. I believe it is to my credit that I climbed into a cab rather than attempt to drive home. Or it would be to my credit if I had actually remembered that my white Camaro was at the airport. I hadn't.

In my condo I left my expensive new suit in a pool of silk on the bedroom floor and changed into a long satin gown and matching robe. Then I got the wine out of the suitcase and sampled it—half of it being what I considered a sample. It seemed to be a nice little wine, but when I went to pour another tumblerful, I couldn't find the bottle.

I put on my reading glasses and tried to make sense of the retirement proposal I'd brought home, but couldn't. For a while, I sat in the living room and stared at nothing, wondering how one's life could change so completely in such a short space of time.

The whiteness of the apartment was depressing. What had made a person like me, one who enjoyed and thrived on color, decorate her home in shades of white? The silence was as oppressive as the décor, so I finally went to bed and tried to go to sleep.

When I couldn't get to sleep, I took a couple of sleeping pills. When they didn't knock me out, I took a few more. Not many, just a few. I think. And then, when my heart felt as though it was going to burst through my chest, I knew I was going to die. And no one knew. There was no one to tell me they loved me, to beg me not to go. No one to say goodbye to.

So I called Vin.

Vin

If Suzanne survives, I'm going to fly to Indiana and forny kill her. Only I'm going to do it slowly. First I'll take away all her makeup, then the hair color, then the acrylic that makes her look as though she has real nails. I'm going to tell her she can't have any more plastic surgery because if she does her nipples are going to be in her eyebrows. I'm going to take all the snow-white caps off her teeth and hide the wax so that she has a moustache. Then I'm going to make her look in the mirror until the goddamned thing breaks and gives her seven years of shitty luck.

Oh, dear God, Andie and Jean, please call back. Please.

Chapter Four

Andie

If I hadn't been so damned scared, I'd have laughed when Jean met me on the sidewalk in front of Suzanne's condo. Her hair was flat on one side, wild on the other, and she was wearing a faded red nightshirt over the ugliest orange sweatpants I'd ever seen. She was wearing slippers—those little things that look like ballet shoes—but one was pink and one was lavender.

We were all running, and we arrived at the door at the same time, banging on it and yelling Suzanne's name.

"What are we doing? She's not answering," said David. "Does anyone have a key?"

"Oh," I said, startled. "A key." Yes, I had one, but where in the hell was it? I dumped my purse out on the porch floor and handed the key chain to David. "That one."

David got the door open and we did a Three Stooges rendition of trying to go through it at the same time. Paul yelled, "Stay!"—sounding for all the world like Dr. Kildare would have if he'd flunked out of med school and never known Dr. Gillespie—and ran in ahead of us.

Stay, my ass. He was a firefighter, for God's sake, not an EMT, and he wasn't carrying an ax or wearing a helmet or anything. We trundled right along behind him.

Suzanne was in bed, looking gorgeous against silk sheets, and I thought for a near-hysterical moment that at least she'd be happy that she died looking pretty.

She couldn't be dead. I wanted to kill her.

Paul sat on the bed beside her, laying his hand on the side of her throat. He reached for a bottle on the round bedside table and shook it, then handed it to me. "Count these. David, come around to the other side and help me lift her into a sitting position, okay?"

I poured the tiny pills into Jean's cupped hands and we both bent our heads to count.

"Seventeen," said Jean.

"Eighteen," I said at the same time, and shot her a look. "For Christ's sake, Jean, can't you count?"

She looked back at me, her light brown eyes fatigued and frightened, then we both looked down again. There were seventeen pills.

"How many to start with?" asked Paul when I reported the number. The right number. "Come on, Suzanne, wake up."

I held the bottle out to arm's length and squinted. Jean picked up Suzanne's reading glasses from the table and put them on. "Thirty," she said.

"Good. Even if she took all thirteen tonight, which she probably didn't, it won't do any lasting damage. Oops, David, she's coming your way." Paul put his hands on Suzanne's cheeks and yelled right in her face, "Suzanne, wake up!"

I'd never seen Richard Chamberlain do that when he played Dr. Kildare on television.

Her eyes opened momentarily and she stared fixedly at Paul. "You're Paul Lindquist, aren't you?"

she said clearly. "Andie should have gone out with you. She wanted to, you know." Then she closed her eyes again and her head lolled to the side.

I'm pretty sure David chuckled—sure enough to give him a look like I'd given Jean a few minutes before. "Do we need to call 911?" I asked.

"No." Paul smiled at me over his shoulder. "She's going to be all right. David, you want to come around here? We'll get her up and moving."

She didn't want to move at all, and the first few trips across the fluffy white carpet of her bedroom, the men were pretty much dragging her. By the third trip, she'd found her feet—at least part of the time—and Jean and I leaned on each other, too weak with relief to hold up our own weight.

On the fourth excursion, when Suzanne was beginning to protest being manhandled, Jean asked, "Should I make some coffee? They always do that on television."

"Good idea," said Paul. "If she doesn't want it, we can all drink it."

"I want," said Suzanne in a muffled voice, "some wine, but someone hid the goddamned bottle."

"We'll find it," David promised.

Paul was looking at Suzanne's face. "We should probably move our walk into the bathroom," he said, turning her.

But it was too late. She lost the contents of her stomach forcefully and suddenly on the puddle of turquoise silk that lay on the carpet.

"Well," said David, turning white.

Jean hurried over to replace him at Suzanne's side. "You make the coffee. Or if you're going to pass out, do it on Suzanne's bed. I'll have Andie take pictures."

"We'll use them for blackmail if you ever decide you want to leave Jean for a woman who doesn't wear ugly red nightshirts and orange sweatpants," I said. I looked with distaste at the mess. "Since we've known her longest, I guess this is where we take over. David, will you call Vin and tell her Suzanne's going to be fine...if we let her live?"

We got Suzanne into the shower, soaking ourselves in the process. Reluctantly, we cleaned up the bedroom floor, tossing the plastic bag full of soiled silk into the trash. Suzanne sat at her dressing table creaming her face.

"It's too bad," I muttered, scrubbing at the damp spots on the carpet, "you didn't have a pair of Birkenstocks in this mess."

Jean giggled first, sitting there on the floor with a rag in her hand and her half-wild hair hanging in wet strings around her face. A soft snort of laughter followed from the dressing table, and then we were all howling. Suzanne joined us on the floor and we held onto each other and laughed and held our knees together against the attacks of our weak bladders.

Paul and David ventured into the room to see if everything was all right and to offer us coffee. It was a good thing they came in, because Jean's right knee had locked up and she had no hope of getting up on her own. I was in mid-crawl to the bed to use it for leverage to pull myself to my feet. Suzanne's laughter had moved predictably, and in this case understandably, to tears.

"Vin wants you to call her back." David helped Jean up and stood with his arm around her waist. "I believe the quote was, 'I don't give a forny fart in hell what time it is.'"

Paul drew me to my feet and held me there in the loose circle of his arms. "Maine?" he said, raising his eyebrows at me.

I nodded. "For a month. We're going to work on that book and we're going to be ourselves. Jean, are you going?"

She exchanged a long look with David, took a deep breath, and said, "Yes, I'm going." She gave me an evil look. "But I'm not cooking the whole time, and I'm not cleaning up after you slugs."

I looked over at Suzanne, still sitting on the floor, and felt a wave of emotion sweep over me. I remembered her handing me that fancy-dancey journal and coming to my house every single day after I came home from the hospital.

She and Jean had taken turns, with my children, driving me to chemo and radiation treatments. When my hair fell out, she drew on faultless eyebrows and tried to attach false lashes to my naked eyelids. She brought me a new hat every day for a week when I refused to wear a wig.

I left Paul's arms and went over to where she sat, offering a hand to help her up. Jean came, too, her hand outstretched. I cleared my throat. "All right, you pain in the ass," I said to Suzanne, "are you coming to Maine, too?"

She looked up, her still-beautiful face a mask of hopelessness, then her gaze moved to our hands. Jean's with its long fingers and the wide white gold band she'd worn for nearly thirty years along with the newer etched one David had given her on their twenty-fifth anniversary. Mine with its short nails and all the tiny scars I'd gotten when I ran a restaurant. Suzanne placed her hands in ours—hers were soft and pretty and she wore rings on nearly every finger.

"Yes," she said, "I'm coming."

Jean

"I can't believe you're really going to do this, Mother." Carrie watched as I put shorts and tank tops into my suitcase. "You can't leave a man alone for a month. What will you do if he gets lonely and finds someone else?"

I added three cotton sweaters. "If your father's and my relationship can't stand a thirty-day separation, it's not much of a relationship, is it?"

She wandered around the room, picking up bottles on my dresser and putting them down, straightening the picture frames that formed the family gallery in one corner, opening my jewelry box and sifting through its jumble.

"What if you get lonely? What will you do?"

Something in her voice put me on mother alert, and I looked over at where she stood, her arms folded under her breasts in a defensive gesture. It was a position I saw her in more and more these days.

"Well," I said with a lightness I didn't think I felt, "if I get lonely for your dad, I'll just call him and get him to talk dirty to me." I waited for her to roll her eyes in disgust. I wasn't disappointed. "And if I get lonely for you kids, I can call or I can come ahead home. But if I get lonely in my soul," I went on slowly, putting three pairs of short white socks in the suitcase, "I'll have to work that out on my own."

I waited for her to call me on it, to assert that I'd

never done anything on my own in my entire life, but she didn't. She just gave me a brooding look and said, "When are you leaving?"

"Tomorrow morning. Your dad's taking us all to the airport. We're going to meet Vin in Bangor and go from there. We have to ride a ferry to the island and then take a taxi. Vin doesn't keep a car there—she says hardly anyone does."

I closed the suitcase and hefted it off the bed, placing it beside its partner near the bedroom door. "There, that's done. I sure hope there are a washer and dryer in the house. Going to a Laundromat on foot doesn't sound like much fun."

"Well." Carrie looked down at the clock on the bedside table. "I have to pick up the kids at Kelly's and head home. Tim will be there soon. He and Brian were playing golf with Daddy."

I walked her to the door. "I hope you and Tim have a good time in Florida," I said.

"Thanks." She gave me a hug and kiss. "Call, okay?"

It made me sad that she didn't wish me a good time, too, but Carrie was twenty-eight. It was a little late for me to work on her manners.

Still dressed in the sundress I'd worn to church that morning—I wear them because David likes them even though I don't like my flabby arms hanging out—I wandered through the empty house. It was cleaned within an inch of its life, which it suffers every time I finish a manuscript.

The cupboards and the freezer side of the side-by-side in the kitchen were stuffed with things David could prepare for himself. All of his clothes except for the khaki shorts and polo shirt he was wearing out on the Fallen Tree Golf Course were clean, pressed, and put away.

When I couldn't avoid it any longer, I sat down at the computer. I always had a new project on the back burner waiting to come forward when I finished a book. Until now. There it was on the screen in front of me: *Chapter One*. That was as far as I'd gotten.

What was that term people used when they talked about writing exercises? I couldn't think of it, but I knew what it was. I laid my fingers on the keys and let them move.

They were four little girls living in house trailers on a forgotten Indiana lake. They didn't have anything and the social workers who visited the lake families whispered among themselves that they never would. It was too bad, too, they said, because that Sharon was sure a pretty little thing and Althea was smart as a whip. Leona had an air about her that would give her stature in a place that promised good things to those who stood tall. And Joanne, well, she was a nice little girl. Such a shame nothing would ever come of any of them.

They didn't know, those social workers, about the dreams...

I didn't stop writing until I heard the back door open and close. I looked up, startled, realizing that the dining room had darkened around me and I was sitting in the little pool of light afforded by the desk lamp.

"David?" Where in the world had he been? It was eight o'clock, for heaven's sake, and he'd left to play golf seven hours ago. "David, are you all right?"

"Don't turn around till I say to," he called from the

kitchen.

"Okay." I faced the screen again. "Since when do you play golf in the dark?"

I heard the rattle of a plastic bag and felt a slight thunk when something was set on the dining room table, then David said, "Okay, now."

Half irritated, as much because of the interruption of my writing as with his lateness, I swiveled in my chair.

Sitting on the table was a new notebook computer.

"I know you've never really wanted a laptop," said David, "because of the smaller keyboard. But you can't take the desktop computer to Maine with you." He sat in the dining room chair closest to me and looked into my eyes. His were very, very blue.

"You said you didn't plan on writing in Maine, that it was going to be a vacation from life," he said, "but you may as well stop breathing. You wrote your first book sitting on the bleachers at football practices, your second one sitting beside my mother's bed for days and nights on end because she was afraid she'd die alone, and this last one even though you're unhappy. You're always going to write."

"I'm not unhappy." The protest was automatic.

He grinned at me. "Right, and I can drive a ball as far as Tiger Woods and putt like Phil Mickelson."

I'd watched enough golf on television to know better than that. "Really," I said, touching the keyboard of the laptop, "I'm not." I leaned in to kiss him hello, feeling the brush of his day-old beard on my cheek. "What do I have to be unhappy about?"

"I don't know that," he said. "Maybe if I did, I could do something about it."

I shrugged. "Menopausal women, honey. You know what they say." I kissed him again. "I love the laptop, though. Does its software match mine so I can work back and forth?"

"Yes, it does. Tim and Brian went with me to get it, and Josh even drove up to meet us with a list of stuff Laurie said you would need on it. It was like Keystone Cops in the computer store, with all three of them telling the salesman what we needed." He reached across the computer for another plastic bag. "Kelly sent orders to get you this. Said it wasn't something you'd buy yourself, but that you'd need it."

The leather attaché was small, slim, and soft, with room for the computer and whatever other writing paraphernalia I carried with me. I could actually put my wallet and keys in it and forego carrying a purse for the first time since entering junior high.

I could suddenly see myself getting on the plane. No purse holding everything but the kitchen sink, no canvas tote I always used in lieu of a briefcase. I felt excitement shiver along underneath my skin. It would be a new kind of freedom for Jean O'Toole.

Freedom.

Free writing, that's what it was called, what I'd been doing on the computer all afternoon!

I turned toward it with every intention of deleting it, but a look in the corner of the screen informed me I had written fifteen pages. I shook my head and named the file before saving it. Then, with a little "why not?" shrug, I saved it to a jump drive, too, and tucked it into the new attaché along with several others.

Later, David and I sat on the couch together and watched an old movie. At one point, he turned to me and said, "I just want to be sure you'll come back to me when it's over." He rubbed a hand up my arm and ran a finger under the armhole of my dress.

I knew he wasn't only talking about the trip to Maine when he mentioned "it" being over. He wanted his cheerful wife back, the Pollyanna who had a smile and a good meal for him on the worst of days. Well, I wanted something back, too; I wanted a husband with a direction that took him further than the Fallen Tree Golf Course.

We were in a trap, I realized. He kept thinking he was going to come home to Carrie, Josh, and Kelly's mother, the good daughter and daughter-in-law, the dutiful wife, and instead he returned to a woman who went through the motions on automatic pilot. As for me, I kept expecting the company vice-president I'd known for so long: in command and in demand and never falling short in either category.

We loved each other, these two virtual strangers on a leather couch in a custom-built house in the Willow Woods subdivision. We had loved each other through early marriage poverty, children's emergencies, a brief affair on David's part, the deaths of all of our parents, and the empty nest. But was it enough? Would it ever again be enough?

Suzanne

Andie was yelling again. I sighed and continued to lay out my underwear in sets.

"How could you?" she shouted. "How could you be so stupid? How could you try to kill yourself? How could you forget for one forny frigging minute how precious life is?"

"Okay." Done with the underwear, I counted out

shorts and shirts. "Number one, it was an accident. Number two, it was an accident. And number three, it was an accident."

She wasn't listening. Sometimes I thought she never listened.

"What did you expect us to tell Sarah and Tom? 'Well, hey, kids, she's dead, but she looked real nice lying there.' That would have been a great comfort to them."

I laid socks up against the tops that matched the shorts, coordinating their colors, and thought about my kids. Sarah, the beautiful veterinarian at the clinic on the edge of town, who seldom gave me the time of day. And Tom, who twelve years ago had moved in with his father as a troubled thirteen-year-old. My son had been in and out of detox so many times I could hardly keep track of his address. The only time I was sure of it was when he called and asked me to send money.

"Somehow," I murmured, "I don't think they'd have needed a lot of comfort. Are you taking anything to dress up in?"

"No! Why are you worried about clothes when you damned near died less than a week ago? I swear, Suzanne, sometimes I think—"

"Shut up, Andie." I got into the bottom drawer, searching for sweatshirts. When I straightened and looked at her, she was staring at me.

"What?"

I almost grinned, but not quite. "I said shut up. And listen. I did not try to kill myself. The end."

"But all that booze and those pills," she said. "Suzanne, you don't do that kind of thing. None of us do. Remember the pact?"

Of course I remembered it. We'd made the pact the day Vin's stepfather's old Mercury had found its way to the bottom of Tonsil Lake. We'd sat on the bank and watched the men fish the car out of the lake with a winch attached to a wrecker. The men had looked up at where Vin's mother stood and shaken their heads.

Mrs. Hardesty hadn't even looked over at where her daughter waited with Andie, Jean, and me. She'd just turned and gone back to her trailer, supported by Jean's mother and mine—which was like the blind leading the blind.

We'd moved closer to each other so that all our shoulders touched, and we'd watched as they loaded Mr. Hardesty into a black bag and zipped it closed before carrying him up the bank to where an ambulance sat.

I looked at Vin and saw that Andie and Jean were looking at her, too. I wondered if I looked as sick as they did. Although there was no emotion showing on Vin's face, I understood the relief in her eyes. We'd all done our share of eluding Mr. Hardesty's advances when he had a snootful; we also knew Vin had been unable to escape.

Actually, we knew a lot of things; it had been a very long day that had started in those darkest hours before dawn. A day that had started bad and gotten worse, ending on sins and secrets.

Jean finally spoke. "I think we should make a pact," she said quietly.

Andie snorted. "We're thirteen, Jean, not little third-graders or something. And what good's a pact going to do anyone?"

"It could do us some good," said Jean. "I think we

should agree we'll never let ourselves get out of control because of alcohol or drugs, and if we find ourselves heading that way, we should call the others."

I liked this, even though I couldn't say things as well as Jean did. "And the others can't get mad or refuse to come." I scowled at Andie when I said that. She was always mad.

Including now. "It's dumb," she had said angrily, starting to get up. "This whole thing isn't because of drugs or booze. It's because—"

Jean's next words stopped her. "And there are things we'll never tell another living soul unless we all agree."

"I'll agree to it," said Vin quietly. "I'll swear."

Jean put out her hand and Vin laid hers on top of it. I put mine on, resplendent with Passionate Plum nail polish.

Andie scooted back into her position, passed a disgusted look all around, and laid her sun-browned hand on top of mine.

"It's done," said Jean, "until we die."

"Until we die," I repeated.

Vin nodded, just one jerky motion of her head. "Until we die."

"Fine," said Andie. "Until we forny die."

"It was an accident," I now repeated to Andie, for what seemed like the hundredth time. "And the pact worked. I called and you came." This time I did grin at her. "Of course, you got mad, which you weren't supposed to."

She grinned back. "Hey, you ruined the end of my date."

I put each complete outfit into a zippered plastic

bag, smushed the air out, and laid the bags into my suitcase. "Ruined it or delayed it?"

Her smile widened. "Oh, well." And then she wouldn't say anything more.

I laid the folder with the retirement plan on top of the bags of clothes. Andie looked at it.

"What are you going to do, Suze?" she asked.

"I don't know."

Then I was the one who wouldn't say anything more, because I couldn't talk with panic pushing up into my throat. I just shook my head and leaned over the bed to zip the suitcase closed.

I went to get my cosmetics case out of my closet and spied one of the bags my company gives away during promotions. I brought the bag with me back to the bed. After clearing my throat to get my voice working again, I said, "These are for you guys. I sent Vin's to her then forgot to give you and Jean yours."

I pulled the flat black cases out and looked at the pressure-sensitive labels on the edges that told the color combinations of the makeup inside. "Here's yours. They're travel cases, so you don't have to take everything with you." I gestured at my own bag; it was the size of a weekender.

Andie opened her case and gave its contents a cursory look. "Thanks," she said, closing it and looking from it to my big blue one. "I think you should leave that here and just take one of these."

"Oh, but..." I stopped. If I didn't take my full battery of cosmetics, I probably wouldn't be able to cover the fine lines around my eyes and mouth. The light tan spots on my hands might begin to darken. I wouldn't have samples with me to offer other women who showed an interest in makeup.

I would have nothing to hide behind and nowhere to run.

I put my cosmetics case back in the closet.

Vin

"Would you be wanting me to go with you, Mrs. Stillson?"

I looked up from my packing. Archie stood in the doorway of my bedroom, holding a long-handled duster like a staff.

"The Maine house hasn't been opened since last summer," she said. "The guest rooms and bathrooms aren't ready, there's no food, the linens need to be re-washed because it's so damp up there."

Martha Mary Archibald had been Mark's housekeeper when I married him. Although she'd never been less than gracious to me, I knew she had not approved of his marriage to a woman twenty-five years younger than himself. We had been married several years before I realized that she was as in love with my husband as I was.

I had understood that, and respected it, and life had gone on. Her grief at his death had been sharp and sustained. We had stayed out of each other's way. When the dust settled and Mark's children had returned to their accustomed pretense that I did not exist, Archie had stood in my bedroom doorway just as she did today.

"Would you be wanting me to leave?" she had asked.

"No," I replied.

And that was that.

"You don't need to come, Archie," I said, slipping

the makeup case Suzanne had sent into the side of my bag. "What will you do while I'm gone?" I'd never inquired into her personal life before; minding our own business had been part of our unspoken agreement to live in the same house and love the same man.

She hesitated. "If it would be all right with you, I would like to close the house and go to Ireland to visit my sister. I haven't seen her in all these many years, and I believe I have enough money saved."

"Of course. And you must stay as long as you want. I'm sure we owe you months in unused vacation time."

"A month will be enough," she said impassively, dipping her head. "Thank you, ma'am."

She turned to leave, and I said impatiently, "Wait a minute."

"Yes, ma'am?"

"We've shared this house for twenty-some years, Archie. I'd like for you to call me Vin. No more ma'ams, no more Mrs. Stillsons. Now, do you have your passport up to date?"

"Yes, ma—Vin. I've always kept it up in case I needed to go home quick-like."

"And when would you like to leave?"

She looked surprised, and I all but tapped my foot waiting for her to answer. "A week," she said definitely. "That gives me time to close the house and prepare for the trip."

"Fine. Come with me."

She followed me into Mark's office, where I got on line and procured a plane ticket to Ireland and arranged for a car rental. "You'll leave in six days," I said, getting up from in front of the computer and handing her the confirmation and itinerary.

"I will write you a check for this cost," she said sturdily, waving the printed sheets at me.

"You'll do no such damned thing. Come with me," I said again, and went back to the bedroom with her following in my wake. I could feel her antagonism smacking me right between the shoulder blades.

This was fun. I felt strong again.

I opened the door of Mark's closet, nearly going to my knees when the unique and distinctive scent of him assailed me. So much for feeling strong. "Oh, God," I muttered, and looked over my shoulder in time to see Archie crossing herself. "We need to do something about this," I said, touching a cashmere sleeve.

"Yes."

"Soon, but not now."

"Thank you."

I looked over my shoulder again, and we exchanged small, tentative smiles, then I walked into the closet, coming out with three pieces of luggage. I set them at her feet and delved into the closet again.

It had been so long since I opened the safe that I no longer had any idea what all was in it, but I knew there was cash. There was also jewelry in a black velvet bag. I tucked the bag under my arm.

I brought out three thousand dollars and slapped it into Archie's hand. "If he were here," I said flatly, "he would do no less."

She was pale. "Are you firing me?"

"No." I touched her hand. It was the first time I'd ever touched her in any way. We hadn't even shaken hands when we met. "Please don't think that. Is there any coffee?"

"I can make it. I'll have it up here in ten minutes."

"No, I'll come down. Here." I thrust two of the suitcases at her and picked up the third, keeping the black velvet bag in my other hand. "You can keep these bags," I said on the way down the stairs. "God knows you've packed and unpacked them enough times to know every fold in the leather."

In the kitchen, I took a seat at the bar while Archie made coffee. I noticed that she tucked the money carefully into her purse and was glad she hadn't refused to accept it. While I waited for the coffee, I poured the contents of the velvet bag onto the marble counter in front of me. "Forny."

"Mr. Stillson's mother's," said Archie, bringing sugar, cream, and a spoon over to where I sat.

There were sapphires, emeralds, diamonds, all in old-fashioned, ornate settings. They were extremely valuable, I knew, and uniformly ugly.

"You should have them reset and wear them." She brought my coffee.

"Bring yours over here, too," I ordered, "and sit down. Today, Archie, we are two women, not lady of the house and housekeeper. Okay?"

"Yes, ma—Vin."

When I'm grown up, I'll be rich, and I'll wear jewelry like all the rich people do in the books, like Queen Elizabeth and Princess Grace, like Jackie Kennedy did at the inaugural documentary thing that was on TV. I'll have servants and three houses and a car with a chauffeur who wears a uniform and calls me ma'am. And no one will ever be able to make me do anything I don't want to. No one.

The memory rose up unexpectedly, attacking me in

the same manner as Mark's scent had when I opened his closet, but with a very different kind of pain. I'd been ten, and my stepfather, the second of four, had just shown me in graphic detail exactly what he could make me do.

Mark had always been careful to let me do whatever I wanted. When, as it often happened, I didn't know what that was, he led me in what always turned out to be the proper direction. When I wanted to go back to work even though I didn't need the money and he didn't really want me to work, he had called Liam Gunderson and told him his wife was looking for a job. Could Liam help?

Now, without Mark, I knew I no longer wanted the brownstone, the house in Miami Beach, the hideous jewels that splattered the counter with jarring colors. Princess Grace and Jackie Kennedy were dead and Queen Elizabeth hardly ever paraded around in jewels anymore.

I didn't want to be "ma'am" to a woman who was no less than I was just because I'd loved and married a wealthy man and she had only loved him. For right now, I wanted—no, needed—to go to Maine with my three best friends and just be one of the Tonsil Lake girls.

"If you'd like," said Archie, helping me scoop the jewelry back into its bag, "I could drive you to the airport."

I met her eyes across the cups and the black bag and the years of our acquaintance. "Thank you, Martha," I said. "I'd like that."

Liz Flaherty

Part Two

"There was no getting around it—she was lost."

Jean O'Toole
The Price of Pride
Cupid's Bow Books, 2009

Liz Flaherty

Chapter Five

Andie

"Do you have any concerns that we should talk about?"

Carolyn Murphy, who's been my gynecologist since our kids were in kindergarten together, never sat behind her desk. She always came around it and sat in a chair beside me. When I'd been too sick to drive myself to see her, she'd dragged a chair from the corner for the person with me rather than sit behind the desk.

"I'm still tired," I admitted. "I thought I would have bounced back by now."

"Your body's been attacked from all angles. And, truth to tell"—she shrugged, with a rueful smile—"we ain't twenty anymore. Your counts are all in good shape, but you're bouncing back like a fifty-year-old, not a teenager."

"Well, it kind of pisses me off."

"I hear that. Did you see the new associate in the practice? She's twenty-nine. Looks like she should still be in elementary school. She's very good, but I'm having to really work at liking her." She leaned forward in her chair, pinning me with her gaze. "Are you scared, Andie? That it'll come back? That we've missed something?"

Deep breath. Another. In. Out. *Where are you when I need you to help me breathe, Jean?* "Yes."

"Good. It'll keep you vigilant." She looked down at the notes in her lap. "Maine, huh?"

"Yes, with Jean and Suzanne and our friend Vin. Maybe you should give me a quadruple prescription for Prozac. I'll just pass it around when we start fighting."

She laughed before an expression of concern crossed her face. "Jean doing all right?" she asked.

"Sure," I said, thinking positively. Then I frowned. "Shouldn't you already know that?"

"I just haven't seen her for a while," she said. "Maybe she's changed doctors, although no one's called for her records. At any rate, give her my best when you see her."

I did, hissing at her in the hallway of her house so that David wouldn't hear. "Why aren't you going to Carolyn for your annual checkup? What did your mother die of, Jean? Do you remember? And who discovered my cancer? It wasn't me."

Jean's mother had died of ovarian cancer. At the age of fifty-one. And Carolyn had discovered the lump in my breast.

"What's that?" she'd said.

"It's nothing. I think you have this thing for women's boobs," I said. She pressed harder. "Ouch."

There were a lot more ouches before we were done.

Jean stopped at her bedroom door and glared at me. "I'll take care of it," she promised in a loud whisper. "Now please shut up. We're going to Maine. We're going to have a good time. We're not going to fight."

"The hell we're not."

The telephone rang, and a moment later, David called, "Andie, it's for you."

We met halfway and he handed me the cordless phone. "It's Paul," he said. He raised his voice. "Tell him we're on for the women tonight."

"I heard that, David O'Toole," called Jean from their bedroom. I heard her laughter when he went in, closing the door behind him.

"Did he say we were on for the women tonight?" asked Paul, after I'd said hello.

"Yes, he did, but you're out of luck. The women down at the Senior Center are on to you guys."

He laughed, and the sound ran along my nerve endings in a way I found altogether too pleasant. I was fifty-one, not seventeen, which meant I was no longer prepared to deal with that kind of feeling. Except maybe in my stand-up breast, which doesn't have much feeling at all but does look like it's seventeen. Oh, I already said that, didn't I?

"I just wanted to say goodbye again," he said, "and to tell you to have a good time."

"Thanks," I said, sounding as breathy as Suzanne at her worst.

He waited the space of the three loud heartbeats I was all but certain he could hear over the phone. "I'll miss you, Andie."

Jake had said those words the day our divorce was final. If I closed my eyes, I could still see him standing there outside the courthouse while his lover waited in the car. He'd traced a finger down the side of my face and tugged gently at the little gold hoop in my ear he'd bought me the day young Jake was born. "I'll miss you, Andie."

I had turned and walked away. I'd gotten into the car and driven to Lewis Point to Jean and Suzanne.

Miranda had ridden beside me, young Jake in the back with the dog. We did not speak until I stopped the car at Suzanne's house.

"We'll be all right," I said, looking from one of them to the other. "We all will."

It had taken me a year to convince them, longer than that to convince myself. The dog never had come around.

"Is it okay if I call you once a week or so?" asked Paul, bringing me back to the present.

"I'd like that. Did I give you the number?"

"Last night."

Thinking of last night made my blood start rushing around crazily, and I knew beyond all doubt he could hear my heart beating then. "Oh," I said, "yes. Last night."

I am not prepared to write about last night, even in this coil-bound journal no one will ever see. Let it suffice to say that losing one breast does nothing at all to lessen the pleasurable sensations that can be felt in the other.

I don't know whether I am getting prudish in my old age or simply paranoid, but that's absolutely all I'm going to say on the subject of last night. God knows, if I chose to tell the whole story, Jean would probably send this journal off to her publisher.

My blood was still thundering. I could hear it.

David walked past, carrying Jean's luggage, and I looked at the grandfather clock. "I have to go," I said.

"Have fun."

"I will. Thanks for calling, Paul." I waited a second, maybe two. "I'll miss you, too. Bye."

I hung up before he could answer.

Jean

Dear David:

As I said on the phone, the trip was uneventful except for my motion sickness, which took us all by surprise. I'm fine now, although it left me a bit weak in the knees for a while.

Vin looks well. She's thinner than she was when I saw her last, and maybe she has some new lines around her eyes, but so do we all except Suzanne. She still has those wonderful cheekbones and the longest legs this side of the NBA.

It was quite a scene when we all came together at the airport in Bangor. I think we all ended up crying, except maybe Andie. You'd have been appalled! *smile*

The house is wonderful. We each have our own room, and we share two bathrooms. There are wraparound porches, upstairs verandas and everything is very light and cozy with mismatched beachy-looking furniture and plenty of old-fashioned lamps so that you never have to look around for a bright spot.

I don't know why I'm writing you when I'm sure we'll talk nearly every day. I guess I need the written word. That's not bad as vices go, being a written word junkie.

I love you, David. Be safe.

I slipped the letter into an envelope on the little white desk in my room and climbed into bed, leaving the windows open. The sea breeze was wonderful, soothing, and cool, and I was exhausted. I fell asleep immediately, with the bedside lamp still burning and Elisabeth Ogilvie's *Rowan Head* lying on my chest.

I woke before dawn with tears on my face, burning up even though the room was cold. I thought about going downstairs, but was reluctant to move in case I got sick again. This was not a good beginning to a vacation.

The fears that usually stayed in the back of my mind came right straight to the front when David wasn't in bed beside me, and for a moment I considered getting on the phone and asking him to come for me. Carrie had done that every year at camp.

"I'm lonely here. Can't you and Daddy come and get me?"

"Just give it a day, sweetheart. If you still want to come home tomorrow, we'll come and get you." She never called back, and was in fact always reluctant to come home when camp was over.

So just give it a day, Jean.

I wished Andie hadn't mentioned my mother the other morning. Thinking of her illness and death only added darkness to my shadowy fears.

I had been thirty-two when she died, so busy with the children and the house that there hadn't been any time to think much about the disease that killed her. I'd done that later, as I sat beside David's mother's bed and did for her what I'd never done for Ma.

"You're always going to write." David's words came back to me as I lay there, and I reached for the notebook computer I had hooked up earlier, just in case. I stacked the feather pillows behind me, wincing as the movements hurt my stomach, and opened the computer.

I wrote until I noticed that the letters weren't very

bright on the screen, and when I looked up I discovered that it was full daylight. There were five new pages of manuscript and my stomach had stopped hurting. Well, almost. My bladder, however, was a different story.

A few minutes later, I followed the smell of coffee down to the kitchen. Vin was there, looking exotic in a long sleeveless black gown that appeared opaque until she moved, when you could the shadows of what was underneath. I spent a moment resenting that what she had underneath wasn't nearly as lumpy as what I had.

"I've decided"—she poured a mug of coffee and pushed it across the counter to me—"that hot flashes are our punishment for skinny dipping in Tonsil Lake." Her auburn hair was damp at the temples despite the cool morning.

I made my eyes as wide as I could and stared over at her. "I never did."

"Liar."

We laughed softly. "Well, most of the time we didn't have bathing suits that fit," I defended, "and we got in trouble if we swam in our clothes. We didn't really have any choice."

"Did you take David back there when you were going together?"

I looked down at my cup, remembering. "He insisted. When we decided to get married, he said it wasn't right that he'd never met my parents, never seen where I came from. So we drove up from Bloomington one Friday after we got out of class.

"When we got there, Dad and Ma were on the couch on that porch he started but never finished. David walked right up and introduced himself and said, 'I want to marry your daughter.'"

Vin smiled. "I can just see him. He was such a handsome devil, wasn't he? What did they say?"

"Dad looked over at me and said, 'How far along are you?' Since David had spent the last three months insisting I was probably the only junior at Indiana University who was still a virgin, that struck me funny, and I started laughing. Dad came up off the couch like he was going to backhand me, and David stepped between us. He said, 'No, sir'—just that quiet."

I sipped the coffee, hoping my stomach would accept its good intentions. "Then we got back in the Mustang—remember that red one, David's pride and joy?—and left. We didn't go back until Dad died, what, five years later.

"He was handsome, wasn't he?" He still is, for that matter, but I was thinking about him as he had been. I missed the boy I'd fallen in love with a lot more than I was missing the man he'd become. In the clear light of morning, with my stomach no longer trying to turn me inside out, I could forget how much I'd longed for him in the dark hours.

Andie and Suzanne came into the kitchen arguing. Andie was whining that her hair looked like dandelion fluff because Suzanne had thrown her out of their bathroom before she'd had a chance to put stuff on it to make it lie down.

Suzanne was obsessing about a zit that had appeared overnight when she had, in a moment of madness, left most of her extensive collection of skin care items in her closet at home. She never would have done this, of course, if it hadn't been for Andie talking her into it.

I thought for a minute about what I'd be doing if I

was home. The breakfast dishes would be in the dishwasher. David would have already left for the golf course. I would have been at the computer for an hour or so before he got up, and I would go back to it when he left unless Carrie needed me to watch the kids.

For now at least, I thought as Andie's and Suzanne's voices swirled around me, *this is better.*

Suzanne

I called Jake last night, just to let him know the phone number here. We talked for fifteen minutes or so, and since I was lying in bed anyway, I indulged myself with a few fantasies. I feel almost guilty about this, because of Andie, yet I know there's been nothing between them for years and years except friendship. Well, I sort of know that anyway. Andie's never been all that forthcoming about her personal life.

My ex-husbands are not my friends. Trent Taylor, who is Tom's father, is a doctor in Indianapolis, and you just cannot imagine a more cold and distant human being. I will admit that I married him for the wrong reasons, most of them involving showing the inhabitants of Tonsil Lake that one of its girls could gain success. There were no professionals living on Tonsil Lake, unless you counted Andie's Aunt Rosie, whose practice of the oldest profession isn't exactly what I'm talking about.

Trent and I lived apart five days a week. He was doing his residency in Indy and I was building my reputation as a sales rep with my company, based out of Lewis Point. One Friday when Tommy was three months old, Trent called to say he wouldn't be home for the weekend because he had to work.

Thinking to surprise him, I left Tommy with Jean,

packed the sexy red lingerie the company had given me as some kind of bonus, and drove up to Tom's apartment in Indianapolis.

Well, he wasn't at the hospital, and he certainly wasn't working. I threw my red underwear at him and the nurse he was playing doctor with and left. I filed for divorce the following Monday. And, if the story weren't full enough of soap opera clichés, I married my lawyer six months after my divorce was final.

In all fairness, Phil Lindsey was a decent husband. He was a good father to our daughter Sarah and tried to be a good stepfather to Tom—who wasn't having any, thank you.

We were married for ten years, a typical suburban couple. We lived just two blocks from Jean and David in Willow Wood Estates and did all the right things. We went to barbecues and had barbecues. We belonged to the country club and the big Methodist church out on the edge of town. We went to Sarah's dance recitals and Tom's Little League games and to parties held by other lawyers.

To tell the truth, I hated my life. I was a half-assed mother, not born to it like Jean or even Andie, and I wasn't that great a wife for a lawyer, either. I was supposed to behave properly at least until he'd been made partner. "Properly" didn't include being a cosmetics company sales rep, not even when I was promoted to the more prestigious title of consultant.

Phil was not the type of man to force me to quit, but he did request that I keep a low profile about what I did. I tried to, and things went along okay. But then the Rivers family moved in next door.

They were a nice couple. Ben was a stockbroker

and Kate was a teacher. They had two children and a Dalmatian named Sidney. And they were black.

Well, this may have been the beginning of the twenty-first century, but let me tell you, some creepy faction in Willow Wood Estates hadn't yet heard of integration, enlightenment, or diversity. Less than a month after the Rivers moved in, we got up one morning to find their yard totally trashed, windows broken, and an effigy hanging from a willow tree. Someone had spray-painted "niggers, go home" on their white garage door. All that was missing was the burning cross.

I saw Ben and Kate the same time I saw the mayhem. They were just standing there, hands hanging limply at their sides. I called Jean, yelling, "Get over here now," and stomped out of my house and into the neighbors' yard. Jean was there in two minutes, and we got started. Two furious women in pajamas and bathrobes soon became most everybody in the neighborhood and we cleaned that mess up. David even stopped on his way to work and took a can of white spray paint out of his trunk to try to obliterate what had been done to the garage door.

The picture on the front page of that night's paper was of Jean and me, flinging broken glass into a trashcan held by Kate Rivers.

Phil was not pleased. Actually, he was irate. What was wrong with me, he wanted to know. Did I want the neighborhood to be taken over by blacks, gays, and other subversives?

The kids and I spent the night at Jean's. The divorce was particularly messy, since Phil was a lawyer, but I ended up with enough money to buy my condo.

Sarah never forgave me for leaving her father, and Tom never forgave me for anything.

So why am I digging up all this old history? Maybe because I'm confined in a house with two women who are close to their children in a way I'm not. Maybe because—and let me admit right here and now that Andie's right when she swears I fall in love at the drop of a zipper—I'm afraid I'm going to fall in love with Jake Logan, who is someone's ex-husband. No, he's Andie's ex-husband, and if there hadn't been a good reason for divorcing him, she wouldn't have.

I'll just keep telling myself that.

When I woke this morning, I had a pimple the size of a small city in Vermont on my cheek, right dead in the middle. I panicked, picked a fight with Andie, and covered it as well as I could with the little pat of concealer supplied in the travel-pack of makeup.

Sitting in the kitchen eating yogurt, looking at Jean's flat-on-one-side hair, Andie's dandelion fluff, and the little curls at Vin's temples that spoke of night sweats or a hot flash, I thought how little some things had changed since Tonsil Lake. We still sat in the kitchen in our nightclothes, still dreamed of the perfect man—whether we'd had him and lost him, still had him, or were sort of hoping—and still got zits.

Vin

Jean looked terrible this morning. Although we laughed together over David's meeting of her parents and that laughter became outright hilarity when Suzanne and Andie came into the room, I sense that all is not well with her. I am not a particularly intuitive person, but this feeling is as strong as it is frightening.

Because Jean is always all right.

I remember when the measles came to Tonsil Lake. While Andie, Suzanne, and I were in our beds groaning and certain we were near death, Jean was sitting beside the lake, spotted but unbowed. She wrote us stories in her tablet with lined yellow paper that sold for a dime in the store at the end of the lake, and stuffed the folded missives between the cracks in the jalousie windows of our trailers. The stories all centered around the dreams we discussed among ourselves and they all ended with the words "they lived happily ever after."

When the rest of us had recovered from the measles and were once more terrorizing the residents of the lake, Jean was still a little weak. She sat lakeside while we swam and she went in earlier than we did at night. Her case of measles had been every bit as bad as ours, we all figured out later; she had simply refused to give in to it.

I wonder if she's still doing that.

Andie and I worked on her book this morning, fighting over every changed word. It was exhilarating, frustrating, and fun. Afterward, we all walked into the village and ate lunch at the café.

And then I wanted to be alone.

I was startled by that. I've spent so much time alone since Mark's death that I looked forward to the company of my friends, but less than twenty-four hours after we all arrived on the island, I wanted them to disappear for a while. What kind of friend and hostess did that make me?

I was stewing over that question when Jean said, "I think I'm going to spend a little time in that bookstore. I'll be home later."

"I'm going to the pharmacy." Suzanne stroked a finger down her cheek. "I'm sure they have some kind of concealer that comes in a quart jar. Does anyone want me to pick up anything?"

"Not for me," said Andie. "I'm going to the beach. It's been too many years since I've seen an ocean. I know it's thataway, Vin, but is there anything I should know?"

I stopped gaping in order to answer. "I don't think so, but it's rocky getting there and the water's freezing in case you had skinny-dipping in mind. Penobscot Bay has iced up many a mainlander."

"Oh, hell no. I don't know if this fake boob will float." With a grin over her shoulder at the rest of us, she headed toward the sea.

"She already seems better," said Jean, watching her. "She's been so tired since the radiation that it was scary sometimes. It was a good thing, Vin, getting her to come here."

I hoped it would be as good for Jean. For all of us. "Well," I said, "I think I'll walk around town. I haven't been here for a year, so I need to reacquaint myself."

"You'll be okay on your own?"

To my surprise, it was Suzanne who asked the question. I saw concern in her soft brown eyes. It made me swallow hard before I answered.

"Sure. Everything is hard the first time without him, but I think I'm better doing it alone."

"Okay. Just remember you don't have to be." Turning toward the pharmacy, she grabbed Jean's arm. "Come on. I'll drop you off at the bookstore. You want to pick up this week's *People* for me in case they don't have it at the pharmacy?"

I had walked less than a block when I heard someone call my name. Only it wasn't "Vin" or even "Vinnie" I heard, but a loud "Lavinia!" I turned toward the sound just in time to be swept off my feet by a bear of a man, the only person who ever called me by the hated name on my birth certificate. My delighted cry was muffled by Lucas Bishop's faded blue denim shoulder as he scooped me close.

Other than a hug from Jake Logan when we'd had dinner on his last trip to New York, it was the first time I'd been held by a man since Mark had become too ill to do such things. I was a little nonplused that it felt so good, even with his stethoscope gouging me between my breasts.

"When did you get in?" he demanded, pushing me back from him and looking me over with a critical gray eye. "Why didn't you call, how have you been, and how about dinner?"

"I just got in yesterday, I have three friends with me, I've been fine, and dinner will have to wait a few days."

"Oh, well." He stepped to the outside of the boardwalk, stuffed my arm through his, and continued on the way I'd been going. "Three friends, huh?" He stopped momentarily to stare at me with sparkling eyes. "Be still, my aching heart. Not the infamous Tonsil Lake crowd?"

"The very same. And how about you, Dr. Bishop? Still working on that two years?"

Hope Island had sent Lucas to medical school. In return, he had promised to spend his first two years of private practice on the island. Twenty-five years after his return, he's still saying the two years aren't up yet.

89

"Still working on it. Just when I think it's about time to pack it up and move to a city where I can make enough money to buy a house on Hope Island, I have a day off and go out with my brother on his lobster boat and realize I couldn't leave here for that long."

I laughed into his open, handsome face, thinking that it was so nice to look up at someone. God, I sound like Suzanne, but it was. Women who are five-ten in their bare feet don't get to look up very much. "You have a house on Hope Island," I reminded him. "It's next door to ours."

"Well, yeah, but I bought that before mainlanders started figuring out that the island was out here. You may have been the first New Yorkers, Stillson, but you weren't the last. Hell, I'm prescribing as many antidepressants these days as I do plain old blood pressure medication."

"Oh, phooey, as if Prozac consumption was confined to city-dwellers," I scoffed, thumping his arm with the hand that wasn't confined in the crook of his elbow. "Still not married?" I quirked an eyebrow at him, knowing he lived under the speculative eye of every unmarried woman under seventy-five on the island, and a few married ones as well.

"Lavinia!" He looked injured. "You know I'm saving myself for you."

I thumped him again, for calling me Lavinia twice in one day, and maybe for something else I didn't want to identify, then rubbed his arm where I'd hit it. "I hate it, Luke. I want him back."

"I know you do." We had reached the end of the business district of Hope Village—both blocks of it— and we went across the street. "Coffee? There's a new coffee bar here next to the bookstore."

"I just had lunch," I protested, which was, as Jim Croce had described so well in a song, just like spitting into the wind. Within two minutes I found myself sitting on a tall barstool with my sandaled feet hooked into the rungs, sipping an admittedly delicious mug of hazelnut coffee.

Luke looked at me, and for the moment he was as much a doctor as a friend. "But you're better, aren't you?" His hand, large, blunt, and rough and gentle at the same time, reached for mine.

I thought to draw away, but I didn't. Because it felt too good. It was warm and solid and—where his broad thumb rubbed my palm—sexual. Maybe he was right. Maybe I was better.

Chapter Six

Andie

At first, the rocks bothered my feet. My beach time had previously been confined to the white sands of Florida that are like a siren call to so many of us landlocked Hoosiers. Islands off the Maine coast were apparently quite different.

But good. Very good. Forny good.

I couldn't resist the call of the surf, and negotiated the rocks to get to it, only to have my feet frozen so instantly I was afraid they might fall off—and I was damned if I was giving up any more body parts. I beat a hasty retreat, deciding the water would be just as beautiful from a safe distance.

I settled myself on a flat rock that had been partially warmed by the sun, setting my commuter cup of coffee and Jean's latest book beside me. I was wearing so much sunscreen I was pretty sure all my pores were clogged and I was probably going to suffocate, plus a wide-brimmed straw hat from the selection that hung in an artlessly artistic arrangement inside the back door of Vin's house.

The doctors had been so insistent that I avoid the sun's rays that I overcompensated and looked like a bag lady in my plaid cotton pants and long-sleeved shirt, with the hat flopping with gaudy ostentation over the whole ensemble.

Down the rocky shore, far enough that I couldn't determine their gender, two small children played. Chasing waves and then running shrieking away from them, their squeals a kind of music. I remembered Miranda and young Jake on the sand at Pensacola, chasing waves, chasing crabs, chasing their father down so they could bury him in the sand.

Jake Logan had been the very best of fathers. No concern had been too insignificant for him to listen to and try to offer resolution. He had lived in Indianapolis while the kids were still in school, making the two-hour round trip several times a week so that he didn't have to miss ballgames, recitals, or awards nights.

"Why can't Daddy just stay?" Miranda had asked while she was still in junior high, still in love with her father. "You laugh together all the time and you kiss him goodbye every time he leaves and tell him 'for God's sake be careful.' Why can't you be married?"

I'd looked at her, absorbed the fury and the questions in her eyes, and exchanged a helpless look with Jake. I'm not really into helpless looks, but that one came naturally.

"I'm not good at being married, punkin." He stood her in front of him, his hands on her shoulders and his gaze holding hers. "I try to be a good dad, and your mom and I are great friends, but I'm not a good husband at all. I'm a slob, I snore, I forget to call when I'm gonna be late, I never change the tires on the car till the rubber's peeling off."

What a genius he was, giving a twelve-year-old reasons she could understand, reasons that didn't make me into the bad guy. Later on, when both the kids were in high school, they heard some things, and we sat them down at the table in our cluttered dining room and gave them the real explanation. The nitty-gritty.

I don't know what we expected from the kids, but it wasn't what we got. It wasn't Miranda's screams of 'I hate you, How could you, I wish I'd never been born.' It wasn't young Jake's sullen silence, his shaking off of his father's hand from his shoulder, his retreat into his room and the bag of pot he didn't even try to hide when I confronted him.

Jake had aged before my eyes, the toll taken on his mind and heart as great as the price later demanded of my body by cancer.

"I'll leave them alone," he promised when he left the shaken-to-its-soul house that night. "They've lost who they thought their father was. They need to grieve."

"No, you won't," I said. "They haven't lost a thing except some of their innocence." I hugged him hard. "Call this week just like you always do. Come to Jake's game. You're still their dad." I was crying. So was he. "For God's sake, be careful."

It hadn't been that easy, of course, but I've learned that there's truth to the axiom that worthwhile things seldom are.

Our children were good kids, raised with values that fell somewhere between Tonsil Lake and Jake's suburban Indianapolis roots. Eventually, they came around, and life went on. Ob-la-di, ob-la-da.

Suddenly new grief welled up to combine with old, creating a maelstrom of emotion that stuck in my chest like a rock with tentacles, heavy and constricting at the same time. I remembered the times during my illness when fear would come up the same way, squeezing and choking.

"Breathe deep," Jean would say. "You're not alone. Even if we're not in the room, we're always here. Breathe deep."

A few deep-breathing exercises later, I sipped my forgotten coffee and frowned toward the horizon. I was spending more time thinking about my ex-husband than I was about Paul Lindquist. What in the hell did that mean?

"Are you stuck to that rock, like some large plaid barnacle?" a voice called from behind me.

"Hi, Suzanne." I looked over my shoulder. "You coming up here?"

"Unless it's your own private rock."

She was wearing a brilliant turquoise bikini and looking like a million bucks in it. There's something wrong with that, I swear. She doesn't even have any stretch marks, at least none that I could see.

"Come on up," I said, "but if anyone comes along and thinks I'm your mother, I'm shoving you into the drink."

She slipped her *People* magazine—complete with an underdressed starlet on the cover—under Jean's book and crawled onto the rock, managing to look graceful as she did it.

Her nail polish matched the bikini. "Do you have any plaid polish?" I asked, gesturing at her turned-up toes. "Maybe you could get me as color coordinated as you are."

She grinned. "Smartass."

"I try."

We sat in companionable silence for a few minutes, then she said, "So, what about Paul Lindquist?"

I gave her a look, one I'd practiced on my kids and perfected on recalcitrant chefs in my restaurant days. It generally worked. "What about him?"

"Is he good in bed?"

Well, it worked on anyone who hadn't grown up on Tonsil Lake, anyway. I intensified it, glowering at her from under the shade of my hat. "Why?" I said. "Thinking of trying him out?"

I was sorry the instant I said it, but she appeared not to notice that my bitchiness was more overt than usual. She just kept looking at the horizon, her blue-tipped toes raising and lowering on the rock.

"I talked to Jake last night," she said.

"Did you? How is he?" I kept my voice even.

"Fine. He said if he had to come east while we were out here, he might come to the island. Just for a day, you know, not to encroach on Vin's hospitality. Is that all right with you?"

"Of course." *Oh, Suzanne, stop now. Don't go there.*

"Andie?"

Oh, hell. "Yeah?"

"Would you mind if I started seeing Jake? I mean really seeing him."

Damn you, Jake, you sonofabitch. You could have prevented this. Why didn't you tell her? Now it's up to me, and that's not fair.

But when I opened my mouth, the ugly words wouldn't come out. I sat in silence for a minute, looking at my own bare toes. When I answered, the words I did say weren't right, either. Not really.

"Yes," I said quietly, looking at her until she met my gaze, "I'd mind, Suzanne. I'd mind it a lot."

Jean

I love bookstores, especially small independent ones like the one on Hope Island. I've learned not to visit them when I'm shopping with anyone else, because no one seems to understand that it takes more than fifteen minutes to buy one book and scan the spines, back cover copy, and teaser pages of hundreds more.

The romance section was in the back, as it often is, but the shelves were well kept and my last book was displayed with its front cover out. I picked up a copy, remembering when I used to run out and buy one the first day a new book hit the stores.

"She's very good." A woman with a duster in her hand and a nametag identifying her as "Meg" pointed at the book, the feathers from the duster tossing little dust motes into the air. "Oh, sorry." She tucked the duster under her arm.

"Thank you very much." I extended a hand. "I'm Jean O'Toole. Would you like me to sign the copies you have?"

"That would be very nice." She shook my hand, and we exchanged the usual pleasantries. Then she said, "Actually, you can do more than sign these."

"Oh?" I looked up from the book I held.

"Yes. I wonder if we could have a book-signing with you while you're on the island, if you're free. Vin's always kept us up on when your next one's coming out, so we feel rather as though you're an islander-by-adoption. We have several customers who would be thrilled."

"Vin's done that?" I was touched. I knew she read my books, that they all did, but I had always thought

Vin looked down on them from behind her desk at Gunderson's, where even the mention of a romantic novel caused lips to curl in disdain.

"Oh, yes." Meg smiled. "She's very proud of you." A look of compassion crossed her face. "We've missed her since her husband died. It's good that she's back." She placed the signed books on a table with the titles on this week's *best-seller* lists, which is probably the closest I'll ever get to them. "So, would you mind?"

"Not at all. I'd be pleased."

That wasn't strictly true; I hated book-signings. Sitting there at a table while people walk past you with pitying looks or queries as to where they can find the most recent Stephen King blockbuster is not exactly an ego-builder. But having Vin tell people about my books was.

When I walked past the French doors that led into the coffee bar adjoining the bookstore, I saw Vin sitting at one of the high tables. I started to go through the doors, then noticed she wasn't alone. A large man with a thick mane of silver hair sat across from her, and he was holding her hand. I stepped away from the doors, going to hide in the sports section, where I found David a book on Maine golf courses.

When I left the bookstore, I walked back to the house slowly. My stomach was hurting again.

I took some antacid and put on my bathing suit, then headed for the beach, wearing flip-flops to negotiate the stony path. I saw Andie in navy blue plaid sitting on a rock and raised my arm in greeting.

"Come on up," she said when I got closer. "You won't look as good climbing up here as Suzanne did, but you're welcome."

I grabbed her extended hand and scrabbled up, then looked around, squinting. "Where is she? You haven't drowned her, have you?"

"No, but she's mad." Andie sighed, looking off into the distance. "And the hell of it is I don't blame her."

"Why? What did you do?"

She answered my questions with one of her own. "Jean, is there anything that would make you leave David?"

That's when I found out that while it's one thing to have hurt, rebellious ideas of getting a divorce, it's something else again when someone asks you what would make you get one. You have to think about it then.

"If he fell in love with someone else," I said, "or if he turned on the children or became abusive."

"What if he were unfaithful again?"

"I don't know." I shrugged. "I never thought I'd stay the first time, but I did, and I've never been sorry." Unhappy sometimes, unforgiving sometimes, bitter sometimes, but not sorry. Not really.

"What if you knew you still loved him, but you just couldn't...oh, shit, what am I trying to say?" Andie slapped a hand against the cover of the book beside her.

I waited, my stomach twisting. Andie was never at a loss for words. What she had to say wasn't always appropriate, and if you happened to be on the receiving end of her anger, it might not be too pleasant, but there was never silence created by her uncertainty.

The antacid wasn't working yet, I was starting to wonder if I'd been lying to myself about not being sorry I'd stayed married, and I didn't need stress on top of indigestion and pointless self-examination. "I don't know," I said sharply. "What *are* you trying to say?"

She shot me a surprised look, then returned her attention to the surf. "Forget it. It's nothing."

"I'm sorry," I said immediately. See? This is why I can't confront people; I always end up feeling bad. "Come on, Andie, give. What's bothering you and why is Suzanne mad?"

"She asked if I'd mind if she started seeing Jake and I said I would."

"You would?"

Andie and Jake had been apart for twenty years, since Miranda was eight and young Jake, six. They were the friendliest divorced people I knew, but I didn't think they still had that kind of connection.

In truth, though, Andie had been closemouthed about the divorce from the very beginning. Even the day it was final, when she drove down to Lewis Point, she didn't talk about it as we all sat in my back yard watching the kids play in the pool.

What had we talked about that day?

I didn't mean to say the words aloud, but I must have, because Andie said, "Crabgrass, mascara, and was it true Suzanne was the only girl in first grade who wore a bra."

"She wasn't. Cindy Hathaway wore one." Vin spoke from behind us. "Scoot over, Andie. You're hogging."

Wearing a black maillot, a tote bag over her shoulder, she joined us on the rock, grabbing our arms to pull herself up. "Of course," she said, "Cindy was twelve, I believe, by the time welfare figured out her folks had never sent her to school."

"Nine," I corrected. "Poor thing. I wonder what ever happened to her."

"I don't know. They left the lake a couple of years later." Andie grinned wickedly. "I think Cindy was pregnant."

We laughed guiltily. "We're being mean," I protested. "She couldn't help the way she was."

"She beat the hell out of every other girl on the lake, plus both the Henderson girls from the farm down the road," Andie argued. "She could help that."

Vin gave her arm a swat. "You're just mad because she beat you up, too, and you had to spend all summer making everyone else afraid of you again."

"Well, there is that."

Suzanne walked down the beach toward us and we stopped talking to watch her. Wearing a bikini and with her hair pulled up into a high ponytail, she looked gorgeous.

"It would serve her right," said Vin, "if she woke up with another zit tomorrow, right on the end of her nose. No one should look that good at our age."

Vin looked pretty great herself, but I knew what she meant. Suzanne had never lost her youthfulness. The rest of us had. The thought crossed my mind that we had grown up in ways she had not, but fortunately the memory of cleaning up Kate Rivers' yard in our pajamas, even though Suzanne was sealing the casket on her marriage, stopped me from voicing it.

She climbed up onto the rock with us and settled herself beside Vin with her back against mine.

"Now that we're all here..." Vin opened her tote bag. She pulled out a bottle of wine and four glasses.

When we all held full glasses, Andie squinted at

hers. "I don't believe I've ever drunk from actual leaded crystal while sitting on a rock."

"No, we always drank our Kool-Aid from the glasses peanut butter used to come in," I remembered.

"And we made toasts," said Suzanne, her voice soft. "To our dreams. Remember?"

"And to each other," said Vin.

"And to the republic," said Andie, "for which it stands."

Suzanne

I don't know what I thought Andie was going to say, but that she'd mind me seeing Jake wasn't it. At first I was mad—after all, hadn't she gone to the senior prom with the guy I'd dated the entire first semester?

Then I was hurt. It wasn't as though I were planning to marry Jake, for God's sake. I just...liked him. A lot. Okay, a whole lot. He made me feel hopeful. Who understood more about hope than Andie? But maybe she only cared about it for herself.

Rather than say something I'd be sorry for later, an unfortunate habit of mine, I mumbled something about taking a walk and jumped off the rock.

It's hard to walk very far on a beach with your stomach sucked in, so when I got out of sight of Andie's perch, I found a seat of my own and sat down to feel sorry for myself. Children played in the sand around me, their mothers watching them with eagle eyes, and I remembered when Jean, Andie, and I had sat around Jean's pool in Willow Wood Estates and watched ours.

The kids had been so cute, all seven of them born in a four-year time-span. Now they were grown and I didn't know where the time had gone. Miranda had been a godsend to her mother during Andie's illness, and young Jake had made her laugh when no one else could. Even Jean's kids had helped. Carrie and Kelly brought meals and Josh and Laurie came and just sat by her bed when she was too sick to do much more than lie there.

Sarah had sent her a get-well card with a note in it after I'd called her in tears, certain Andie was going to die. Although she hadn't had any sympathy to spare for me, I was glad my daughter had given some to Andie.

I hadn't heard from Tom in months. I didn't even know where he was.

I hadn't been with a man since a relationship with an ad executive from Indianapolis had fizzled last winter and the only one I was interested in had been declared off-limits by his ex-wife.

My job, my career, the one thing in my life I was proud of, was going to hell in a hand basket.

And I had a forny zit.

After awhile, bored with my own admittedly crummy company, I headed back toward Vin's house. I approached the flat rock where I'd sat with Andie earlier and saw that all three of the girls were on it now. I stopped for a minute, my feet in the freezing shallows, and watched them.

How splendid-looking they all were. Vin with her sophisticated New York looks, Jean all neatness and sweet smiles, Andie with her dandelion fluff hair and eyes like shining blue pieces of the sea in her thin face.

I wanted to cry, no longer because I felt sorry for myself—though I still did—but because I was so happy to have those women in my life.

I climbed back up on the rock.

We stayed down there for over an hour, sipping wine and laughing loud and often. It wasn't over between Andie and me yet, but if it came right down to it, her friendship probably meant more to me than dating her ex-husband did, so we'd just have to see what happened.

"Who's going to cook tonight?" asked Vin.

"You are," said Andie. "You had the bright idea to bring those damned cookbooks. You should be the first one to use them."

Vin frowned. "Well, if I'm cooking, I say we walk down to the harbor and have lobster."

With a heavy sigh, Jean pushed herself off the rock. "Fine. I guess I can do the dishes."

For some reason, that struck us all funny, and we laughed all the way to the house, shoving each other off the path and working our usual way into bladder jokes. Which aren't really jokes anymore but we laugh at them anyway.

There were messages on the answering machine at the house. David for Jean. Paul for Andie. Kelly for Jean. Marian Nielson for Vin. Jake for me.

Andie and I looked at each other. She smiled, just a slight tilt of her lips. "Tell him I said hello."

Vin

I never would have thought one could get into the habit of rising before dawn. Even for a self-professed morning person, five o'clock is borderline ridiculous. Nevertheless, it's when I'm getting up these days.

Usually Jean's already up, sitting at the kitchen table with coffee, her laptop, and a bottle of antacid. When I suggested that a little less coffee might mean a little less white chalky stuff, she gave me a distracted look and said, "Good. You want to warm mine up?"

I wasn't sure what she thought she'd heard me say, but I refilled her cup anyway, feeling like an accessory to a crime.

Andie's always the next one up. You don't say much to her in the morning unless you want to have your head bitten off. "Good God, Andie," I said this morning, cowering behind the refrigerator door, "if you hate mornings so much, why don't you sleep in?"

"Leave her alone, Vin," Jean mumbled, staring at her computer screen. "It's the only fun she has."

"Bitch," said Andie.

Jean gave her a sidewise look. "Scum of the earth."

"Slut."

"Tramp."

"Dick licker."

If anyone else had said that to Jean, she would have lapsed into hurt silence, her bottom lip stuck out in just the slightest of pouts. When Andie said it, she only gave her a pitying look. "Really, Andie, you're going to have to do better than that."

"Give me some time." Andie sat down, holding her coffee cup in both hands, warming them against the morning chill that finds its way to Maine even in June. "It's early yet."

Suzanne wandered down when we were midway through the second pot of coffee. With murmured good mornings, she poured herself some and sat in the remaining chair. She tucked a foot up on the seat— which I'm not sure I can do anymore—and began painting her toenails a shiny plum color.

When she was finished, Andie asked acidly, "Do you have a purple bikini?"

"No. Purple shorts. Give me your foot."

"Oh, shit."

But she stuck her foot out, and Suzanne took it in her lap. "Grab me the lotion off the sink, will you, Vin?"

We all walked down to the village for breakfast with purple toenails sticking out of our sandals. Our feet had been lubricated and massaged and our cuticles trimmed. The whole thing had felt wonderful.

Halfway there, I stopped walking and hugged Suzanne. "Thank you," I said.

Jean gave her a squeeze. "Me, too."

Andie said, "Give me a break."

"I already have," said Suzanne. "I haven't killed you yet." She gave Andie a pat. "But I'll make sure your nails look real pretty in your coffin."

Jean snorted, which got us all started. We were standing in the path with our legs crossed, howling with inappropriately loud laughter, when a male voice called, "There they are, visions of feminine pulchritude, the girls from Tonsil Lake."

Before I could answer Lucas, Andie said, "Well, no, it's actually the Weak Bladder Society of Hope Island," and off we went again.

"You know what's bad," said Jean, leaning against me and wiping her eyes on the tail of her shirt, "is that Toby is into potty jokes right now and I keep telling him they're not nice. I'll never be able to look my grandson in the eye again."

When we had settled down and Suzanne's hand was clamped over Andie's mouth to keep her from setting us off again, I introduced Lucas. I saw speculation coming into Jean's eyes. She exchanged a furtive but significant look with the others, and I felt like smacking all of them.

"Would you like to join us for breakfast?" asked Suzanne.

"I don't know." Lucas's gaze was on me. "Is that all right with you?"

What would he think of Suzanne's obvious flirtation? Would he be attracted to it or would he pity her efforts to stay young? Would he be repelled by Andie's raucous humor, uncomfortable with Jean's eagerness to please?

Mark had liked my friends only one at a time and in very small doses, preferring that I visit them on my own when I went to Indiana to see my mother. It had been one of those little sore places that seem to find their way into every marriage. I'd put it into a mental folder with my inability to be in the same room with his two children without wanting to scream, and tried to leave it there.

But Mark had been my husband. Why did I care what Lucas Bishop thought? He was only a summertime friend, not someone I lived with and loved, even if I did allow him to call me Lavinia.

"Of course you should join us," I said, taking his arm, "and you should buy our breakfast, too."

He exchanged a twinkling look of shock with Suzanne. "All of you? I'm just a simple island doctor who still gets paid with lobsters and blueberry pie, when he gets paid at all."

Andie shook her head. "Forget it, Doctor. No one's buying it."

Breakfast was as usual. Andie had forgotten her medication, which earned her a scolding from Jean, and

Suzanne was obsessing over the two pounds she'd gained. Jean mentioned needing another bottle of antacid and I went into a little tirade of my own concerning her dependence on it, subsiding in embarrassment when everyone stopped talking and stared at me.

Just then, Meg from the bookstore stopped by our table and, after greeting everyone, proceeded to discuss Jean's book-signing which was to take place this coming Saturday. Something Jean had neglected to mention.

When Meg left, there was silence at the table. Suzanne, Andie, and I all favored Jean with an accusing stare that should have shriveled her up right where she sat. Lucas's eyes danced between the four of us, a look of expectancy on his face. "I'll watch the clock for you if you want to go at it," he offered.

We ignored him.

"My goodness," Andie drawled, "one would think she was ashamed of us, wouldn't one? I mean, after all, we might show up at her autograph party with tobacco on our teeth, saying 'ain't' and spitting on the floor."

"Shut up, Andie," Jean muttered, her face red. Jean didn't blush well, and her skin looked mottled. It served her right. "You know that's not true."

"Do we?" Suzanne's voice was a little high, and the red spots on her cheeks were becoming. Her eyes were wide and bright. "You never even mention your signings till they're over."

Jean tossed me a beseeching look, and I lifted my shoulders in a shrug. I wasn't even going to examine the thoughts I'd had an hour earlier when I introduced them to Lucas. This was Jean, not me. She had spent a morning—with Suzanne—cleaning a neighbor's yard in her pajamas with her hair looking like a fright wig. I would have called and hired a cleaning crew, anonymously and on the spot, but I doubt I'd have gone myself.

"You don't understand—" Jean began patiently.

"You got that right." Andie sipped her coffee, her blue eyes glaring over the top of the thick restaurant cup.

"They're boring, is all," said Jean. She looked down at her plate, which she'd hardly touched. "You sit there and people come by and say things like 'when are you going to write a real book?' and 'do you know John Grisham?' and then they don't buy your book. You smile till your cheeks shake and you apologize to the store manager because you've screwed up her entire day and only sold six books."

"Oh, Jean, you've done better than that," Andie scoffed.

"Sometimes, yes, especially when I've signed right there in Lewis Point. I guess the thing is that writers are supposed to have thick skins, because rejection is such an inherent part of the business, but you know me." She laughed, an entirely unconvincing sound. "I get my feelings hurt if the clouds obscure the moon; imagine what it does to me when no one wants to buy my book."

"I still don't understand why you don't tell us," said Suzanne. "We'd at least be a support group."

"Yeah," said Andie, "we're good at that."

"Because I'm always the strong one," said Jean, and none of us disagreed with her. "I don't want you to see me being rejected and embarrassed." She laughed again, sounding a little more like herself. "It's bad enough you're seeing me being embarrassed now."

"Do David and the kids come to them?" I asked. I'd been at book-signings that were attended by the author's entire extended family as well as every friend she or he'd had since kindergarten. I'd also been at ones like those Jean described.

"No. They did the first one I ever had, of course, but not since then. I've asked David not to come and I don't tell the children until they're over. They don't like it, either," she admitted, "but it's the easiest way for me to cope with it."

Lucas said, "I hope you don't mind if I come and bring my sister-in-law. If I don't, she might never let me go out on their lobster boat again and that's about my favorite thing to do."

"I'd be pleased if you would," said Jean. She passed a warning look around at the other three of us. "But not you. You stay away."

Chapter Seven

Suzanne

I'm worried about Tom. More than usual, I mean. Sarah hasn't heard from him in nearly a month, his father in longer than that. Trent has pretty much thrown up his hands when it comes to his only child, but he still grows concerned when a period of time has gone by with no contact just like I do.

I told Jake about my concern. He said, "Let me check with young Jake. Unless his mother already has?"

When I said I hadn't talked to Andie about it, Jake hung up and called me back a half hour later.

"He saw him a few weeks ago, Suzy-Q. He said he was pretty messed up."

The sympathy in his voice had tears rolling down my cheeks in a heartbeat. "I swear," I said, sniffing, "it was easier when he was in jail. At least I knew where he was."

I called Sarah back to tell her young Jake had seen her brother.

"I knew that," she said, "but it doesn't help us to know where he is now."

"How did you know? And why didn't you tell me?" I probably sounded accusing, but I couldn't believe Sarah's dislike of me went deep enough that she would withhold information about Tom just to hurt me.

111

"I knew because Lo told me—young Jake, I mean—and I didn't tell you because I didn't want you asking questions about him and me." She sighed. "Also because it would just make you worry more. Tommy was in pretty bad shape."

"That's what Jake said."

"Are you seeing him? Old Jake?"

I didn't like the reference to him as old, though I guessed that was no different than referring to his twenty-six year old son as young. "Sort of."

"Mother, maybe..." She stopped.

I waited, looking down at a crescent-shaped chip in a nail, then said, "Maybe what?"

"Maybe you shouldn't."

"Why not?" I reached for a cotton swab and the nail polish remover, holding the phone between my ear and my shoulder. "It's just a good time, Sarah. Nothing serious."

"Does Andie know?"

I could feel myself blushing and turned my back on the bathroom mirror. "She knows."

"What does she say?"

"Well, she's not happy about it, but—"

"Never mind. I understand." Her voice was flat and bitter. "You're only concerned about other people's happiness as long as it doesn't interfere with yours. What made me think you could change?" She hung up with an abrupt "goodbye."

I disconnected the phone and laid it down and began to fix my fingernail. It would only take a minute and then they'd all be perfect. I needed to repair my makeup, too, because I'd cried when I talked to Jake. Where were my cosmetics? Andie made such a mess in here I couldn't find anything when I wanted it. Jean's book-signing is tomorrow and I will need to help her with her makeup.

Sarah, Sarah, Sarah. Oh, for God's sake, my hands were shaking. *Oh, Tommy, where are you? Sarah, what have I done to make you hate me so?* The questions kept hammering. But I couldn't listen to them. I needed...

I opened the door to the medicine cabinet, holding the newly polished nail away from the others. Surely there was something in here that would help take the edge off, silence the questions for a while. I knew I had some left. I had only been taking one a day, just as the prescription said, so I knew there was another two-week supply in the bottle.

Well, not quite that many. I looked at the bottle of antidepressants in consternation, trying to remember if I had doubled up on other days.

Tommy, please call. It's okay if you need money. I don't mind, really I don't.

The bathroom door opened. "Suzanne, are you in here? I knocked, but you didn't answer."

Vin looked down at the bottle in my hand, then at me. I saw an expression cross her face that looked horribly like pity, and her green eyes went dark. "Don't," she said. "Don't."

Andie

We've been here two weeks now, and I feel better than I have for a couple of years. I find it odd that I am not homesick for the house where I have lived for fifteen years, or even for my kids and grandkids.

"I don't miss mine, either," said Jean when I mentioned this. "I think it's because they're always inside us, wherever we are. And our children are grownups now. We don't see them every day."

Which is a mushy thought but probably accurate.

I don't really miss Paul that much, either, though I enjoy talking to him when he calls. It will be interesting to see if this relationship develops into what I've avoided ever since divorcing Jake. If it does, I'm going to have to explore a whole bunch of mind and emotion things, which exhausts me just thinking about it.

That book business is going along just fine. Vin tells me what she wants, I bitch at her, then I do it. I can't say I want to spend the rest of my life doing it the way Jean does, but it's certainly an interesting diversion.

It reminds me of exercise. When it's new and different, you kind of enjoy it, but once you find out it takes real discipline and makes you sweat in the bargain, it's not near as much fun.

We spend a lot of time on the beach, both together and separately. It will be hard to go back to being landlocked. We've always laughed about moving back to Tonsil Lake in our retirement days and I must admit the idea doesn't sound as ridiculous as it once did.

Although we all avoid going there during daylight hours, I did make a lonely trek there when I first got sick, driving around the lake, past the church and cemetery, all with my hands white-knuckled on the steering wheel. When I looked at the lake, it was as though I could see—but of course I couldn't.

The trailers are gone except for a couple of doublewides that have been put on permanent foundations, and everything looks pretty respectable these days. One end of the lake doesn't have any houses at all, just trees and well-tended grass. The other has the pub and the general store that has been there since we were kids, though it looks better now.

The trees have matured and given the whole area a park-like look. The road to it has been improved enough that it's much easier to get to. If you're there about twilight and you squint a little, it's downright pretty back there.

One morning last week, while we were having coffee, Suzanne said, "I think we should have a question a day that we all have to answer and we have to tell the truth."

We are all enjoying it here, but to Suzanne it's one long slumber party. I didn't want to answer a question a day, but when Suzanne wanted to know why not, I didn't know how to tell her it was because I didn't want to talk to her about Jake. Which, knowing Suzanne, would probably be Thursday's question, as in, "What kind of attachment do you have to former relationships in your life?"

At any rate, I got voted down, which I should be used to after forty-some years of knowing these women, and as much as I hate to admit it, the questions have been fun.

We now know that Jean's all-time favorite book is *Little Women*, Vin's is *Gone With the Wind*—which surprised the hell out of me, Suzanne's is *The Price of Pride*, which Jean wrote. We all accused Suzanne of sucking up, but then she listed a whole bunch of really good reasons why it was her favorite. Tickled Jean to death and shut Vin and me right up.

My favorites are Sue Grafton's alphabet mysteries, which only recently replaced the Nancy Drew books in my reading heart. I like knowing what I'm getting when I open a book.

The next day, the question was favorite movies. After breakfast, we went to the video store and rented them all, and as soon as we got in from the beach that afternoon we made popcorn and started watching them. We never had supper, which was good because it was my night to cook.

I'm pretty sure Jean got sick in the middle of the night, but she was okay in the morning. I really wish she'd gone to see Carolyn Murphy before we came here.

Lucas Bishop comes around occasionally. Not enough to get in our way or to dilute the all-girl atmosphere, just enough so that we've all gotten to know him. He's a truly nice guy, I think—like David and Paul and Jake are nice guys, but different, too. He's in love with Vin and I think everyone knows it but her.

I can see Jean missing David when Lucas is around. This pleases me, because theirs is the only true love story that I'm sure of and I know she's been less than happy for the past year or so. Although this worries me for her sake, it worries me for my own, too, because I need a happily ever after story to believe in.

Curiously enough, Lucas's presence doesn't make me miss Paul. I think maybe I've spent too much time alone. Now that I've finally allowed him into my life, I want him to stay there; I'm just not sure how far in I want him to be. Oh, hell, I think this boob that looks seventeen has affected my mind and made part of it seventeen, too.

I'm not sure how Suzanne feels, which is curious, too, because she's the original wearer of her heart on her sleeve. I know she talks to Jake almost daily, but he's a subject I avoid and I hope she does, too. She doesn't look good today. The face that is always all light seems to be in shadow. I touched her shoulder as I walked by, and she clutched my hand for a moment.

Jean's book-signing is today. She was in a real flutter all morning. She hadn't brought any suitable clothes, her hair needed cutting, and she was almost out of that antacid crap she takes all the time again.

Vin brought out this thing that looked like a wadded-up sheet, but when Jean put it on, it was a white gauze dress with a scoop neck and little cap sleeves. It was probably calf-length on Vin, but it went to Jean's ankles and looked like that was exactly what it was supposed to do. Suzanne did her hair, makeup, and nails and she looked great, if a little thin.

I scrounged in my suitcase and found the abalone necklace and earrings I'd bought with the vague idea of giving them to Miranda. I carried them into the kitchen and thrust them at her. "Here," I said. "If you don't like them, don't worry about it."

But she put them right on and they completed the outfit perfectly. I felt like an idiot because it made me so happy, but when I looked at Vin and Suzanne I saw that they were beaming, too. And Jean looked a little less anxious, sliding her thumb over the smooth setting of the necklace and smiling at her reflection in the mirror Suzanne had set on the kitchen table.

Fine, so we're all idiots. I don't care.

Jean checked her leather attaché for business cards, bookmarks, and flyers, lifted her chin, and went to the back door. "Remember," she said, "you're not to come. I'll be fine."

"You bet," I answered.

"Break a leg, sweetie," said Suzanne.

Vin just smiled and waved. "See you later."

We crowded together at the windows in the door and watched her until she was out of sight.

"Okay," said Vin. "I'm going to the dock. Andie, you're checking with the florist. Suzanne, what are you doing?"

Suzanne rolled her eyes. "Calling the photographer at the *Island Voice*, although I don't know how she could forget since we've called her almost every day."

I looked up at the clock. "Should we synchronize our watches?" I asked, grinning.

Vin didn't miss a beat. "Andie, you're such a bitch."

Jean

Sometimes I am so ridiculous. I didn't want David to come to my book-signing at the island store, but when he said he couldn't come to Maine this weekend, it hurt my feelings.

We haven't seen each other for two weeks, although I've written him four letters and he's written me two and we've talked every day. We haven't been apart for this long since his early days with the company, when his superiors thought nothing of sending him away for weeks on end.

It's so different being apart now than it was then. I can remember preparing his favorite dinner no matter what time his flight was due in, sending the kids to Andie's or Suzanne's for the night, and meeting him at the door in something sexy. Although I never wrapped myself in plastic wrap or aluminum foil the way I've read about, I wore about everything else. I'd fly into his arms like a love-starved woman—which I was—and we'd invariably have a long evening of good food and even better sex.

I don't think I'd fly into his arms now, though a part of me would be very glad to see him. I'm ready for some sex, and he's the only one I want to have it with, but there's no sense of urgency.

It's as though this sojourn has given me a look inside myself, a closer look than I've ever taken, and what I've seen is a murky impression of David's wife, the kids' mother and grandmother, and the strong one of the Tonsil Lake girls. Surely there is more to me than that.

It was David's wife who always flew into his arms when he came home, near tears with the relief of having him back. I think Jean stood back a little, wondering if he was really glad to be home, wondering if he'd been unfaithful again and terrified of finding out, wondering what she would do if she ever didn't have him.

Here on the island, I am Jean. I am going to a book-signing this afternoon in a gauzy white dress that feels heavenly, with silver and blue jewelry that is warm against my skin, and as scared to death as I was the first time. But now I am scared for myself, not that I will disappoint or embarrass anyone else.

My kids went through a time in junior high school when they were very uncomfortable with what I did. They didn't want to answer the leering questions about how their mother researched love scenes or did she pose for those lurid book covers. I told them just to tell everyone she didn't do anything different; she stayed home and kept house and drove in carpools, and that is what they did.

At a dinner party once, I learned that none of David's associates knew about the books when I mentioned one in passing. After they knew, they were curious—respectfully so at that—but I demurred talking about it. I'd seen the look in David's blue eyes and knew the pride he'd professed to have in me was only lip service. He'd been ashamed to tell his friends what I did.

That left one of those scars that never completely heal over.

But today, walking by myself on the path that leads to the island village, I will not think about that. I will not care about it. I am going to sign the books I have put my heart and soul into writing.

Because that's who I am. Jean O'Toole, romance novelist.

Vin

"What if we've done the wrong thing?" I stood with my hand on the ornate handle of the bookstore door. "What if she never talks to us again? What if this makes her stomach worse?"

Andie shrugged. "We'll tell her it was all my fault. She expects such things of me and, besides, I owe her one for sending you that damned book."

"We won't find out any younger." Suzanne opened the door.

It was a madhouse. Islanders and tourists were all over the bookstore and spilling into the coffee bar next door.

"Oh, Vin, isn't this wonderful?" Meg inched around a cluster of customers to greet us. "She's so gracious, and we've already sold out of every book of hers in the store, including the ones I special ordered.

She's up there signing bookmarks, bookplates, and napkins from the coffee bar. Plus, she's recommending all kinds of books to everyone and they're buying them. The flowers you sent are just beautiful. The people from the *Voice* are here now."

"She sold out?" asked a male voice.

"Yes, sir. I'm sorry. But she'll sign a bookplate for you." Meg beamed past my shoulder and I exchanged grins with Andie and Suzanne.

"That's okay." He walked past us. "I have a copy already."

We followed, skulking along in his wake. Jean was talking to the reporter, her face and voice animated. I was so happy for her I could feel tears burning at the backs of my eyes. I heard Suzanne sniff behind me and knew I wasn't alone in that.

The man in front of us spoke. "Excuse me. Could I get this signed?"

Jean's cry of "David!" brought the whole store to a standstill.

A moment later, the *Voice* photographer was snapping pictures of the most passionate reunion the island had seen since the end of the Vietnam War, when Lucas's brother Zeke had come home minus one eye. His eighteen-year-old wife had met him at the wharf.

"This is our boat that you've bought for us," Maggie told him. "It will support our family and it's a good place for a second honeymoon, especially since you shipped out before we got to have a first."

Zeke swept his bride into his arms and carried her onto the boat. The picture still hangs in various places on the Island, including Lucas's office.

Once they figured out this was another happy

occasion, the occupants of the store burst into applause, and we joined them.

I felt an arm come around my waist and looked up at Lucas. "If that's not her husband," he murmured in my ear, the vibration of his voice tickling, "the island's got the biggest soap opera on its hands since that one filmed a storyline here in the eighties. We all came to a standstill at one o'clock every day to watch it."

I laughed. "No such luck, he's her husband. For almost thirty years. Come on, I'll introduce you."

The men shook hands, but David kept his arm around Jean the whole time.

"I thought you weren't going to be able to make it this weekend," said Lucas.

"No, I wasn't coming because Jeannie never wants me to come to her signings. Then Andie gets on the phone and says"—he raised his voice into a falsetto—"'Jesus Christ, David, when are you going to stop listening to what she says and listen to what she means?' After that, I knew I was in trouble no matter what I did, so I figured I'd rather be in trouble with Jean than without her." He brushed a kiss over the top of her head.

Jean gave the three of us a mock threatening look. "I thought I told you not to come, either."

"It was Andie's fault," said Suzanne instantly.

"She made us do it," I added, sounding as righteous as I could.

"Well, to punish you, I'll cook dinner," said Jean, "even though it's not my night."

We all beamed at each other, and I'm sure my expression was as self-congratulatory as Andie's and Suzanne's. This was our Jean. The nurturer had only needed her self-confidence restored a bit.

"After this, the star's going to cook?" Lucas looked around at the people still milling throughout the store. "Doesn't sound right to me. How about if everyone comes over to my house about six and we'll have lobster?"

He didn't understand; the star *wanted* to cook.

Then I looked at Jean's face. No, she didn't, and who did we think we were? I could feel my cheeks burning. *Jesus Christ, when are you going to stop listening to what she says and listen to what she means?*

"That sounds great," said David. "Anything I can do to help?"

"Sure can. You can walk right down to the market with me and help me choose the screamers. You any good on the grill? We could do some steaks, too. Have us a real saint-and-sinner supper. We can buy salads from the deli and put them onto real dishes, and no one will know we didn't slave all afternoon over them."

David's smile went from Jean around to the three of us. "Work for you?"

"Absolutely," I said. "We'll bring the wine and the scintillating company. Will that do?"

"Perfect," said Lucas.

We watched shamelessly as David and Jean exchanged a lingering kiss. Then the men left the store.

"I don't know about this," said Suzanne.

Andie frowned at her. "Don't know about what?"

"Jean and Vin both have dates. Back in high school, we wouldn't have dreamed of encroaching on their privacy. We'd have sat at home and been afraid our social lives were over forever." She sounded so serious, then her shadowed brown eyes lit with laughter and she grinned at Jean and me. "Too bad for you two we're not in high school anymore."

Chapter Eight

Andie

We were all going to wear dresses we'd bought on the island, shapeless floaty things that were slit thigh-high on the sides. We were quiet as we got ready, and I wondered if our slumber party atmosphere had ended with David's arrival. Even though I'd teased Suzanne about it, I'd loved it, too, that camaraderie that seems to exist only between women.

But now David was here. He would sleep in Jean's room tonight, so none of us could barge in and sit on her bed to talk or borrow clothes because she was the only one who kept up with her laundry.

In the morning, would he suggest that Jean go home with him? Would she go? It would still be fun with only the three of us, but not the same. We would miss her steadying presence, her unexpectedly wicked sense of humor, the tapping of her fingertips on her laptop at all times of the day and night.

We would miss her cooking, too—her meals were the only palatable ones we ate here in the house—but that didn't matter. I hoped she knew that didn't matter.

We met in the kitchen in varying stages of readiness. Suzanne was pulling her hair into a high, sideways ponytail and I was still looking for the thongs that protected my feet from the rocks on the paths when Jean said, "Oh, poop, we forgot."

Vin looked up from where she was kneeling before the wine rack. "Forgot what?"

"The question of the day. We haven't had it. Whose turn is it?"

"Mine." Vin was still for a moment, her hand on the edge of the counter for balance. Finally, she straightened, bringing two bottles of wine up with her. She turned so that her eyes met ours in turn. "Do you think people actually get second chances, or do you think if your first chance runs out you're just out of luck?"

We all had to think about that one. Suzanne braided her ponytail then combed it loose with her fingers. Jean lay on the kitchen floor with her hands behind her head and did crunches in brand new white eyelet underwear from a boutique on the island. I counted for her.

"I think we all get second chances," said Suzanne. "And thirds and fourths, if that's what it takes. What we do with those chances"—her laugh was soft and self-deprecating—"that's another story altogether." For a moment, she looked sad, her pink-tipped fingers flashing as she braided her ponytail again. "And you just keep hoping and praying you have one more. That's all you can do."

"I don't know," said Jean, coming to a panting stop. "Sometimes I think you have only one, but different people's chances come at different times. I don't believe a chance ends because something bad happens…because you get a crummy deal. You just have to hold your cards close to the vest sometimes and play conservatively until the luck of the draw comes your way again." She frowned and I could tell she wasn't completely happy with what she'd said. "But you have to work hard at the game. You can't just wait for the good cards; you have to look for them."

"Andie?" said Vin.

I looked down at my chest, at Jean's too-thin face, and thought of Paul and Jake, and said, "Yes, I believe in second chances."

Vin smiled, and there was a lightness in the expression that made her appear younger, almost happy again. "I do, too."

Jean

The men had laid a fire on the beach. After we all ate far too much steak, lobster, rice, salad, and cake, we walked down to the ring of stones surrounded by folded blankets and unopened bags of marshmallows.

David and I left for a walk almost immediately, a blanket tossed over his shoulder.

"It's nice here," he said, looking around in the star-studded darkness. "You won't want to come home."

"Oh, I don't know." I gave him a teasing look. "You're still going to be there, aren't you?"

"Oh, yeah."

When we'd gained enough distance from the others that we could no longer hear the words in their voices, we moved to a grassy, protected area and spread the blanket.

I sat down, arranging the fluttery skirt of my dress. "Do you want me to come home now?"

David lay on his back and pulled me down on top of him, not at all concerned about my dress, unless it was with how he was going to get it off of me. "No."

His hands were moving, gliding, finding all the places he knew so well. Did I mention a lack of urgency earlier? I lied.

"No?" I spoke between kisses, my voice hitching in my throat.

"No."

Then I couldn't think any more for a while. Although there are many things about being fifty-one that aren't as good as they were ten, twenty, and thirty years ago, sex isn't one of them. It deserved all of my attention and I was glad to give it.

It was only when we lay sated and sweating, my head in its accustomed place on his shoulder, that I said again, "No?"

"When I retired," he said, "I thought I couldn't wait. Remember how we'd planned for it all those years before? And we did the things we intended, I guess. We've traveled a little, made plans to travel more, and God knows I've played golf."

He sighed, his fingers stroking up and down my arm. "We got Kelly married and the nest emptied except for the boxes of dolls, trophies, and baseball gloves in the attic."

His fingers continued up and down in a light, sweet caress that made me turn my lips to his shoulder. I loved this man so.

"And I hate it," he went on heavily.

I stopped all movement, gazing up at him in the starlight.

"I hate not having a purpose when I get up in the morning. The only thing in my entire life that's still okay is you. There with coffee first thing in the morning; there at your computer when I come in from outside or, up for air from the television; there for the kids when they need something." He leered at me and squeezed my shoulder. "There for the best imaginable sex and some we couldn't have imagined twenty years ago."

I chuckled because I knew he wanted me to. "So," I said, laying a hand on his chest, tangling my fingers in the soft brown and silver hair. "What are you trying to tell me, David?"

"That it's time I found something to do and that I need to do it on my own, without you making things easy for me."

"What if you're not ready at the end of two more weeks? Do you want me to stay longer?"

"Oh, honey." He captured my face between his hands and kissed me hard. "I don't want you to stay now, but I really do think I need to work a few things out on my own. And, to be honest, I think it's good for you, being here with the girls." His hand moved from my arm to my breast, then over my ribs and down my hip. "But you're losing weight, Jean. Are you feeling okay? Should you come home just long enough to pay Carolyn a visit?"

"No, I'm feeling fine." And I was right then, so I wasn't lying to him. Not really. "Do you suppose we should go back to the fire? They'll know what we were doing."

"Well, hell." He hauled me against him, laughing, and I felt his laughter against every inch of my skin. "Do you think they'd know if we did it again? We've been saving up."

Suzanne

I'm much better today. It's Sunday, and everyone's off doing their thing. Jean and David went to church this morning and are having lunch at the café before he

Liz Flaherty

takes the afternoon ferry in order to catch a plane from Bangor. Vin and Lucas took the morning ferry to the mainland to shop for things not available on the island. (Vin's going to get me more concealer.) Andie's sitting on our rock on the beach writing letters. Jean offered to let her use her laptop, but Andie said she'd probably just break it when she tried to erase something.

Lucas and I had a chat about my antidepressant use. He said Vin was absolutely right to stop me from doubling it up. I don't like relying on anything at all, and it's scary when I look at the arsenal of pills I've built up. He suggested I get a physical, which Carolyn's been after me to do, too, and he said I should put all my pills into a baggie and take them in with me.

I've been thinking, sitting here on the porch, wondering if I'm the reason Tom's the way he is. I don't mean his drug use, because I never took more than an aspirin while the kids were growing up and I spent as much time repeating "just say no" as anyone.

But did I do something else horribly wrong? I was never the consummate mother that Jean was or the fun one that Andie was—my children always preferred their houses to ours—but I always loved them. Didn't they know that? Did they know it even now?

Then the questions got harder. Did the fact that I had loved men—always the wrong ones—always right where the kids could see it happening, cause the distance between the kids and me?

I had thought it was wrong that Jean damned near martyred herself raising her children, that she never took any time for herself, that she always put them first. Always.

And I thought it was wrong that Andie kept her

relationships and her children separate. They knew she dated, and as they got older, they probably knew she had sex. But she never had anyone spend the night when they were home and never spent the night with anyone else when they were even in town.

"Do you want them to grow up believing in fairy tales?" I asked once.

"It's okay with me," said Jean, watching David and Josh tossing a baseball back and forth. "I think maybe I still do."

"I'm not a fairy tale to Jake and Miranda," said Andie. "I'm just Mom, and they don't need to know I'm human till later."

Their children are all right. Young Jake's a cop, Miranda and Carrie are teachers, Kelly's a photographer, and Josh is a medical resident. My Sarah is a veterinarian, and I'm so very proud of her, but she's also alone and bitter.

And then there's Tom.

I stare blindly toward the sea, not even seeing Andie come up the path.

"Suzanne?"

I jumped. "Holy shit, Andie, you scared me to death."

"Sorry." She stood in front of me. Her white hair was longer than it had been when we came, and it lay in soft waves that she pushed back from her face. She looked healthy and fit, and I sent up a little prayer of thanksgiving. "I'm starved to death," she complained. "What do you say we go in there and rape that cake we brought home from Lucas's last night?"

"Works for me. We got any ice cream?"

"I think so. Jean never lets us run out of staples."

We grinned at each other and went inside.

A while later I put our dishes into the dishwasher while Andie brewed coffee. We returned to the porch, perching ourselves in rockers with our feet on the porch rail, a small round table between us holding our cups.

"You know…"

She hesitated, which isn't at all like Andie, and I turned my head to look at her. "Know what?"

"We need to talk about it."

The back of my neck prickled, and I could envision the fine hairs back there standing straight out. "About what?"

"We need to talk about Jake."

Vin

Lucas took my hand on the tabletop between us. "Did you know I fell in love with you that first summer you and Mark came to the island?"

I felt my eyes go wide.

"That's always the way of it, you know," he said, his smile reaching out like a caress. "Country doctor without a pot to piss in falls in love with rich woman who just happens to be married. Only the husband isn't supposed to be a nice guy—he's supposed to be a loser with mafia connections and a blonde mistress who lives in a penthouse somewhere and wears leopard-skin pants."

"You've been watching too many movies."

"That's what we do on the island in the winter. We read books and watch movies, and by the time April gets here, the movie pickings are getting pretty slim. I watched the *Star Wars* series three times last winter."

He held my hand up to his, measuring their differing lengths. "Maggie—you know my brother

Zeke's wife—has three different versions of *Little Women* and we watched all of them. Every time Beth died, Zeke and I had to go to the kitchen."

"You couldn't stand it when Maggie cried," I guessed.

"No. She made fun of us when we did."

I laughed over at him. "You're such fun, Lucas Bishop. I'll miss you when I go back to New York."

He didn't laugh back, and his eyes were the color of fog. "Don't go back," he said.

"My home is there, and my job. People depend on me."

"*Is* your home there?" he asked gently. "Without Mark, is it?"

I looked down at where my hand rested in his. The warmth went all the way up my arm.

There was no warmth in the brownstone, just two lonely women who'd loved the same man rattling around in its opulent and empty splendor. I realized with sudden and brutal clarity that I hated it. It had been a good and beautiful home for the wife of Mark Stillson. But when he died, his widow became once more just a girl from Tonsil Lake who no longer fit her own skin.

"I don't know," I admitted.

"Do you love your job?"

"Sometimes." When I'm sitting in the island house with Andie, arguing over syntax, I do. Otherwise... The thought trailed away. "But I can't give it up. It's all that's left, really, of my life with Mark." I met his gaze again. "I loved him so much, Lucas."

But I couldn't see my husband's face clearly anymore. I no longer started when I saw medium-height men with thinning gray hair. And I could scarcely hear his voice in my head. Even if I played the old answering machine tape with his crisp, "We can't come to the phone..." it didn't sound like it did in my fading memory.

The man who'd made the tape had been Mark Stillson, man of business and massive wealth. I wanted to hear Mark, my husband, who'd sung Irish ditties in the shower and told the most awful jokes in the world.

"He called me Vincent," I said. "He said Lavinia was such a pedestrian name for someone he loved, whereas Vincent brought to mind beauty and grace and...something else. I don't remember what else."

"Power." Lucas's voice was devoid of expression, his eyes opaque.

I stared at him. "Yes, that's right. Power." I didn't ask him how he knew, or guessed. Something told me I wouldn't like the answer.

"We'd better go, or we'll miss the ferry." He reached for the check in its unobtrusive leather cover, raised his eyebrows when he saw the price of our lunch, and pulled a wad of bills out of his pocket.

We were on the sidewalk outside the restaurant before he spoke again, and then he didn't look at me. He just tucked my hand into the crook of his elbow and said, "It was Lavinia I fell in love with."

I stopped walking, right in the middle of the sidewalk so that people had to go around us. I looked up at him and all I could think was that the man who loved Lavinia, who I knew for a fact really was occasionally paid in lobsters and blueberry pie, was a bigger tipper than the man who'd loved Vincent. An unselfconscious tipper who'd left the bills crumpled up when he put them inside the leather folder.

Lucas pulled his arm loose from my hand and put it firmly around my waist, holding me full-length against him. "I still love Lavinia," he said, and kissed me as though we had all the time in the world and we weren't standing in the middle of a Bar Harbor sidewalk.

It was forny wonderful.

Liz Flaherty

Part Three

"Life is simply one damned thing after another."

Elbert Hubbard

Liz Flaherty

Chapter Nine

Andie

Suzanne and I watched from the porch as Vin and Jean negotiated the path on either side of Lucas Bishop. They were singing "Hey Jude" at the top of their not-very-tuneful voices and all of them were carrying plastic shopping bags from Vin and Lucas's trip to Bar Harbor.

Oh good, we won't have to talk about this now. The relief I felt was immense, and a sideways glance at Suzanne showed it mirrored on her face. God knows what I'd been thinking when I brought it up in the first place.

"Look at Vin," she said, pointing. "She's all lit up." Her relieved expression slid into a frown. "And Jean's white as a ghost." Fear threaded through her voice. "What do you think's wrong with her, Andie?"

I shook my head. I wouldn't go there; I couldn't say out loud the thing that was hammering at the back of my mind. Ovarian cancer was still among the sneakiest and most lethal of killers. Jean's mother had been fifty-one when it had claimed her. And Jean turned fifty-one in May.

Lucas greeted Suzanne and me and set his share of the bags on the porch. "I'm going to go home," he said. "Jean, please remember what I said."

"I will, Lucas," she said, sinking into a rocking

chair beside Suzanne and setting her bags on the porch floor. "Thank you."

Lucas took off on the path to his house and Vin sat in the fourth chair. I gave Jean a hard look. "This is ridiculous," I said. "You look like warmed-over death."

"Thank you, Andie. I needed that."

Her withering look was interrupted by a flinch, and I wanted to run after Lucas, yelling for help all the way. I absolutely do not know how I used to make people afraid of me when I am the biggest chickenshit in the world.

"Did David enjoy the island?" Vin's fingers were light on my arm, but I recognized a signal for me to shut up.

Jean's eyes got kind of dreamy, and she seemed to look a little healthier because of it. "Yes, he did."

"You two need to come back sometime on your own. You can use the house any time," said Vin. She flushed. "Even if I'm in it, you can use it. I hope you all know that, that I want you to come to see me when this time is over whether I'm here or in New York. I'd love for it to be an annual thing, sort of like our drunken brawls at the Tonsil Lake Tavern only longer and soberer. We owe it to your children and grandchildren to show them fun can be had without throwing up on your Birkenstocks."

Oh, we had come a long way on this sojourn.

"I think we always have known it," said Jean quietly. "Even though you never invited us, and we did wonder why, we knew we were welcome if we ever came."

Suddenly I understood. It was as though someone had written the truth in the stars and I could finally read the message that had eluded us for years. "Mark didn't like us, did he, Vin? Or at least one or two of us, and when he died you would have felt disloyal if you'd let us come to you."

Vin was silent for a long moment, and when I looked over at her, I saw that a tear had trickled from the corner of one eye. Damn, I had done it again. I really do get tired of feeling like a shit because I've hurt someone's feelings. "I'm sorry," I said.

This was something new with me, apologizing for my bluntness. I wasn't sure I liked it, but I was positive I didn't like making a good friend cry, even Suzanne who wept at the drop of a hat. "I didn't mean..." I stopped. Exactly what didn't I mean?

"No," she said, putting her hand on my arm again and leaving it there. "He didn't dislike you, but he didn't feel comfortable with you or with our friendship. You knew he called me Vincent sometimes, didn't you?" She looked down the row of us and we all nodded. "It was because he didn't feel comfortable with Lavinia, either."

The tears came fast then, heartrending in their silence. "After this afternoon, with Lucas," she said, "I realize that perhaps Mark never loved me at all, but this version of me that was only real in his mind. He was happiest when we were in New York or Palm Beach, only tolerating the time we spent here, and this was the place I loved best. He wouldn't even come to Indiana, remember?"

"Oh, Vin, of course he loved you."

It was Suzanne speaking, and we all looked at her. I felt familiar "oh, Suzanne, what do you know?" impatience welling up inside, but I had learned in the past few weeks that she knew a lot, and if I'd kept my mouth shut a little more often, it wouldn't have taken me so long to figure it out.

"Okay," she went on, "so he didn't like the island, but he bought you this house and handed you the deed with just your name on it so that it was yours no matter what happened. And he wasn't crazy about us, but he never tried to stop you from being with us." She grinned. "His not loving us only showed that the man's character had limits, not that he didn't have any."

I remembered Suzanne's first husband, Trent, who'd thought he could have one life in Indianapolis and another in Lewis Point. And then there was Phil, who had hidden from his colleagues the fact that his wife was a beauty consultant. She knew what she was talking about when it came to men's characters.

I just wish she knew about Jake.

"You know, she's right," I said. "And let's be honest here, you hate Palm Beach and I don't think you're really happy in New York. Does that mean you didn't love Mark?"

Vin snatched her hand from my arm. "Of course not," she said indignantly, spoiling her hauteur with a sniffle. She looked down at all of us again. "Do you think he did?"

"Yes," Suzanne and I said together.

"Sure do," said Jean, who seemed to be getting a little color back. I don't know whether it was the conversation or the roll of antacids she'd pulled out of her purse. "After all," she went on, "the man thought you were a C-cup when he met you. If he still wanted you when the falsies came out, I'm sure it was love."

Our laughter seemed to bounce off the rocks

below, coming back to us in the stillness of the night. We stayed on the porch, going in only for sandwiches or glasses of something cold, until darkness crept in and slid into the water. We slapped at mosquitoes, but none of us wanted to go inside. Jean finally found a can of repellent and we sprayed each other down and resumed our seats.

It's been said that time heals all wounds, but sometimes friendship does, too.

Jean

The story is flowing so rapidly it's as though I can't type fast enough. I was afraid David's visit would stop that flow, or at least impede it, but if anything it accelerated it. I'm writing nearly all the time that I'm awake.

The pain in my abdomen is worsening, waking me sometimes with the gasping fear that I'm going to die on the spot. I can't though until I finish this book, make things right with Carrie, and separate myself enough from David to ease his grief.

Sometimes, when I'm not feeling so bad, I wonder if I'm wrong. Maybe it's a misplaced appendix or a bad gall bladder or just a cyst that's attached itself to something. I am not, after all, particularly intuitive except where my children are concerned. I've never felt the foreshadowing of bad things or "just known" when something was wrong. Andie's cancer was as big of a shock to me as it was to her, or nearly.

My own, however, is not. It is as though I've known since the dreadful days of my mother's illness that her end would also be mine. I have schooled myself for years not to be angry, as she was, or afraid, as David's mother was.

Sometimes I am anyway. After making love with David, I raged that I couldn't grow old with him, couldn't stay with him until we were fragile little people who knew only our memories and each other. And in the night, I'm frightened. I believe in the afterlife, but the people I love are still here. Common sense tells me I won't be alone, but without my family and my friends, how can I be otherwise?

Lying in the soft, feathery bed in Vin's house, I remember the nights when I was small. My parents would leave for days at a time, looking for a different job, a place to live, or just a good time. They'd leave a row of canned chicken and noodle soup on the cluttered counter along with a crank can opener. "Don't tell anyone we're gone," they'd say. "You never know who or what might come in here looking for a little girl like you."

I was so scared. I'd go to bed as soon as the nine-o'clock TV shows were over, lying silent and afraid beneath scratchy old military blankets until sleep overcame both my dread and me. If a storm or just the creaky sounds of night woke me later, I learned to make up stories, telling them out loud to stave off the noise and the fear.

The other girls found out about me being alone at night—I don't remember how. They didn't tell anyone, but Andie would drag me into her trailer. "Jean's staying with me," she'd say to Rosie, the aunt she lived with.

Rosie would nod and give me a smile. "Keep the noise down."

We knew gentlemen callers didn't like knowing there were kids in the house. Later on, when puberty struck us all at once, Rosie wanted us to be quiet for other reasons we didn't quite understand until Vin explained them.

I've always believed there is a special place in heaven for people like Rosie. She died when an aneurysm in her brain burst our freshman year in college. The four of us stood hollow-eyed over her grave at the back of the Tonsil Lake Cemetery and realized that the only person who'd ever taken care of us was gone.

Maybe Rosie will be waiting for me.

Lucas made me promise to see Carolyn as soon as I return home, and the pain is getting bad enough I will keep that promise. He was angry when we talked about it, but I don't know whether the anger was at me, disease, or fate. He is such a nice man.

We are down to our last few days of this month on the lake. Vin and Andie have finished the editing of what Andie persists in calling "that book," and the mood has been both celebratory and sad.

I don't think Suzanne has made a decision concerning her job. We all put on our reading glasses one night and pored over the retirement offer made by her company. It was adequate if not generous, but she really doesn't want to retire.

"You don't seem to understand," she said patiently. "I *am* a beauty consultant. It's not just something I *do*."

Looking down at my laptop and thinking of the pages I have written in this idyllic place, I understand very well. Very well indeed.

Suzanne

Jake came yesterday. It was a real surprise to all of us. We were eating our breakfast on the porch, which has become a habit the past couple of weeks, when we saw a tall, lean man coming up the path. He was even thinner than he'd been when I saw him last month and he was wearing sunglasses and a baseball cap that covered his dark hair.

I didn't recognize him right away, but Andie did. I saw a smile cross her face before she lifted an arm in greeting.

"Good Lord," he said, stepping onto the wooden porch, "if you women get any more beautiful, they're going to have to make this island into the eighth natural wonder of the world." He clasped a column as he spoke, and even though the movement was casual, it was as though he needed the post's support as much as the porch roof did.

"I believe that's being considered," said Vin. "Jake, you old dog, how are you?" She got to her feet first and went to meet him with her arms outstretched.

He hugged us all indiscriminately, telling us the whole time about all he'd gone through to get here in time for breakfast. His arm lingered warm at my waist when he was done. I looked up at him—probably with a goofy smile all over my face—and intercepted a look that passed between him and Andie.

It was like standing at the edge of the ocean and feeling the tide washing the sand out from under your feet. You start out ankle-deep in water and end with the surf lapping over your knees while you try to keep your balance against the surge.

I'd always known at some level of thinking that getting interested in one of your friends' ex-husbands was a bad idea, made even worse when the friend tells you she minds that interest. I had told myself that

Andie's friendship was more important than a romance with Jake, but I hadn't believed it.

Men who were an integral part of your lives were always more important, weren't they? And Jake had become, through the months and the whirlwind time together we'd had, a very integral part of my life.

I thought Andie wouldn't stay mad when the relationship deepened. Friends just didn't. They fought about things and moved on. That's what the girls from Tonsil Lake had always done.

But with the look exchanged between Jake and Andie, I knew how wrong I was. Their connection went much deeper than their children and the friendship they'd always shared. I had always thought Andie never married again because she was embittered and couldn't fall in love again, but that wasn't the case at all.

She couldn't fall in love again because she was still in love with Jake.

And he with her.

Vin

I showered before I went. I sprayed expensive cologne into the air and walked through it, shaved my underarms and legs for the second time in the same day, and slipped into the apricot bra and panties that had been my part of a shopping trip to the boutique in the village a week ago. If that's not premeditated, I don't know what is.

So?

I pushed my bare feet into scuffs, belted my silk robe at my waist, and slipped away through the darkness.

When Lucas opened the door after my knock, it was as though he'd been waiting for me. He took me into his arms without so much as a "hello" and I went willingly. Later, lying half on top of him in the king-size bed that took up most of his first-floor bedroom, I realized I'd been waiting for him, too.

We didn't ask each other the obvious question: What now? We didn't speak of love and forever and New York and Hope Island. There were no flowers or wine or seductive fragrances or candles flickering on the windowsills.

This was not a carved antique bed with imported linens and a heavy spread that coordinated with the window appointments, but a cherry wood four-poster he'd bought on the mainland and hauled across the bay on Zeke's boat. The sheets were soft cotton—Lucas thought Maggie had bought them at Wal-Mart on the mainland—and the quilt had been a gift from a grateful patient. There was only Lucas and me and the night we gave each other.

It was everything.

Chapter Ten

Andie

I had flown in a day early to surprise him. We'd planned the long weekend for months in advance. Jake would already be in San Francisco on business and I would come on Thursday's earliest flight and be there in time for a late lunch. Miranda was staying with Jean, young Jake with Suzanne.

It seemed as though he'd been gone for months, though it had been less than a week. He traveled a lot as half of a manufacturing consultant team, and sometimes the trips seemed to run together. I told him he spent more time with Ted, his partner, than he did with me. He told me he knew that was true, though he couldn't get Ted to do his laundry.

I was able to get a flight on Wednesday afternoon, so I drove my kids over to Jean and Suzanne in Lewis Point and went on to the airport. On the flight, I had a few second thoughts that skittered through my mind like air turbulence. Suzanne had sought to surprise Trent once, too, but she'd gotten the surprise, finding him with another woman.

But Jake wasn't Trent. He was the best of husbands, the best of fathers. He hated our separations as much as I did and he loved surprises. It was more fun throwing a birthday party for him than for one of the kids.

It was nine o'clock San Francisco time when I reached the hotel. I showed my driver's license to the desk clerk and was given a key to Jake's room. The elevator to the third floor was slow, and I remember thinking I should have taken the stairs, but I was too tired to look for them. Nine o'clock in California time meant midnight and exhausted in Hoosier hours.

I knocked lightly on the door before unlocking it. The safety chain wasn't on—Jake never remembered that—and I stepped inside, surprised to find the room dark and the television off since he'd said he was staying in tonight. We had laughed that he was saving himself for my arrival, and I giggled again there in the dusky vestibule of his room as I remembered the conversation.

And then I didn't laugh for what seemed, even in memory, like a very long time.

Jake was in the queen-size bed in the hotel room, but it wasn't me he had saved himself for.

It was Ted.

****

I'm not sure Suzanne believed me at first. "But you're still in love with him," she said. "I saw you look at each other yesterday when he got here. It was one of those David and Jean looks, like a silent secret."

I sat with my legs drawn up into the chair. I'd gotten chilly while I told the story I had never told another living soul. Jean went into the house and came out with a knitted blanket. She gave it to me, letting her hand rest on my shoulder for a wordless space of time.

"Oh," said Vin. "Oh, Andie, why didn't we know? Why didn't you tell us?"

"Because we didn't tell anyone. That was how we

decided to do it. Because we didn't want the kids to know till they were much older. Because, at that time, it probably would have cost Jake and Ted both their jobs had it gotten out. And because"—I stopped, meeting Suzanne's gaze—"because sometimes the love doesn't stop just because the marriage can't go on. I couldn't live with a bisexual once I knew he was one, couldn't bear the idea of sharing my husband with a man, but I loved Jake Logan with every breath I breathed."

"And you still do," said Suzanne.

I heard the wonder in her voice and smiled at her, though none of it was the least bit funny. "I'm not in love with him anymore," I said. "Being in love isn't static, it requires forward motion, and that all stopped that day. But I've loved him for thirty years and I don't know that I can ever love someone else as much as I do him." I thought of Paul and realized there was a chance I'd just spoken a lie. "Or that I would subject myself to that kind of pain again." That part was the truth.

Vin's voice slipped into the silence, so quiet it barely disturbed it. "Andie, is Jake sick?"

I hadn't wanted to tell them this, had wanted to spare Suzanne if no one else, but Vin's question left me little recourse. "Yes."

"AIDS?"

"Yes." I took a deep breath, then another, and almost laughed when I noticed that we were all doing the same thing. In. Out. In. Out. If we kept up with this heavy breathing, we could go into business as crank telephone callers.

"He's been HIV-positive for some time, but it's gone into full-blown AIDS in the past two years. There isn't much time left." It hurt so to say those words, to imagine life without Jake Logan, but the relief at having them said was almost greater than the pain. "Suzanne, I—"

Her hand gripped mine, and I held on.

"How could we have helped you through any of this?" asked Jean. Tears trembled on her lashes. "What could we have done?"

Before I knew what was happening, I was crying. Oh, hell, no, I was blubbering like a baby. "Oh, Jeannie, you guys always helped me. God, that day around the pool, talking about—all I can remember is Suzanne being the only first grader with a bra—but it kept me from thinking my life was over."

I tried to laugh, but it spluttered into a sob. "Vin, you sent me money, remember? And I sent it back. So you sent it again, the same bedraggled check, with lots of cuss words in a note, and you paid book rent and bought my kids' school clothes that year because even with Jake helping beyond the limits of child support, I couldn't do it all on a hostess's salary."

The blanket fell from my shoulders to my lap, and I left it there. I wasn't cold anymore. "And the past two years, between Jake's illness and mine," I said, "I don't believe I would have survived without the three of you."

****

We left the house on Hope Island the next day without looking back. None of us wanted to cry again. Vin flew out first, after long, hard hugs all around, then Jean, Suzanne, and I got on the plane to Indianapolis. David met us at the airport and drove us home. Paul was waiting at my house with dinner ready. We invited Suzanne to stay, but she said she wanted to go and see

Sarah.

It was almost dawn when the phone rang.

Jean

David took me through the house blindfolded, but he tickled me in the hallway and ended up walking me into a wall. By the time we finished laughing, my blindfold was askew and so were our clothes. Reunions, we decided, were great things.

He straightened the sweatband covering my eyes, turned me around in circles a few times, and led me on. I heard a door open and close, but I had no idea which one it was. "Are you taking me into the linen closet to have your way with me?" I demanded. "Because you wouldn't need to. The hallway floor's just fine with me."

I felt so good today, so alive, that I truly thought I might be mistaken. Maybe it was an ulcer, or—never mind, I wasn't going to think about it now. I was having too good a time.

"Hush, woman." His breath tickled my ear, and he paused to kiss the side of my neck, little butterfly kisses that sent sensation curling through my whole body, before moving us forward again. "Okay, here we are." He pulled off the sweatband. "Voila."

We were in Carrie's room, or what used to be Carrie's room. The French provincial furniture was all gone, as was everything that had hung on the walls, the windows, and in the closet. Even the purple carpet Carrie had chosen, and I'd hated, had been removed.

"We were going to just move Carrie's stuff out and bring yours in," said David, "but when we were getting your desk ready to move, Laurie found this folder full of pictures and notes about what you wanted in an office. Since none of us had a clue what 'BIBCIC' meant, we decided we'd wait."

I looked over at the closet, roomy enough to have been a playroom in bygone days. "Built-in book cases in closet," I translated, "with a stepstool so that the shelves can go all the way to the ceiling. It would be my own little miniature reference library with a rocking chair and a little table with a lamp." I looked up at him, not allowing the thought "too late" to come all the way into my mind. "What about Carrie?"

"She's fine. It's time for her to be a grownup. And Megan's thrilled. She wants to sleep in Mommy's bed all the time and give the puppy her crib."

"She's too little," I protested.

"She doesn't think she is."

"And they don't have a puppy."

"They will have. Kelly and Brian's dog got out and went whoring around."

"Oh, David, it's perfect." I put my arms around his waist. "How did you know I was so upset about it?"

"Well, it sure as hell wasn't because you told me." He scowled at me, but it wasn't an angry look. "I just had a lot of time to think about what Andie said about listening to what you meant instead of what you said. And one time while you were gone, Josh and Laurie had a spat and he looked at me in total bewilderment and said, 'Damn, Dad, why didn't you tell me you had to be a mind-reader to be a husband? I thought that was the wife's job.'"

I walked the perimeter of the empty room, mentally placing my desk here, the filing cabinet in that corner, a small table and two chairs under the window. I grinned over my shoulder at him. "And you said?"

"That I'd only just figured it out myself. You always did such a good job of reading my mind, I didn't even know you were doing it. It'll take me some time to acquire the skill. Can you be patient?"

I glanced over at where he leaned against the doorframe with his arms crossed over his chest. His hair, more gray than brown these days, flopped over his forehead, his eyes sparkling bright blue below. He was smiling at me, but it wasn't a public smile. It was one of those looks Suzanne called a silent secret.

"I love you," I said, "so much." My chest ached with it, and it occurred to me that I couldn't die; there was too much yet to do. I had to finish what was proving to be the book of my heart, put this office together, and weed the flowerbeds that had gone mostly untended in my absence. I wondered if my mother had felt that way, if everyone did.

David crossed the room, pulling me unresisting into his arms. "Me, too, Mrs. O'Toole."

I was sitting at my computer in the corner of the dining room when the phone rang the next morning. It was five-twelve.

Suzanne

I didn't really want my Camaro anymore. It was a pretty car, and a convertible, but it sat so close to the ground that it didn't ride very well. If it snowed more than a teaspoonful, you could forget it, because it would rear up on its wide back wheels and say it wasn't going anywhere. It was hard to get into, even harder to get out of, and no amount of plastic surgery changed the fact that my hips were starting to get arthritic. I'd been more comfortable sharing the back seat of Jean's Buick with Andie and Jean's laptop than I was in the flashy little car I'd once loved so much.

Sarah lived on the edge of Lewis Point. It was just a little shotgun house, but she had a small barn and a few other outbuildings that made it easy for her to keep and care for the stray animals that gravitated to her.

I wondered, as I pulled into the carport beside her SUV, if I'd be welcome. Or would she be "on her way out" or "just going to bed" or "too busy to talk now, Mother."

She was busy—being the junior partner in her veterinary practice kept her on call more than off—but I knew it wasn't the busyness that kept her from wanting to see me. The time had come to find out what it was.

She eyed me from behind the wooden screen door that led to her front porch. "Mother. I was just—"

"You weren't 'just' anything," I interrupted. "You 'just' want to avoid me."

She was silent. God, how that silence hurt.

"I've lost your brother," I said baldly. "I don't know any way I can get him back, or any of us can get him back, for that matter. I've pretty much lost my job, my condo's all white and boring, and I hate my car. I'm not losing you, too—whether you like it or not." I glared at her through the screen. "And if you think you're already lost, you can just think again."

She pushed open the screen. "What do you mean, lost your job?"

I walked past her into the cozy living room. "I'm too old," I said briefly.

She gestured toward the couch, and I sat down, jumping back up again when a kitten squealed in protest. "Sorry." I made sure the seat was clear this time, and sat with the small black cat in my lap. "There,

there. You're not hurt."

"Want some lemonade?"

"Thank you." I held the kitten up to my face, relishing the soft feel of its fur. "What's its name?" I called.

"Elmer." Sarah came back into the room with two frosty glasses and handed me one before sitting in the recliner at right angles from me. "Your job?" she urged.

I started to tell her, surprised by her interest, then stopped abruptly. "That's not why I'm here." I took a long swallow of lemonade and met her eyes.

She looked like me with darker, not-so-round eyes. Her streaky blonde hair was almost the same color as mine, but hers was natural, as were the extremely long eyelashes that no one ever saw because she flatly refused to wear makeup.

"You have the most beautiful skin," I blurted.

Sarah grinned, and I saw vestiges of my little girl in the expression. "Cowshit, Mother. It does wonders."

I grinned back at her. "You talk like Andie."

"Thank you."

I hope I didn't flinch. "You've spent a lot of time making sure you're not like me, haven't you?" I asked slowly, setting my glass down because my hands were suddenly so cold.

"Sure, I have." Her gaze didn't waver. "But that's not just me, Mother. Miranda tries not to be like Andie—I swear, she has as much makeup as you do. Carrie and Kelly never even considered being like Jean. Everybody does that."

"It's not because you hate me?"

Elmer was tired of being stroked, he was ready to go to sleep, but I kept my freezing hands buried in his fur.

She leaned forward in her chair. "I don't hate you," she said. "You drive me crazy, but I don't hate you. Did you hate your mother?"

"Yes," I said instantly, thinking of the woman who had sat in that filthy trailer for years on end, hearing voices and seeing shapes and screaming out in the night.

"Only when you were young, when you just knew she wasn't like other mothers. Not when you found out she was paranoid-schizophrenic and couldn't help it." Sarah smiled, but there was an unkind edge to the expression. "Then she just drove you crazy."

"Is that how I lost your brother, by driving him crazy? Is that what pushes you away from me?"

She hesitated, and she wasn't looking at me anymore. I followed the line of her vision and saw that it rested on a picture on an end table. It had been taken the day she graduated from high school. Phil and I had reluctantly posed with Sarah and Tom standing between us. We were all smiling dutifully for David's camera.

"It should have been that way," said Sarah.

I looked from the picture back to her, seeing the sheen of tears in her dark eyes. "What way?" I asked, although I knew.

"We were a family, but you tore that apart without ever looking back. It's always all about you, and you never gave a damn what the divorce did to Tommy or me, or even Daddy. At least you never appeared to, and that's more than a kid can understand." Sarah gave a self-deprecating little shrug. "I guess I still don't understand."

"Don't you know why we got divorced?"

She shrugged again. "Because of your job, because your needs always came before everyone else's."

"Is that what your father told you?"

"Not in so many words. That's what I observed on my own."

"Do you remember Ben and Kate Rivers?"

She rolled her eyes. "The infamous picture of you and Jean on the front page of the paper. Of course, I remember. Jean's kids and Tom and I were popular for a whole week because of it. Kate and Ben bring their dogs to our clinic now. They still have Dalmatians."

"Do you remember your dad's reaction?"

"You fought about it," she said, "but you guys fought a lot, so it was no big deal, was it?"

"Sarah, think about it. Why would we have fought about something like that? Jean and I did the right thing, didn't we?"

"Well, sure, but—"

A knock at the door interrupted her, and she got up to walk across the room, looking back over her shoulder at me with a puzzled expression. The watch on my wrist, a gift from my company as part of a bonus one year, said it was five minutes past midnight. In my lap, Elmer rose to a sitting position and eyed me expectantly. I stroked his head.

Later on, I would play this scene over and over in my head, till I felt like screaming. Maybe if the plane from Maine had been late into Indianapolis instead of early. If I'd stayed away from Sarah's and minded my own business the way she preferred. If I hadn't been there, young Jake Logan might have come earlier and no one would have said what he came to say. There was nothing in it that could have warned me, nothing I could have changed, but I still felt responsible.

I heard him murmur, "Hi, hon," as he stepped inside, pulling Sarah into the curve of his arm.

He was in his state police uniform, which only added to the movie star looks he'd inherited from his father. I could see his side and part of his back, and I noticed he'd just gotten a haircut; his tanned skin was lighter at his hairline.

"Mother's here, Lo," said Sarah.

I wondered why she called him that.

He turned toward me then, and my greeting was halted in the middle by the stricken expression he wore. I said, "No."

But he told us anyway.

Vin

I heard the telephone, but rolled over and ignored it. That was, after all, why God had invented answering machines, wasn't it? And if God hadn't done it, surely he'd intended to, to make up for allowing the emergence of telemarketers.

Then there was a knock on my bedroom door. I muttered something unintelligible into my pillow and rolled again so that my back was to the door. The prescription Lucas had given me was working—I hadn't been awakened by night sweats in over a week—so why wouldn't outside forces let me sleep?

The door opened. I supposed I couldn't ignore that. Since only Archie and I were in the house and she never disturbed me needlessly, I'd better open my eyes.

Archie held a cordless receiver in her hand. "It's Andie," she said. "You'd better take the call."

I took the phone and watched Archie go into Mark's office and turn on the light. A moment later, as

I tried to absorb what Andie was telling me, I heard Archie's voice from the other room, speaking softly but authoritatively on the other line.

When I said, "Thanks for letting me know, Andie," and laid down the phone, Archie came back into the room.

"Do you need me to pack for you?" she asked. "Or will you just take what's still in the bags?"

"I'll just take that," I said, pointing at the smaller of the two bags that sat in front of the closet doors. If I needed more, I could buy it there.

"The plane leaves at ten. There's an afternoon commuter to Lewis Point, so I booked that, too. Will you need a hotel room?"

"No." I got out of bed and pulled on a robe, stopping to give her a curious look. "How did you know I'd go?"

Archie smiled at me, and I thought how the expression softened her features into prettiness. Suzanne would have a heyday with that face. *Oh, Suzanne.*

"When I went back to Ireland," Archie said, "I learned that you can't always go home again. When you went to Maine with your friends, I think you learned that sometimes you can."

She left the room, carrying my suitcase and the telephone, and I dressed in jeans and a cotton sweater, wondering how Suzanne was doing. I would have liked to talk to her, but Andie said the doctor had given her a sedative and she was sleeping in Kelly O'Toole's old room at Jean's house.

I thought of young Tom Taylor, who I hadn't seen since the summer he and Jean's Carrie graduated from high school. He had been out of control even then, although charmingly so. And now he was dead at twenty-nine, the victim of a hit-and-run driver on the street outside Suzanne's condo.

I felt an ache in my chest as I tried to imagine the depth of her grief. Was this what our fifties were going to be? Was it all going to be about loss and pain and suffering?

Archie had coffee and a croissant ready for me when I went downstairs. I sipped the coffee and reached for the phone.

He answered on the third ring.

"Lucas?" I said.

Chapter Eleven

Andie

We gathered at Jean's after the funeral. The house was full, what with friends, family, and ex-husbands. Had we not been so sad, watching Trent Taylor and Phil Lindsay try to avoid each other would have kept us entertained. As it was, the years-old enmity seemed to deepen our sorrow.

I stood in the dining room with Paul at the sliding glass doors and looked at all of our surviving children together beside the pool. Carrie's and Miranda's little ones frolicked in the water. They had probably not all been together since the last wedding in one of our families. Or the last death.

Young Jake stood with an arm around Sarah, and I wondered how far beyond friendship that had gone. My son was not what one would call forthcoming, and Sarah was downright closemouthed.

"I'd like to see that," said a voice beside me, and I looked up at Jake, Sr. "She's a terrific young lady, and our boy isn't so bad, either."

Paul spoke from my other side. Turning, I realized he was talking to Jake more than to me. "We wondered, didn't we, back when they played Little League, how they'd all turn out. We talked about it then, and I think we grieved a little bit ahead of time for days like this."

"I remember," said Jake, and he wasn't talking to

163

me, either. "I never thanked you, Paul, for how good you were to young Jake when I couldn't be there."

The melancholy in his eyes was overwhelming, and I had to look away, back toward the group of twenty-somethings gathered at the pool. They were laughing uproariously, holding onto each other. It was nice to see, even though it was the kind of laughter that masks pain.

"You were always there, Jake," said Paul. "Maybe I was your mouthpiece sometimes, but you were always there."

Jake nodded, accepting the compliment with the same grace with which it had been delivered. "Well, so were you."

Their eyes met somewhere past me, and I sensed there was more being said than I heard, which is not a new thing for me. I miss out on a lot. Jean says it's because I'm always making so much noise, but I was quiet now.

"I'd like to think you'll always be around," said Jake casually.

"Me, too," said Paul.

They shook hands, and, slow though I may be to catch on, I had the feeling Jake had just let me go.

"I should go see if Jean needs any help," I said, and left them there together, the only two men other than young Jake who'd ever had a definitive place in my life.

I found Jean in the kitchen with Vin. They were standing at the sink, their heads together at the window over it. I poured myself a cup of coffee and hipped my way between them, which was easy to do because I have considerably more hip than either of them. "What are you two doing?"

"Look out there," said Jean, washing glasses without looking at them.

Suzanne stood in the yard with Trent's arm around her. They'd been together a lot the past few days, grieving for the son they'd lost, and I wasn't surprised to see them together now. The addition to the picture was Phil Lindsey. Whoa.

"I thought he left after the funeral," I said.

Vin shook her head, rinsing glasses and setting them upside down on a dishtowel—she wasn't looking at them, either. I was glad I was drinking from a mug.

I became as involved in watching the tableau as they were. Pretty soon David and Lucas were snickering behind us and Vin hissed, "Shh!" as though the three on the lawn could hear them.

"Oh, shit," I said. "Here comes Phil. Look busy."

"We are busy," said Jean. "Get another plate of sandwiches out of the fridge."

I buried my head in the side-by-side, coming out again quickly so that I wouldn't miss anything. Sometimes I am just not a very nice person. When I closed the refrigerator door, I hit my head with it. *Shit.*

Phil looked surprised to see all of us crowded into the kitchen. He nodded indiscriminately. "I have to be going. Does anyone know where Sarah is?"

"Out by the pool," I said, thinking with snotty satisfaction that he was going to have to walk into another crowd of people who made him uncomfortable in order to say goodbye to his daughter.

"Thanks." He started toward the door that led into the dining room then stopped and turned back toward us. "Do you know if there's anything I can do for

Suzanne?"

"Why, yes, there is," I said immediately and sharply. I met his eyes across the space of the kitchen and fancied that our mutual dislike made a dark cloud somewhere under the overhead light fixture. "You can tell Sarah the truth. She needs to know that her mother wasn't the only bad guy in the end of your marriage."

He hesitated. "I suppose you're right."

"She certainly is," said Vin, her voice crisp and cool. She folded a dishtowel, its corners snapping droplets of water all over the place. We all ducked in unison.

"It might not help Suzanne, though," said Phil quietly. "What if Sarah thinks I was right?"

Jean gave him her best hostess smile, although I could see definite overtones of superiority in it. "She won't."

"Try the truth," Vin advised. "It often works wonders."

I remembered something Suzanne had said within the past few days and beamed at him. "Just like cowshit."

Jean

In the end, Tommy was a hero. The car hit him after he pushed a child to safety. I don't know how much comfort that is to Suzanne, but I must admit it makes me feel better, if it's possible to feel better so soon after you bury someone you've known all his life. Whose diapers you changed and who you helped teach to do the swim and the frug for the sixties dance when he was in junior high.

This evening, we ended up as we have so often in our lives, the four of us around a kitchen table. David and Paul went to take Lucas to the Indianapolis airport and Jake went to Miranda's.

Trent had left when they did. He and Suzanne had held each other for a long time before he left. We watched, and our hearts broke a little more.

We didn't say much at first. We were all very tired and Suzanne's wounds were too new and too raw to take the chance of throwing salt on them. "It was nice of Lucas to come," she said. "I appreciated it."

Vin nodded.

"He's a nice guy," I said.

They all nodded.

We were silent.

"I believe," said Andie in a strangled voice, "this is the scene from *Steel Magnolias* where Sally Field lost it and earned herself another Oscar nomination. Or should have. I don't remember which."

I stared at her, aghast. Vin dropped her head into her hands. Suzanne got up from the table and pulled a bottle of wine out of the refrigerator. She set it in front of Andie with a thump. "Here, Weezer, open this."

Andie fluffed her white hair. "I look more like Olympia Dukakis than I do Shirley McLaine."

"Yeah, but I can't remember what Olympia's name was in the movie," said Suzanne.

I reached behind me for the corkscrew and tossed it to Andie. I ended up getting up anyway to retrieve four glasses from the dishtowel beside the sink.

After the first glass, I said, "I really hoped we'd never have to share a day like this."

No one said anything until Andie spoke into the silence that wasn't silent at all. "Do we all wonder the same thing?"

Yes, we probably did. The look we exchanged acknowledged that, but this was Suzanne's conversation to lead, not ours. It was, as horrible as it sounds, her day.

"He left a note on my door," she said. Her eyes were bright, her voice wistful. "He said he was sorry to have missed me. He knew I'd been worried about him but he was going to be okay. He said he was on his way to Sarah's but if he missed her, too, to give her his love. Do you think he really was okay?"

"Sure, he was," said Andie.

Vin and I nodded. "Absolutely," we said together.

Suzanne smiled around at us as huge tears spilled from the corners of her eyes. "You're all such liars." She reached for Andie's and my hands and we automatically grasped Vin's. "And I love you all so much."

Suzanne

Two weeks after Tommy's funeral, I drove to Chicago and turned in my retirement papers. I had lunch with Jake and drove home. When I got back to Lewis Point, I went to the only realty in town and listed my condo. I stopped by the dealership and traded my Camaro in on a nice dark blue midsize that had four doors and built-in GPS that might keep me from getting lost in my own backyard if I could only learn how to use it.

The next morning, I went to Willow Wood Daycare, where Miranda and Carrie both took their children while they taught school, and applied for a position.

I was hired on the spot and went home with finger paints in my hair, paste on my sleeves, and unidentified residue on the front of my skirt. I had read *Green Eggs and Ham* seven times, changed six diapered butts three times, and given three bottles of nasty-smelling formula that left yellowish stains on the shoulder of my blouse.

I called Sarah when I got home and asked her to come over for supper.

"What are you having?" she asked doubtfully.

"Pizza. I'll call for it when we hang up." I hesitated. "You can ask young Jake to come if you like."

"Don't forget the black olives." Her voice became muffled, as though she'd covered the mouthpiece, then she came back. "He says he doesn't like them, but get them anyway. He can just pick them off."

I took a shower, and when Sarah rang the doorbell, I answered it wearing sweats. My wet hair hung in strings around my face.

Young Jake looked stunned, Sarah uncertain.

"Mother?"

I drew them inside, kissing both their cheeks and herding them into the dining area. "Pizza just got here, so it's hot. Who wants beer and who wants soda? Jake, why is it you're not working? Did you get to go to day shift?"

"No, ma'am. Days off." He came into the kitchen and took me by the shoulders, looking down at me with his father's face and his mother's eyes. "It is you, right, Suzy-Q?"

My bravado wavered under his scrutiny, and my voice wobbled a bit when I said, "I don't know whether it is or not. I just know that who I was wasn't working out worth a damn."

He gave me a squeeze. "Good luck. Beer, Sarah?"

Her affirmative drifted in from the living room. I looked up at Jake. "Is she doing all right?" I whispered.

"I think so."

When the pizza was nothing except a few dried crusts and all the breadsticks were gone, I brought three more bottles of beer from the kitchen and said, "Young Jake, do they ever call you anything else? Are you destined to go through life as young Jake?"

He laughed. "No one calls me that except family. Everyone else calls me just Jake or Lo."

"That started in junior high," said Sarah, "when he'd come out on the football field and people would chant 'Lo-gan, Lo-gan.'"

I took a sip of beer and tried out the name. "Lo. I like that."

"You listed your condo," said Sarah. "I saw the sign. What are you going to do if it sells?"

"I don't really know," I said. "But this place is too white, just like the car was. Did you see the new one? It's the same color as yours." I took a deep breath because I felt like crying and I didn't want to do that anymore. "I need that, I think…more color."

"I saw it when I saw the sign." Sarah turned her beer in a wet circle on the table. "You can stay with me for a while, you know, if you need to." She smiled self-consciously. "Elmer likes you."

"Thank you, honey. I'll remember that."

They got up to leave an hour or so later. Lo gave me a bear hug and a damp raspberry on my cheek that made me laugh and swat him. Sarah stood, looking uncertain.

"Daddy told me," she said. "After the funeral, he told me the truth about the day the Rivers' house was trashed. He told me some other things, too. Like that he didn't want me to go to vet school so you footed the whole bill."

"I didn't want you to have to work too much," I said. "It's such a hard course." I beamed at her. "I'm so proud of you for doing so well."

I don't know which one of us reached first; all I know was that in the next moment, my daughter was in my arms and we were both weeping buckets. We cried so hard and so long that Lo put his arms around us both and we stood as a small quaking circle on the sidewalk in front of the condo.

We cried for Tommy, for times lost and times wasted, for the great gaping holes his death had left inside us. I think we cried for our own and each other's pain because of our estrangement, too, but maybe I place too much weight on a few tears.

When the weeping finally subsided and we were sniffing into crumpled tissues Sarah pulled from her pockets, she said, "I'm very proud of you, too, Mom."

It was the first time since Tommy died that I thought I might actually live. It was the first time I wanted to.

Vin

My work at the office was so backed up that Gunderson's actually broke down and hired me an assistant. He's a brand new college graduate who's spent the last few months interning at another publishing house. He's smart and eager and he wants my job.

Most days, I'd like to let him have it.

I don't believe I've ever known such discontent. I've been unhappier—I've just come off the worst two years of my life—but I've never been so restless.

It would be so easy to chuck it all and move to Hope Island, bag and baggage. I love it there, I believe I love Lucas, and I could do free-lance editing to stave off boredom. It would be easy, yes, but something holds me back and I don't know what it is. At least I didn't till I talked to Andie.

"You're afraid Hope Island will become Tonsil Lake," she said bluntly when I told her. "What if it doesn't work out with Lucas? What if you can't stand the winters there? What if you wake up and you're facing the same dead end we were facing back there in those trailers?"

"I guess so." I leaned back in Mark's leather desk chair and stared at the ceiling. "I think I'm scared of starting over."

"With good reason," she said. "It's a forny bitch."

"How's Suzanne?"

"Scary."

"What?" I sat up.

"She retired and went to work at a daycare center, sold her car, and put her condo on the market. You knew all that, but, Vin?"

"Yeah?"

"We all had lunch today because Jean's working too hard and looks like a dishrag, and I saw Suzanne's roots. I saw Jean's earlier this summer, but I think that was just a fluke because her hair was a mess. But Suzanne didn't have a hair out of place and I could still see them."

"Get real." Andie and I had teased Suzanne about her perpetual blondeness ever since she'd discovered a peroxide bottle in our freshman year of high school. I wanted to keep doing that.

"No, I'm serious. She doesn't seem miserable or anything, but when her lipstick disappeared while we were eating, she didn't put more on. And she was wearing sweats. Jean and I were, too, but we always do. Suzanne always wears skinny pants with a shirt tucked in. I'm afraid she's doing some kind of self-imposed penance because of Tommy. You know that game everybody plays when somebody dies."

"The 'if only' game? Yeah, I know it well." I had been at a writers' conference in New Jersey when Mark died. I went against my own better judgment because he insisted. It took me months to forgive myself. I don't think his daughters have forgiven me yet. "Give her time."

"I know. It's just that..."

I waited a minute. "What? Just that what?"

"Time's so damned precious. I hate to see either of you wasting it."

"What do you mean, Andie?" Alarm made the hairs on back of my neck stand up. "Are you okay?"

"Me? Of course," she answered too quickly. "Hey, you should see Jean's office. Actually, you should have been here while we all created it. It looks great, but she worked us to death. David threatened her with a hammer one day, I swear."

I laughed in spite of the prickles of unease I still felt. "What did she do?"

"I'm pretty sure she offered him sex. We told her that was probably the only thing that would save her. So then all the guys were fighting over the hammer to threaten us with. It was a really mature kind of afternoon."

"I'm glad she got it. The office, I mean." I looked at the clock, surprised at how long we'd been on the phone. "How's Jake?"

"Not good."

"Ah, Andie, I'm so sorry. Is there anything I can do?"

"No. Probably later I'll be calling you screaming my brains out against wicked fate, but for now we're just doing one day at a time."

"Well, call if you need anything." I yawned. "I need to get off here and go to bed. Tomorrow's another forny wonderful day at the office."

"Vin?" Her voice was quiet. "I'm serious when I say time's too precious to waste. Don't let that second chance we talked about in Maine pass you by, okay?"

"I won't," I said. "Promise."

I hung up and went into the bedroom to crawl between the sheets, wondering if that was a promise I'd be able to keep.

Chapter Twelve

Andie

Paul and I had just come back from a four-mile walk. I like walking a lot, but I like sauntering. You know, just cruising along sniffing at flowers and tossing beer cans into a garbage bag and noticing that so-and-so's lawn needs mowing in the worst way.

One does not saunter when she's walking with Paul Lindquist. We do a lot of cardio-vascular stuff and warming up and cooling down. The cooling down part is the only one I really like, and if I had my way, I'd never get hot enough to need it.

Of course, it's August now, which is no laughing matter in the Midwest. All you have to do to get hot is exist. I was all for giving up walking altogether in August, but Paul wouldn't hear of it. Now we go after dark, which is cooler—or it would be if he'd let me saunter.

"How's Jake doing?" asked Paul, when I was leaning against the relative chill of the refrigerator pouring a bottle of water down my parched throat.

He hadn't even broken a sweat, drat his in-shape hide.

"He's had to quit work and go on disability," I said. I looked past Paul and out the kitchen windows at the darkness that lay beyond. In life, I guess there's always darkness just beyond. And in death. "He gets tired just talking on the phone."

Silence stretched between us, not comfortable as it usually was, but tense like the heavy air before a thunderstorm. I knew what Paul was going to ask and what I was going to say. The silence was probably better.

"What's he going to do when he can't take care of himself?" He spoke carefully, his eyes on mine.

I opened the refrigerator door to replace my water bottle and answered with my back turned to him. "He'll come here. We've already made all the arrangements with hospice."

Paul's hand rested on my shoulder. "Andie?"

I turned back to face him, closing the door and leaning against it. "Yes."

"Don't you think you might have mentioned it? That we might have talked about it?"

"It wasn't your decision to make, Paul. It was mine. He can't go to Miranda's because both she and Ben work and because of the kids. Lo doesn't have the time, room, or temperament for it." It was funny how, after twenty-eight years of "young Jake," it was so easy to call my son Lo. I wondered if it was one of those rites of passage, when you see your children as real adult people rather than beloved responsibilities.

"And what about you? You're still trying to get your health completely back." Paul looked angry, and I didn't know whether it was at me, Jake, or himself. "What about you, Andie?" he said again. "How could Jake ask—"

"He didn't," I inserted crisply. "He wouldn't. And he fought us tooth and nail on it. Do you want some coffee?"

"Please."

I made it as I talked. "We discussed it in Maine, and the children and I had talked about it before then. Jake was all for staying in Chicago, but that's too far for them to see him often. So then he wanted to go into a nursing facility down here." I poured the water into the reservoir and turned back to Paul. "None of us could stand the idea. We want him to die among people he loves. People who love him. That's us."

I wanted him to understand, but I'd been on my own too long to plead for that understanding. I had survived without Paul Lindquist before; I could do it again.

He didn't say anything at all until we had gone out to the patio with our coffee and taken our accustomed seats in the two lounge chairs Lo had bought me for my birthday.

"When my wife was sick," he said quietly, "it got to where I couldn't take care of her alone anymore. It was hell on her, me, and the kids. On a good day, she asked me to put her in a nursing home so that we could remember her as the woman we'd loved."

He cleared his throat, staring toward the stillness of the woods behind the house. "I wouldn't do it, so we got help and we kept her at home and took care of her till the end." He looked over at me, and his eyes looked hot and unhappy in the dusky light from the kitchen. "It was the hardest thing I ever did. The last month or so, she wasn't even the person I knew. The medication and the disease had made her into someone else, someone I wasn't in love with. Someone who...I was relieved when she died."

"But you still loved her," I said. I swung my feet to

the ground between the chairs so that I could look into his face. "I haven't been in love with Jake for years, and I know full well that it will be a relief when he dies—the idea of seeing him suffer is unbearable—but I still love him. He's still Miranda and Lo's father. This is something I can do for him and for them."

"You don't think it's above and beyond what you need to do?"

I smiled. "When I was sick, Jake Logan called me almost every day. He sent flowers, and silly presents, and armloads of books he'd go into a bookstore and buy at random. He called from Chicago and had pizza delivered on nights I didn't feel like eating, called Jean and Suzanne to come over when my voice didn't sound right on the phone, had Miranda steal hospital bills right out of my mailbox and send them to him so he could pay what the insurance didn't cover. And he never once came to see me because he knew how low my resistance was. Not once in a whole year."

I felt tears pushing against the back of my eyes and sniffed to hold them at bay before accepting the handkerchief Paul held out to me. "So, no," I finished, "I don't think it's above and beyond."

He sighed. "Well, damn." He reached for me and pulled me over into his lap. His words were muffled against my hair. "I guess the rest of the story of my wife's last months is that it was—I don't know—a precious time, I guess. Those random moments when we laughed together or shared memories. Even though everything had changed, I guess you're right when you say I still loved her."

He gave me a kiss and met my eyes in the near-darkness. "Tell me how I can help."

Jean

I typed "The End" and started the printer. I had written a hundred thousand words in three months and I hadn't any idea whether any of those words were even remotely marketable. What was more, I didn't care. This book, *Dancing in Moonlight*, had come directly from my heart, leaving it both eased and full at the same time.

I looked around my office with satisfaction. The room was everything I'd wanted it to be. Even Carrie had been delighted when it was finished. There was something of everyone I loved in here: the wallpaper the girls had hung, the bookshelves David and the boys had built, the book covers the Tonsil Lake girls had framed for me. One wall was devoted to family pictures and there was a small round table with four chairs for brainstorming or man-bashing sessions. But it was my room. Mine.

A sound from the doorway made me look up. David stood there, dressed in a tee shirt and the cotton pajama pants we'd both taken to wearing around the house as the mornings and nights cooled. "It's done," he guessed.

I nodded. "It may be the end of my career." Then I frowned at him. "Why aren't you dressed? Aren't you going to work?"

David had gone back to work at his old office as a consultant. He worked a few days a week and traveled when he wanted. It was an arrangement that made David, his employer, and me all very happy.

"Not today." He looked at his watch. "I think my wife has a doctor's appointment in an hour-and-a-half. I'm going with her."

"Don't you trust me to tell you what the tests show?"

"Nope."

I had finally broken down and gone to Carolyn the week before. The pain had progressed to the point that I could no longer hide it, and no amount of antacid I took touched it. She had taken some tests and sent me to the hospital for more.

"I know what it is," I told her flatly. "We've talked about it before. You know my history."

"Do you mind letting me do my job?" she asked testily from her chair beside me. "Maybe it is. I'm not going to lie to you about that. But maybe it isn't, either. Those symptoms don't belong exclusively to advanced ovarian cancer. And who are you to just give up without a fight? Your daughters are my patients, too. Is that the kind of example you want to set for them? If it's your history, it's theirs, too. How would you feel if it were Carrie or Kelly deciding to martyr herself?"

"You always were the meanest mom in the carpool," I said.

"Nah. Andie was." She shook my folder at me. "If you're not back in here next week, Jean, I'm coming to your house. You don't have to come to me for this if you feel like we're too close or if you'd rather have a doctor from Indy, but don't let it go any longer. All right?"

And now it was next week.

I was strangely calm as I dressed, did my hair, and put on makeup. David was happy, the children settled, the book done. I could deal with whatever came next.

He held my hand in the car on the way to the doctor's office. We talked about things like bringing in the plants before frost, making sure the cars were winterized, what to serve for Birthday Saturday that week.

When David had parked and we were walking toward the professional building beside Lewis Point Memorial Hospital, he took my hand again. His was trembling.

"David?" I stopped walking and looked up at him, drawing my hand free to lay it on his chest.

His heart beat strong and safe against my fingertips. The leaves overhead fluttered in the breeze so that the sun dappled the ground around us in a dance of lights. I thought, as we stood there together, that life had given me many perfect moments—the children's births, sitting on a rock in Maine with my best friends, time after time with this man that I loved. How could I ask for more?

He smiled and reached to frame my face with his hands. "All I want in this life," he said, "is you."

And one more perfect moment was given.

Suzanne

What am I supposed to say when people ask me how many children I have? Two? One? I had two but now I have one?

I doubt that anyone's asked me that question ten times in the last two years, but now it's asked every time I turn around. The mothers at the daycare center all asked. Now that they know, they give me these soft-eyed looks that mean, "God, I'm sorry for you, but I'm glad it's you instead of me."

I know that look because I used to wear it myself. When I couldn't anymore, when I knew the agony that is the deepest of all agonies, I became someone else. I always said I was afraid there would be nothing left of me if I lost my looks, but now I've lost my child. When I catch myself even thinking about my looks, it makes me sick.

I don't mean to say I have nothing to live for, because I have Sarah and I have friends and I have a new job I like, but the person I was died the day Tommy did. And I don't know what is left.

Trent and I cleaned Tommy's things out of the apartment he'd kept in Indianapolis. It is nice being with Trent right now because he shares my need to talk about Tommy. Nearly everyone else avoids the subject, as though that will make the pain go away. Even Sarah doesn't want to talk about him. I suppose everyone copes in their own way, but coping's never been my strong suit.

We gave most of our son's clothes to the neighborhood thrift store, threw away things like razors and half-used bottles of shampoo, and donated his books and linens to a shelter. Except for Jean's books, all autographed and in a neat row on a shelf over his bed. Trent packed them away carefully and labeled the box for Sarah while I stripped the sheets from the bed.

"I'll wash these before we donate them," I said, but the cotton went right past my nose as I folded them and I stopped moving altogether. It had been so long since I'd smelled the scent that was Tommy's alone, and it nearly brought me to my knees. "Oh, Trent," I said.

He knew. He'd spent a lot of time with grieving parents during his years as an emergency room doctor. "Don't wash them yet," he said huskily. "Wait till you're ready, and if you never are, that's okay, too."

I pushed the folded sheets inside a pillowcase and

set them aside along with photographs we'd found and put into a manila envelope to be gone through when we could bear to look at them.

When we found the bag of pot in his bottom drawer, neither of us commented. Trent flushed the weed down the toilet along with an assortment of pills and a vial of suspicious-looking white powder.

"I keep asking myself where we went wrong," he said, watching the water taking the drugs away. "I was an asshole of a husband, but not a bad father. You were a good mother. Even Phil Lindsey tried. But nothing ever worked, did it?"

"No," I admitted. "Tom always knew he was loved, which I thought would carry him through because it would have me, you know? But it wasn't enough for him."

"Nothing was," said Trent. "Nothing was ever enough for him."

I knew anger was a part of the grieving process, and even though I hadn't gotten there yet, it was obvious that Tom's father had. I went to him and put my arms around him.

"Funny, isn't it?" he said, rubbing his cheek on the top of my head. "We've held each other more in the past month than we did when we were married."

I smiled up at him. "We're grownups now."

When the apartment was clean and empty, we turned the key over to the building superintendent and started toward Lewis Point. It was Friday night and the traffic was terrible. It took us forty-five minutes to reach the outskirts of Indianapolis, normally a twenty-minute drive.

"Did I ever say I was sorry?" asked Trent, when we

were sandwiched between two eighteen-wheelers and moving at the approximate rate of a sedated snail.

"Sorry?" I looked over at him, noting how he'd aged in the past weeks. He still looked boyish, but no longer immature, never again carefree. He'd lost his only child.

The tenderness caught me unawares, and I reached to touch his face. "Sorry for what?"

"Wrecking our marriage." The car moved forward another six feet. He took my hand and kissed my fingers. "For letting you go."

"Well, no," I said, a little breathless. "Most of the time, we hardly spoke at all. But we were kids, Trent. Maybe not chronologically, but in every other way we were. The time for blaming is long past. Like I said, we're grownups now."

"Yes." He released my hand and eased into the left lane. "We are."

We picked up Chinese on the way to my condo and sat on the floor and ate out of little white buckets while we watched *The Quiet Man* for the hundredth time. Watching the sensual interplay between Maureen O'Hara and John Wayne, I was suddenly conscious that my hair was in dire need of cutting and coloring and that my makeup had worn off hours ago. I was glad for the darkness in the room.

Was this the beginning of healing? Instead of making me sick with self-hatred, thinking of my appearance gave me a thread of hope. I considered what Andie's response would be to that and almost laughed aloud.

"I wonder..." I mumbled.

Trent turned a sleepy-eyed glance my way.

"What?"

"How I'd look as a redhead."

Vin

"What in the hell is this?" I waved the single piece of paper around as though that would make it visible to the lawyer on the other end of the line.

"I'd say that was obvious, Mrs. Stillson. Mr. Stillson's daughters, Marie Stillson-Lance and Joanna Stillson-Martin, would like your permission to make use of the Palm Beach house during the month of October. They plan to do some entertaining while there and will of course pay their own expenses."

Randall Naismith talked, as Andie might say, as though he had a corncob up his ass. If the man ever sneezed, I'm sure the top of his head would blow off. He had been Mark's lawyer and probably his closest friend, but, like Marie and Joanna, he still considered me an interloper.

"They've used the house every October that I can remember, Randall. Why did they feel the need to put it in writing?"

"They didn't use it last year."

"They didn't?" I didn't remember. I had still been in a fog of grief over Mark's death and consumed with worry over Andie. "Why not?"

"Out of respect for your bereavement, I'm sure."

I almost snickered. "I'm sure. Well, tell them..." I stopped. "No, wait a minute. Tell them I'll discuss it with them over lunch on Friday. One o'clock. Here."

"Mrs. Stillson, I hardly think that's appropriate given the circumstances. You can just sign the letter where indicated and return it in the envelope included. There's no necessity for difficulty."

185

"No."

"Pardon me?"

"No. Lunch. Friday. Here."

I hung up and went into the kitchen, where Archie was putting the finishing touches on dinner. "Arch, was I what you'd call a wicked stepmother?"

She set a platter with four grilled pork chops on the counter between the two place settings she'd laid, complete with linen napkins, Mark's mother's china, and the crystal we'd bought on our honeymoon. It had taken me the entire month of July to convince her that we could eat together, in the kitchen, and remain civilized.

"No." She still had to bite off the "ma'am," but she was getting better at it, and I grinned at her. "But I believe anyone Mr. Stillson married would not have met with his daughters' approval."

"Really? Even if it had been one of their mother's friends, you don't think they'd have liked her?"

Archie shook her head and set a small serving bowl of vegetables on the counter. "Wine?" she asked.

I nodded and went to the cellar in the pantry to choose a bottle. "Did they think, seriously, that I was going to displace them in their father's affections, or what?"

"Their mother was an unforgiving woman," said Archie carefully. "Even though you didn't even meet Mr. Stillson till long after they were divorced, I'm sure she portrayed you to their daughters as *the other woman*. There you were: pretty and smart and scarcely any older than they were. You would most certainly be considered a threat."

"Oh." I poured the wine and we took our places.

"They're coming for lunch Friday."

"Here?" She looked horrified, but her voice was sturdy and calm. "What would you like to have?"

I shrugged. "Something easy, maybe something a little bit Hoosier so they won't be disappointed in their worst expectations. Think we should eat in here?"

"No!"

I grinned at her again, and this time she grinned back.

"Here, look at this. I want to talk to you about something." I handed her the letter from Randall.

She reached for the reading glasses we kept on the counter for whichever of us needed them and read in silence, then looked expectantly at me.

I plunged in. "I'm thinking of giving the houses—this one and the one in Palm Beach—to Marie and Joanna."

She looked shocked. "Giving?"

"Yes."

"But they're yours."

"No, the house in Maine is mine. Property in Indiana is mine. But these houses, even though Mark left them to me, should go to his daughters. Should have been theirs all the time."

"They'll evict us."

I laughed. "No, the giving will have some strings attached. One of those strings is that you go with this house if you so choose."

Archie nodded, though she didn't look relieved. "What will you do?" she asked, then immediately retracted. "I'm sorry. That's not my business."

"I don't know," I admitted, "but I'm not going to stay in New York."

It was the first time I'd said those words aloud. Even though I'd been thinking them ever since I returned from Hope Island two months ago, I'd been reluctant to commit the decision to voice. I looked across the counter at the woman who had, against all odds, become my friend. I would miss her.

"I'll go to Hope Island or Indiana," I said. "Or both."

Archie was silent a moment, cutting her pork chop into neat bite-size pieces. Then she said, "Ma'am?"

I sighed. "Yes?"

"Will you be needing a housekeeper?"

Part Four

"Not only is life a bitch, but it is always having puppies."

Adrienne Gusoff

Liz Flaherty

Chapter Thirteen

Andie

I cleaned house all morning long. I did windows, mirrors, and windowsills. I went down to the supermarket and rented a machine and came back and began to shampoo carpets. I took down curtains and tossed them into the washing machine.

Suzanne came in at noon, took one look at my house, and began stripping the beds even though no one had slept in the guest room since Vin came back for Tommy's funeral.

"Don't you have to go back to the daycare center?" I asked at twelve-thirty, looking down the length of a long curtain rod at her.

"No. I've cut back to three days a week. I spent the morning packing stuff up at the condo till I couldn't stand my own company anymore. I can't believe David hasn't called. He knows we're worried to death."

"He'll call," I said. "She's probably not even out of surgery yet."

"It's been four hours."

"I know."

Without discussion, we prepared the guest room and bath for Jake's imminent arrival, cleaning out the dresser drawers and the closet, replacing daisy-laden sheets with soft white ones. I hung new black and white towels in the bathroom and placed a new, guaranteed-not-to-slip mat in the bottom of the shower.

"I should probably see about renting a hospital bed," I said finally.

"Do you think?" said Suzanne.

Then we left the room quickly, closing the door behind us.

We ate ham sandwiches sitting at the table and tried not to look at the silent telephone.

"Jean and I did this the day you had surgery," said Suzanne, picking the crust off her bread in little pinched pieces.

"What did you talk about?"

"Tonsil Lake." She looked startled. "We never went back this year, did we?"

"The year's not over yet," I said, keeping my voice light. *But, God, I wish it was. How much more of this year can we take? Will it just go on till we've lost more children, more ex-husbands, each other?*

"God," said Suzanne, "I wish it was."

I blinked. "Me, too."

"I don't know whether I'm more afraid of one of us dying," she said, "or that we'll continue to live and it won't get any better."

I wanted to shout at her that living was better; I'd come close enough to dying to know that.

But I hadn't buried a child. I thought of Lo and Miranda. Of my son-in-law Ben whose endless patience never ceased to amaze me. Of my three little stair-step grandchildren who could undo my spate of housecleaning in six minutes flat. Of Jake.

How much poorer our lives are when we lose those we love; how much richer because we knew them at all, because we loved them in spite of everything.

This Jean-like thought coming from my mind startled me so much I said it aloud, then immediately apologized. "I'm sorry. That was rather pompous, wasn't it?"

Suzanne reached across the table to squeeze my hands. "No, I don't think it was. I think you're right. The worst thing in my life was Tommy dying, but I wouldn't go back and wish I'd never had him."

Into the silence that followed, she said, "She did this when we had measles, too, remember? Just went on till she dropped. Bringing us stuff and—"

"I remember."

We'd yelled at her for her stubbornness against giving in to the blisters. *Little brave heart showing off for the preacher. Do you think it'll get you into heaven or something?* But we'd read her stories voraciously, been glad for the conversations whispered through the jalousie windows.

By the time Suzanne's bread was a bunch of doughy little pills on her plate and the melting ice had faded my iced tea to the color of beer, I was ready to pick the phone up to make sure it was working.

But then it rang, and we sat there and looked at each other. Neither of us wanted to answer it, but since it was my phone, I drew the short straw.

"Hello?" I croaked.

"Andie?" said David. "Is that you?"

I cleared my throat. "It's me. Is Jean all right? How did she come through the surgery?"

"Like a trooper. The mass..." He stopped, and I heard a little gasp, as though he were crying.

Oh, God, no, Jean.

"It was the size of a grapefruit, but they got it all. It

193

was contained within the pelvic region." He stopped again, and I could sense his struggle for control. "And, Andie?"

I nodded, realized he couldn't hear my head moving, and whispered, "Yes?"

"It was benign."

Jean

It hurts like a sonofabitch. Andie says my writing that is plagiarism. I don't give a damn.

Suzanne

The condo sold last week. The woman who bought it, an executive at the same automobile factory where David is still a consultant, loved the furniture. So I sold her most of that, too.

"She's thirty-eight," I told Jean and Andie, as we all sat on David and Jean's king-size bed eating lunch. "By the time she's fifty-one, she'll be sick of all that white."

"Uh, Suzanne..." Jean, two weeks after her surgery, weighed in at about a hundred pounds soaking wet. It was the first time in my life I'd ever encouraged anyone to gain weight.

"What? Here, have some of these. If I eat them, the sour cream goes right to my ass." I handed her the potato chip bag and the dip container. "The chips just gather up on my thighs in perky little dimples."

"Suzanne, where are you going to live?"

"Oh." I gave them the most vacant-eyed, dumb-blonde smile I could come up with. "Probably move in with Andie."

Andie was silent for a moment, exchanging a look with Jean. Then she said, "Isn't there a saying about dead bodies?"

Jean grinned. "Or pigs flying?"

"Or hell freezing over?" said Andie. "Suzanne, I don't have room in my house for your makeup, much less your wardrobe." She looked speculatively at my hair. "Or enough dye to maintain that atrocious color. You look like you should have a mattress strapped to your back."

"Sarah's already offered to pimp for me," I said, scrubbing a hand through my redder-than-I'd-intended hair. "I gave tons of my makeup to Miranda. Ben suggested I stop before they had to build onto their house. And I put a lot of my clothes in the daycare center's garage sale. The owner said my suits, by themselves, probably bought the new playground equipment."

"Suzanne, what are you doing?" asked Jean quietly. "New job, no makeup to speak of, new hair, new car, no clothes, no home. What are you doing?" she repeated.

I was quiet for a minute, thinking. Then I reached for the purse-sized photograph album Vin had sent to Jean. I flipped through it till I found the shot Lucas had taken of the four of us sitting on the rock. "What do you see?" I said, pointing at the picture.

"Us," said Andie, looking mystified and somewhat impatient.

"And who are we?"

"What are you saying, Suzanne?" asked Jean, looking at the photograph with her brow pleated into a frown. "It's a good picture of all of us, something we don't have many of."

"You're right, it is a good picture of us. It's so good, you could look at it and point out which Tonsil

Lake girl is which, even if you didn't know us."

I pointed. "There's you, Jeannie, the strong one, the one who wouldn't complain about anything. See, you're sitting on the edge of the rock, with one cheek about to fall off, and you're laughing."

"Well, it was funny," said Jean, "because I *was* getting ready to fall off right that minute." She arrowed a look at Andie. "Or was being pushed."

"I know," I said, "but it's representative of who you are. And look at you, Andie. The fighter. You've got your hand up on your shoulder like you're daring someone to knock the chip off."

"I was brushing sand off," Andie protested.

"Representative," I said again. "Okay, look at Vin. What do you see?"

They gazed at the snapshot, and I saw realization dawn on Jean's features. "The mystery," she said. "She's looking somewhere other than the camera, and she's just wearing this cool little smile instead of laughing like the rest of us."

Andie nodded. "Lucas hadn't tickled her yet."

"Now," I said, "look at me."

Although Jean had been right when she said it was a good picture of all of us, it was best of me. My hair was tousled, but artfully so. My makeup was intact. My turquoise bikini showed up better than the other girls' dark-colored maillots. I was—

"The pretty one," said Andie.

Jean nodded. "You've always been the pretty one."

"We don't even hate you for it anymore. Much," Andie added. She looked at me, not smiling. "But you do, don't you?"

"No," I said as honestly as I could. "I liked being

196

the pretty one. I still like people thinking I'm nice-looking. But I let that be *all* that I was because it was the only thing I succeeded at. I failed at two marriages, I was never a good mother, I can't *do* anything. I can't write like you two, or make money just by waking up in the morning the way Vin does."

I laughed, although it sounded forlorn to my own ears. "I can't even keep houseplants. They die on me so fast I'm convinced it's a suicide pact between the philodendrons and the English ivies."

I reached for the potato chips and scooped up some dip. "I know I'm not going to change into someone else overnight," I said, "and I'm just feeling my way right now. I'm already discovering I'm too old to be chasing small children around as a way of making a living. I adore your grandkids, but they just flat wear me out."

Jean and Andie both laughed. "Us, too," said Andie. "There are reasons for having your kids when you're young."

I laughed, too, because Jean looked worried and she was still too sick to be worried. "I'm so proud of you guys. Jeannie, being the strong one has gotten you through this illness and surgery with flying colors even though you do need your butt kicked for being so secretive about it. Andie, the way you fought your cancer was inspirational to all of us. And Vin's just wonderful. I guess I want to be proud of me, too, for something besides being able to pick out the perfect shade of foundation for any skin tone."

Jean took back the potato chips. "We always kind of liked the pretty one."

I smiled at her. "I appreciate that, but maybe you'll like whoever I become, too."

197

Andie said, "You do know Tommy didn't die because you're pretty, don't you, Suze?"

The tears filled my eyes before I could stop them. "I know that in my head. But you have to understand that every day, when I walk out of that condo, I look straight at the place where he was killed. I see cars driving over the area of pavement that was stained with his blood. And every day, I remember that he wouldn't have been at the condo if he hadn't come to see me. If I'd been home, he wouldn't have been outside at that precise moment."

I held up a hand to forestall their protests. "You don't have to tell me that's nuts. I know it is. But tell me this"—I leaned forward and met first Andie's eyes, then Jean's—"if it were you, would you feel any different?"

They hesitated before Jean said, "I don't know."

Andie said, "You can stay with me for a while if you need to."

Vin

We had to re-schedule the lunch meeting between my stepdaughters and me twice—once because Marie said she was sick and once because I got too buried at work. My bravado wore off by the Thursday afternoon before the third-time-scheduled lunch.

I sat at the kitchen counter with three unread manuscript submissions in front of me. I should have had them read by Tuesday at the latest; instead, I was two days later than I'd promised and I was obsessing over a luncheon menu.

"You knew them when they were young," I said, glaring at Archie. "What did they like?"

She glowered back at me. "They weren't here that

much, and when they were, Mr. Stillson usually took them out somewhere. But when they were here, they didn't like anything. Mostly, they wanted to go home."

I thought of their bedrooms, still kept as they had been when Marie and Joanna were teenagers. Archie only went in them to dust; I didn't go in at all. "But Mark was so crazy about them."

"That he was." She sighed and looked away. "But being crazy about them didn't make him a very good father. He didn't know what to say to them, what to do with them. He was very proud of them, but long distance suited him fine. He was relieved when they were in college and he only saw them when he wanted to."

I was horrified, but I believed it. Mark had liked his life very well-ordered, and two resentful children who became snarling adolescents wouldn't have fit comfortably into that order.

I called Jean. "What would you serve people who didn't like anything?"

"Are you trying to formalize or in-formalize your relationship with these people?"

"In-formalize."

"Tacos. They're good, they're easy, and they're messy. It's hard to be snotty when you've got taco sauce running down your chin and your nose is running because you got a shot of hot sauce."

"Sounds good. How are you feeling?" I asked belatedly.

"Fine, but no one will let me do anything. I'm just lying here watching do-it-yourself shows."

"Where's your laptop?"

"In my lap." She sounded sheepish. "I have to hide

it under the covers if anyone comes in. They think I'm brain-dead because I had surgery and shouldn't be writing."

I laughed. "Then quit watching TV and get busy, at least till someone comes in."

"Vin?" Her voice was hesitant, and I frowned at the phone. "Can I ask you a favor?"

My God, Jean O'Toole asking for a favor instead of doing one? I was surprised the heavens didn't open up right then and there. I caught myself looking up to check and grinned in spite of my jangling nerves. "Anything."

"Would you look at some of the book I just finished? It's rough. I haven't revised at all. But it's...different. Just a chapter or so?"

I looked at the manuscripts in front of me and crossed my eyes. "You bet," I said. "Why don't you e-mail me the first three? I'll read 'em tonight or tomorrow." Maybe I could print them out and read them in the bathroom. That was the only free time I could see in the near future.

"Oh, there's no hurry. Just wait until you have two minutes to rub together. You want me to tell Archie how I make tacos?"

I covered the receiver and put the question to Archie, who nodded and reached for our communal reading glasses. "Yes, that would be great. Bless you, Jeannie, and take care."

Archie took the phone and sat down with a pen and paper. I started reading, relieved the menu crisis was over, but wishing we had two sets of glasses in here— my arms weren't long enough for me to read without them and I was too lazy to go in search of another pair.

"What a lovely woman." Archie looked at the phone after she'd hung it up.

I smiled, reaching for the glasses. "She is that."

"I'm glad things went well with her surgery. I know you were worried."

"It's been a rough couple of years for all of us," I said. "I think we're all starting to doubt if we'll survive our fifties."

She went to the refrigerator, digging through the crisper drawers. "I think you're all survivors, from what you've said and what I've seen."

****

Marie and Joanna arrived together. Marie wore Donna Karan and Joanna wore Liz Claiborne. I wore jeans, flip-flops, and a cotton sweater I'd bought at Hope Island Knits.

There was a time, not that long ago, when it would have mattered who wore what designer.

The first few minutes were as uncomfortable as they'd always been. I hung their coats in the entry closet and we exchanged tight-lipped pleasantries on the walk from the front door to the dining room. Their husbands were fine. Their kids were fine. I was fine.

"Oh," said Joanna, "tacos! I love tacos, but I hope you've supplied bath sheets. I make a hell of a mess when I eat them."

I stopped dead beside my chair and looked at her. "You've had them before?"

"One of the kids came home from camp one year raving about them," said Joanna. "Our cook considers such things beneath her, of course, so we go into the kitchen and make them ourselves on her day off."

Marie took her seat and looked at the taco fixings

with raised eyebrows, more the reaction I'd expected from her sister, as well. "Somehow, I can't imagine Daddy eating them."

"Oh, he wouldn't have," I admitted. I met her cool gaze and lifted my chin. "There's an old country saying about making a sow's ear into a silk purse. Your father tried, but there's still a lot of sow's ear in me."

Joanna looked between the two of us, and I sensed that she struggled between old enmity and new realization brought on by the appearance of tacos on her father's Italian dining room table. "Well," she said finally, "silk spots dreadfully."

After we'd eaten—Joanna had four tacos, Marie three—Archie came to take away plates and ask if we were ready for coffee. "Yes, I said, "but we'll have it in here."

With the aromatic brew between us, I took a deep breath and plunged. "I know you wonder why I insisted on this lunch, since we've never had much to say to each other. Your request for the use of the Palm Beach house really forced me to consider what I wanted to do with it."

Marie's eyebrows went up again. "Do with it?"

"Yes." I took a sip of coffee, willing it to calm my jumping nerves. "Because I don't want it. Nor do I want this one."

"But they were Daddy's houses." Marie's protest was immediate and heartfelt. "He loved them."

"I know he did. And I loved him." I forced myself to meet her eyes again. "But I never loved these houses, and without him, I don't even like them. No one's been in the Palm Beach house except staff since he died."

Joanna spoke stiffly. "Will you allow us the first

chance to buy them?"

"No." I smiled at her. "You shouldn't have to. Mark should have left them to you in the first place. Since he didn't, I'm asking you to take them. I don't know the legalities involved, so if you need to buy them from me, the price is one dollar each."

"Why?" asked Marie. Her question couldn't disguise the leap of joy that had lightened her dark eyes.

I sighed. "I gave up wondering what made you two hate me years ago. To be honest, I didn't care. You didn't interfere in your father's and my relationship and I sincerely hope I didn't get in the way of yours with him."

I stirred my coffee even though it didn't need it. "I have regrets, of course. I'm sorry I don't really know your husbands and children, sorry we couldn't mourn together for a man we all loved. But there's nothing I can do about those regrets."

Joanna nodded. "One of those lessons in life people try to explain when we're too young to believe them." She reached for my hand. "Believe me when I say the regrets aren't one-sided."

I squeezed her fingers. We actually touched. "One of the things my friends and I decided when we were growing up was that we would always try to do the right thing. Didn't always mean it would be right to anyone else, but it had to be right for us. I haven't always done that, but I'm trying to now."

"But you were Daddy's wife," said Joanna slowly. "You are entitled to the houses, to anything else he wanted you to have."

"Maybe," I said, "but I don't believe he considered

that I'd ever leave New York. He loved it so much here that he couldn't imagine anyone wanting to live somewhere else. As far as he was concerned, he really had made me into a silk purse. But the truth is that even though I love New York, too, I still feel like a visitor here."

"It was difficult," said Joanna, her voice hollow, "living up to his expectations."

Marie said, "He always wanted what was best for us." She shrugged. "But it was hard. You're right about that."

"I hope you both know he adored you," I said. "I don't know much about your relationships with your parents—they're not my business—but I do know that much, that he always loved you and that he was very proud of you."

Marie's head lifted, and her eyes were glistening. "Was he?"

Her expression made me think of Suzanne, and I added to my list of regrets. Why had I waited so long? Was life entirely comprised of "if only I had"? When did one get to the "I'm glad I did" part?

"Yes, he was," I said firmly. I didn't even know if I believed the words myself, but I wanted them to. Although they had done nothing for me during my marriage to their father, neither had I done much for them.

"What are you going to do?" asked Joanna. She leaned her elbows on the table, drew them back, then put them down again.

I thought of the end of Tonsil Lake that had my name on its deed; of my mother, so content in her assisted living apartment; of Jean and Andie and

Suzanne.

I thought of Lucas Bishop and the cozy house on Hope Island, and realized the answer was the same either way.

"I'm going home."

Chapter Fourteen

Andie

The guest room in my house is okay, but it's not very big. A hospital bed and other medical paraphernalia would fill it to uncomfortable proportions in no time. So we spent a bittersweet afternoon preparing the dining room for Jake to occupy. Paul and David brought in a hospital bed, Suzanne and I heaved in the recliner that had sat in her condo, Jean brought over the hospital tray table that had been above their garage since David's mother's death.

"How are you going to do it?" asked Miranda directly. "Do you want me to take a leave of absence? I can, you know. We can live on Ben's salary for a while."

Miranda and Ben were both schoolteachers. The only way they could live on one salary was if they gave up eating and my youngest grandchild stopped getting ear infections and changing shoe sizes every two weeks. "No," I said. "I can do it."

He came the week of Columbus Day. Lo and Sarah drove to Chicago on Lo's days off and helped him close his apartment, pack what he wanted to bring, dispose of or place in storage what he didn't. When they arrived at my house, Jake was gray and sick-looking and Lo looked ten years older than when he'd left.

"They're both exhausted," Sarah said in a low

voice as we carried things inside my house. "I think it's the first time Lo's accepted that he's going to lose his father."

I nodded. "Take him home, Sarah. Jake and I will deal with this."

"Are you sure?"

"Yes. We'll be fine."

She hugged me hard, and I reflected that giving my son up to another woman wasn't difficult at all when the woman was like this one.

After seeing them off I went inside and looked at the clock. It was six o'clock and already growing dark. This was one of the things I hated about winter, that days were too short to do what needed doing. Too short to say what needed saying.

Jake was in the recliner, sitting with his face toward the window. He turned to look at me when I came in. I didn't switch on any lamps, and I fancied the feeble light of dusk would be kind to his ravaged face and my white hair.

"I'm so sorry, Andie. I wish I'd had the balls to take care of things myself before it came to this."

"Don't be an idiot," I said tartly. "The Tonsil Lake girls would insist I drove you to it. You know they would."

He laughed, then began coughing. "Damn!" he said, his voice a shadow of what it had once been. "I couldn't do it," he said, "because of the kids. It's bad enough their old man's going to die of AIDS, they don't need suicide added to it."

Our eyes met in the half-darkness, and I understood what he was saying. That he was asking my permission. *Explain it to them so they'll understand it wasn't because I wanted to leave them. I never wanted to leave them.*

It had been the worst part of our divorce, that the kids had felt as though he were leaving them. Even after they knew why he'd gone, they'd felt the emptiness caused by his leaving and grieved for it. They would grieve for it again soon.

I thought of my chemotherapy days, when I'd prayed for deliverance without caring what form it took. I'd become determined to live only when I was pretty sure I was going to. I still remember that day, when I woke to the sun in my face and Jean saying, "Come on, let's go plant flowers."

She'd done most of the planting, while I'd sat bald and exhausted on a lawn chair, but I knew as I sat there that I would see the multi-colored fruits of her labors. That was the day of my deliverance.

Jake would not have a day like that.

"Are you hungry?" I was unable to face his unspoken question or compose an answer I could deal with.

"No. Nothing tastes good anymore."

"Okay." I wouldn't fight him on it tonight. We were both too tired.

He went to bed early. Paul called, offering to stop in when his twenty-four hour shift ended at seven in the morning. "Would you mind if I said no this time?" I said. "I need…" I stopped. I didn't know what I needed.

"Okay," he said after a moment. "I'll call you tomorrow. Try to get some rest."

"Thanks, Paul."

I couldn't sleep when I went to bed, and finally I gave up. I put on sweats to guard against the chill that permeated the house at night and went into Jake's room. I pushed the recliner all the way back, tucked a small pillow under my weak left arm, and fell into an uneasy doze.

He had coughing spasms a few times through the night. I woke each time, going to sit on the bed beside him and hold him up.

"This isn't going to work," he whispered. "You need your sleep, Andie, and the kids need to live their lives. Let's call the nursing home tomorrow."

"Hush." I stroked his hair and stared into the darkness, knowing he was right. Energy levels at fifty aren't the same as they are at thirty in the best of cases. Throw a little breast cancer, some surgery, and a whole lot of chemo and radiation therapy into the works, and your stamina's pretty well gone to hell in a hand basket.

AIDS patients aren't like people who have heart trouble or brain tumors; people are scared of them, scared of their body fluids, of the hopelessness of the situation. There wouldn't be volunteers coming out of the woodwork to help with his care.

My tears dripped into his hair, and I fell asleep like that, his head pillowed on the breast that was really me. He slept, too, undisturbed by coughing for at least a few hours.

Maybe some deliverances are just shorter than others.

Jean

"I'll be back at noon," David whispered. He gave me a kiss and a squeeze, and left.

I made coffee, nearly as familiar with Andie's kitchen as my own, and cooked oatmeal, putting it in a casserole dish in a warm oven to keep it hot. I didn't know how Jake's appetite or digestion was, but I didn't figure a fried breakfast would be a good thing.

With coffee in front of me, I sat down and opened my laptop to check my e-mail. The first message was from Vin, and it made me grin, sitting there in morning's half-light. "SEND MORE!"

Okay, I could do that.

Andie came in as I worked, wearing faded green sweats. Her hair stood up in frosty spikes. "What are you doing here?" she said crossly, going to the coffeepot.

"Giving you a break. Here, I've made out a schedule." When she sat down, I pushed the worksheet across to her.

She emerged from her cup to stare down at it. "What in the hell is this?"

I got up to prepare her a bowl of oatmeal. "Stop complaining and read," I said. "You can't do it on your own. That's why you have children and friends and friends' children." I plunked the bowl in front of her. "Is Jake awake?"

"No." She read the entries on the worksheet. "Jean, you can't come over this often. You're still recovering."

"Oh, phooey. If I recover any more, I'm going to go crazy. Eat your oatmeal and go back to bed. David will be here at noon. He'll help Jake get a shower and all that good stuff."

Jake was awake when I took his breakfast in, his face turned toward the window. I set the food on the tray along with ice water and his medication. "How are you feeling?" I asked, arranging his pillows behind him.

"Like I should be dead."

I looked at him and thought of myself, of the

benign tumor that I'd thought was my death sentence, of my "second chance." I wondered why I'd gotten one and he hadn't. "Well," I said, "obviously you shouldn't be. Who would charm our socks off if you weren't around?"

"That's the hell of it." The old twinkle lit in his eyes. "You girls always insist on stopping at your socks."

I gave him one of those come-hither looks that look ridiculous on older women but we do them anyway. "Well, darlin', you know how fussy David is about sharing."

When I picked up his scarcely-touched breakfast dishes to take them into the kitchen, he said, "Did you bring your laptop with you?"

I nodded.

"Will you bring it in here when you come back? I'd like to write some letters—private things to different people—and my writing looks as though I'd spent twenty years in medical school." He moved his thin hands restlessly. "It wears me out, though. Would you do it for me, write what I dictate?"

"Of course."

We only got one letter written that morning, to Miranda. I'd barely gotten past "My darling daughter" before tears were blurring my vision, but I typed on.

So many journals have started since those first books Suzanne bought us. I don't know if the other girls have continued theirs, only that I have. And now I'm typing what is essentially Jake Logan's final journal. It makes me sad, but it also pleases me to be able to do something for him.

I watched him as he faded off to sleep, and

remembered when we were all younger, with our children playing together while we talked and laughed and played cards. Had we known the sadness that was in store—Mark's and Tommy's deaths, Andie's and my illnesses, this horrendous disease that was robbing us of Jake—what would we have done? Would we have laughed harder, played more, loved better?

Or would we have slogged on as we did, doing the best we could with whatever we had to work with: dancing in the moonlight in our kitchens, bringing in New Years with beer toasts in our living rooms, caring for our sick on rented hospital beds in our dining rooms.

David came in as I daydreamed, his arm around Andie. "We're running away together," he said in a whisper. "Can we use your car? You have more gas."

"Sure," I whispered back, pushing myself out of the recliner. "Will you be back in time for supper?"

"Depends," said Andie. "You cooking?"

We huffed quiet giggles. I watched David lean over Jake, touch his hand gently, then sit in the recliner. When my husband looked up to say goodbye to me, his eyes were glistening.

We talked this morning, David and I, about Hawaii and about friends. Although we didn't say much, it was enough. By the time I got out of the shower, he'd already canceled the reservations. Hawaii didn't fit into the schedule I'd laid on Andie's table this morning.

I guess, all things considered, I'd stay with dancing in the kitchen, beer in the living room, and hospital beds in the dining room.

Suzanne

Andie was hollow-eyed and had lost at least half

the weight she gained back after her illness. Even with the schedule Jean devised and with everyone taking four-hour shifts whenever they could, the weight of Jake's increasing needs was on her shoulders.

I pushed her out of my way. "I'll just put my things in the spare room," I said over my shoulder. "Good thing we got it all ready for company, isn't it? Not that I'm company, but I am partial to clean sheets even if they are plain white, which we both know I'm sick to death of."

"Suzanne."

Going through the dining room with her hot on my heels, I waved at Jake and Paul, then blew a kiss. "Hello, you gorgeous men, you."

"Hey, Suzy-Q." Jake's voice was so weak I could barely hear him.

"Hi, Suze." Paul lifted a hand.

"Suzanne."

By the time I got to the guest room, Andie was pushing me ahead of her. "I know what you're doing." She closed the door behind her. Rather firmly. "It's not necessary. Things are going all right."

I tugged open the top drawer of the dresser. "Sure, they are," I said. "They're going so well that now Lo and Miranda are worrying about losing both their parents instead of just one." I shot her a look. "You look like hell that's frozen over and thawed out again."

"Thank you very much. Did you know your ass was dropping? You'll be feeling the old slap on the backs of your knees any time now. And all that plastic in your face is melting."

I grinned at her, then turned back to dump my duffel bag into the drawer. "You said I could stay."

"If you needed to. Not as a one-woman rescue unit."

"No one-woman to it." I began peeling off the clothes I'd worn in the daycare center that day. Carrie's little girl had puked all over me. "We're all in it together, kid. I can be more helpful here than from out at Sarah's. Besides that, I think I sort of cramp their style. Hers and Lo's, I mean. They spend an inordinate amount of time checking on the animals in the barn, and it's getting really cold for that sort of thing. Hand me that other bag, will you?"

I rummaged through the bag she tossed on the bed, coming up with some sweats. "Now," I said, "go get Paul and you two go for a walk." I pulled a sweatshirt over my head and fluttered my eyelashes at her. "Find a barn and check on the animals."

She stood still, her gaze and mine clashing as our personalities almost always had. "Thank you," she said.

"Go."

Vin

"You just got here." Lucas nuzzled my neck.

"Two weeks ago," I corrected him, keeping my knees from wobbling by leaning them against the kitchen cupboards, "and now I need to go to Indiana." I turned in his arms. "I'll be back."

He pushed my hair behind my ears, looking down at me, and I finally understood what romance writers meant when they wrote about getting lost in someone's eyes. If I'd ever memorized any poetry after Joyce Kilmer's "Trees" in the seventh grade, I'd have started spouting it.

"Well, I gotta go. Have a good flight and give me a call to let me know you got there safe." He gave me a kiss, long and leisurely enough to weaken my knees again, then tapped the end of my nose. "Love you, Lavinia."

I closed the back door behind him and lifted the curtain to watch him negotiate the path toward the village. He turned to wave before he moved out of sight and I lifted a hand in response. It felt as weak as my knees did, and I let it drop to my side. " 'I think that I shall never see a poem lovely as a tree...' "

Archie came into the kitchen, carrying my bag. "Excuse me?" she said absently.

"Nothing," I mumbled, but I could feel myself blushing. "Are you sure you don't mind being stuck here?" I said.

"Stuck?" She gave me a look of astonishment. "I love it here. Reminds me of home, it does, but with differences."

She looked younger and prettier, I noticed, and wondered if she'd met someone on her daily trek into the village. "Archie, how long have you been widowed?" I asked.

"Twenty-five years. We were only married a couple of years, but we made them good ones."

I almost asked why she had never remarried, but then I remembered how she'd felt about Mark. "What do you think of Lucas?" I asked instead.

"He's lovely." She grinned at me. "Seems more to the point to wonder what you think of him. I must say, I've lived in the same house as you for over twenty years, and I've never heard you recite poetry before. Though I did wonder at your choice in verses."

"It's the only poem I know," I admitted. "But he is lovely, isn't he?"

****

I rented a car in Indianapolis and arrived unannounced at Andie's, too late for supper and too early for bed. I tapped lightly on the back door and went in just as Jean walked into the kitchen pulling on a jacket.

Our hug was silent and hard.

"He's sleeping," she said quietly. "Do you want to see him?"

I nodded and followed her into the dining room. Young Jake, or Lo, as I couldn't seem to get used to calling him, shared a recliner with Sarah. I touched their heads, kissed their cheeks, then turned to the hospital bed.

I'd thought I was prepared. I'd talked to one of the girls almost daily, so I'd expected to scarcely recognize the skeletal man in the bed. But I couldn't stop my horrified gasp, and when I touched my cheek lightly to Jake's, mine was already wet.

Andie and Suzanne came in shortly, and we put blankets around our shoulders and carried coffee to the patio.

"The doctor says it's probably a matter of days," said Andie, her voice low and thin with exhaustion. "Happy goddamned Thanksgiving."

Her eyes glittered in the dim light that flowed from the house. "When he first came, he talked a little about suicide, and I was so afraid he'd do it. Now, I almost wish he had. This isn't living."

"We may not feel like it's living, but this time has been a gift." Suzanne had her face turned away from the rest of us, and her voice was muffled. "He's been able to say his goodbyes, put everything in order. I'd give anything..." The words trailed away unsaid, but we didn't have to hear them to know what they were.

"See that brightest star up there?" Jean's voice was cheerful and strong. She pointed. "No, not the tower lights, the other big one above them."

We all craned our necks and nodded.

She smiled at each of us. "That's Tommy, you know, waiting for Jake."

It was the kind of thing Reverend Parrish said to us in Sunday school at the little church that sat on a hill right in the middle of the Hendersons' farmland. We'd trudge up there every Sunday morning, not putting on our shoes till we reached the churchyard because the road was dusty and we figured dirty feet were better than dirty shoes.

When the minister cut loose with one of those platitudes, we'd all look at each other and Andie would smirk because living on Tonsil Lake taught you better than that. Clichés about God's will and angels on high weren't intended for the likes of us. It was only later, when we attended Rosie's funeral in the little church, that we admitted we'd taken comfort from some of the tired expressions.

"Look," I said now, pointing. "There's Mark, too, and Rosie behind them to watch over them the way she did us. They'll be all right."

We watched in silence for a little while, sipping our coffee, then Andie said, "Goddamn it."

"What?"

"Rosie's star's a forny airplane."

Chapter Fifteen

Andie

Sometimes I feel as though sadness has seeped right through my pores and become a part of my bloodstream, poisoning me in much the same way as the cancer did. Only they don't have chemo and radiation for sadness; there is no prosthesis or reconstructive surgery to replace the part of you the sadness destroys. I look at the shell of the love of my life as he lies in bed, at my children as they lose their father, and think I can't bear another day.

That's when I understand the murder-suicide scenarios you read about in the papers. How easy it would be, if there were no one else to consider, to put Jake out of his misery and then turn the weapon of choice on myself.

What about Paul? The thought dances through my head like a song I can't stop singing, but I don't know that there will be enough left of me when this is over to make real the relationship we only play at in these awful days.

I think all of this as I sit in the recliner listening to Jake's breathing. Sometimes the space of time between sucking in air and shuddering exhalation is long enough that I lean forward in the chair and say his name.

"Still here," he says, his voice little more than a sigh.

It is the Friday before Thanksgiving, though I've given little thought to either the holiday or giving thanks. I feel remorseful about that sometimes, when I think of my loud-but-happy children and grandchildren, of Jean's grapefruit-sized benignity, of my own restored health. But then the sadness overwhelms the remorse.

Lo and Sarah came in as I stared out the window at the bleak November landscape. Suzanne was with them.

We exchanged the kind of silent conversation we'd all gotten good at, with raised eyebrows and headshakes, and went into the kitchen. I turned up the monitor on the counter, and for a moment we stared at it, hearing that shallow breathing.

"Uh, Mom, Suzy-Q, we need to talk to you." Lo was at the coffeemaker, preparing a fresh pot, making it strong enough to cut with a knife. "You got anything to eat?"

"You know where the refrigerator is," I said. "You spent half your life standing in the open door of it complaining."

"True. Sarah, would you make me a sandwich?"

"No. Your legs aren't broken."

I beamed at her. "What a good girl you are." Suzanne rolled her eyes.

He settled for pecan pie, eating it straight out of the pie plate because there was only a third of it left. Seated at the table, he jerked his head toward the dining room. "Any change?"

"No. He sleeps more every day, but you know that."

"Well." He exchanged a look with Sarah. "We thought we'd get married." He fluttered his long eyelashes at her and gusted an unconvincing sigh. "She thinks I should make an honest woman of her."

Sarah rolled her eyes just as Suzanne had, and it was uncanny how much like her mother she looked. "Truth is," she said, "he says he won't sleep with me anymore if I don't marry him."

"But, sweetheart…" Suzanne was all wide eyes and breathy voice—I wanted to smack her one. "You *do* realize who you're getting for a mother-in-law, don't you?"

So then I *had* to hit her, then we held each other close and hard before turning to hug our children.

"We'd like to do it here," said Sarah, when we were seated around the table with cups of thirty-weight coffee, "on Thanksgiving, with just you two and Miranda and Ben and Jake." She met my eyes. "I'd like for my dad to perform the ceremony. Would that be okay?"

"Of course," I said. Although I didn't particularly like Phil Lindsey, he had gained points with me when he told Sarah the truth about his divorce from Suzanne. And whether I liked him or not, he was the father of the young woman who was about to become my daughter-in-law.

I saw in Suzanne's eyes the regret that her only daughter was going to marry in someone's dining room with no guests to speak of. No white tulle or bridal showers or flower girls. Sarah would be married as we had all been.

There had been no money for weddings for the Tonsil Lake girls, and we'd all been too proud to allow our fiancés or their families to finance the kind of luxury we'd lived all our lives without. We'd lived out that particular dream in our children's marriages. All three of Jean's kids and Miranda had had big weddings and noisy, laughing receptions at the country club or the park or, in Josh's case, in Jean's back yard.

Sarah must have seen her mother's eyes, too, because she said gently, "This is what we want, Mom. We want for Jake to be there."

"Of course you do," said Suzanne, her smile instant and bright. "You'll have to watch him, though. You know how he always becomes the life of the party. Remember when you kids were all little? None of you wanted to have a birthday party unless he was going to be there."

"You gotta admit," I said, "playing Pin the Tail on David O'Toole was entertaining."

We all laughed. "And David was so good," said Suzanne, "yelling like a banshee every time a kid even approached the target Jake put on his butt."

"Remember when Carrie wanted a swimming party and Jean said no because it was too cold?" said Sarah. "Jake started pushing people into the pool and it became a swimming party anyway. Jean was the first one he pushed in." She looked anxious. "Will they understand why we're doing it this way?"

"You know they will," I said. "But Jean will have a party for you at some point. You can bet on that." In the silence that followed my comment, I listened to Jake's breathing as it came through the monitor. He would think he was a lucky guy, seeing his son married to a girl we both loved.

I smiled at my son and Suzanne's daughter, willing the sadness—for the moment at least—to go away and leave me the hell alone. How could I do any less? "It'll be the best Thanksgiving we ever had."

Jean

"My editor hates it." I looked down at the sheets of manuscript Vin had printed out. "She says it will disappoint readers who expect a certain thing from me." I frowned at the plethora of red ink on the printed pages; there were slashes and scribbled notes everywhere. "It looks as though you weren't thrilled with it, either."

"Look again," said Vin sharply, pointing at the pages with her butter knife. "Of course your editor doesn't like it. Although you're an excellent writer, your voice is also predictable. If you released a book under a pseudonym, your readers would still know it was you. You've stepped way outside that box on this, and that's not something your publisher wants from you. Doesn't necessarily mean it's a bad thing."

"Oh." Pleased, I went back to looking at the manuscript. "What can we do for Sarah and Lo?"

"I was thinking about that." She sat at the table with her toast. "I thought maybe a honeymoon of sorts. They're off work until the Monday after Thanksgiving."

"They won't want to leave town," I said, "with Jake being so bad right now."

"I know." She looked thoughtful. "The Henderson farmhouse at the lake is a bed and breakfast now, and that's only fifty miles away. What do you think?"

"I think that's inspired."

"Good. I'll call them this morning." She sighed. "And one of these days soon I've got to bite the bullet and go see my mother."

I grinned. "Carrie will be saying that about me one

of these days, if she's not already." I looked curiously at Vin. "Do you ever wish you'd had children?"

"Sometimes, I guess, but most of the time I think it's good I didn't. I'm too selfish for the full-time business. I want to put my toys away when I'm tired of them. I like being the fairy godmother, with all the good stuff but none of the heartache. It was nice of you guys to give me that opportunity."

"We thought so," I said primly. I leaned an elbow on the table and propped my chin in the palm of my hand. "So what's with you and Lucas? You talk to him every day, you blush when David teases you about him, and you've left New York behind you. What comes next?"

"I don't know," she said with a shrug. "I'll just go call that bed and breakfast." She hurried out of the kitchen even though there was a telephone right there, and she was blushing.

Suzanne

"Mom?" Sarah stood in the middle of her bedroom, clad in a silky white slip with scallops around the bottom. Her hair was wrapped in a towel. "Would you maybe do something with my hair? And put some makeup on me that I won't rub off halfway through the ceremony?" She laughed, sounding self-conscious. "I'd kind of like getting married looking as if I had eyelashes."

My first impulse was to get all maternal and teary, but I knew that wouldn't fly with my daughter. "Sure," I said briskly. "Go on in the bathroom. I'll get the makeup."

I got us each a glass of wine while I was at it, even though it was only nine-thirty in the morning.

223

She looked askance at the glass. "Mother, I just finished my coffee."

"Hey, you don't get married every day, kiddo." I put my hand on my chest. "Even *I* don't get married every day."

She laughed, but when she met my eyes in the mirror, hers were worried. "What if we're making a mistake?" she said. "I don't want to be in the situation you and Andie were in, divorced with two little kids. What if this is the wrong thing?"

"There aren't any sure things, honey," I said past the lump in my throat. "I'm sorry I couldn't give you the kind of home and life that Jean and David gave their kids, but things just didn't work. That doesn't mean they're not going to work for you. You and Lo were friends before you were anything else; you're still friends. Good heavens, your dad and I were never friends. Trent and I weren't until...until recently. It would have been so much better if we had been."

I worked my fingers through her soft blonde hair. "Up or down?"

"Down but out of my face," she said. "Lo likes it down, but it drives me nuts if it's in my eyes. Jake and Andie were always friends, though, and look how that turned out."

"That's what I mean by 'no sure things,' " I said, "but they're still friends, they still love each other. They just couldn't be married."

I put white clips in her hair to hold it back from her face. "This is a compromise, leaving your hair down but holding it back, and compromise in marriage is at least half the battle. You can't do that with everything. Andie couldn't with Jake's lifestyle, I couldn't with your dad's...uh...views on things. But Jean and David and Vin and Mark had it down, and had Trent and I been more mature, we probably could have survived."

I tugged at a lock of hair. "But then I wouldn't have you, so I certainly wouldn't want to change anything."

She turned toward me, pulling her hair out of my hands, and put her arms around me, her face pressed against my breast. "I love you, Mom."

There was no stopping the tears then, and we both cried a little before I gave her a last hug and said, "I love you, too. Now, we'd better hurry, or you're going to be getting married in your slip. Lo would probably like it, but your dad's a little stodgy about things like that."

She rolled her eyes. "My dad's a *lot* stodgy about things like that."

We laughed together, and it was like dancing when you feel the music instead of just hearing it.

Oh, she looked lovely. I almost cried again after I dropped the simple white sheath over her head and zipped its back. She'd bought it off the rack, but it looked as though it had been made for her.

She wore the strand of pearls that had been Phil's mother's and a slender, twinkling gold chain Tommy had given her for Christmas one year. Her earrings matched the pearls, a gift from Andie and Jake, and in the second hole in each ear she wore the tiny diamonds I'd bought her when she graduated from vet school.

She'd said, "Diamonds, Mother?" in a voice that indicated she'd really rather have had some heavy-duty rubber boots.

I'd countered with something idiotic about how

every girl needed diamonds sometimes and had bawled all the way home.

"You were right," she said suddenly, touching the little studs as though she knew what I was thinking. "Everybody needs diamonds sometimes."

"But you don't," I said. "You sparkle just fine without them."

She grinned. "You bet I do. I look just like my mom."

Their ceremony was short and very sweet. Jake was able to stay awake through it and hand the ring to his son to place on Sarah's finger. Lo kept staring at his bride with a tender smile on his face that warmed me right down to the toes of my black suede pumps.

Andie and I didn't look at each other until Phil said, "Normally, I would ask who gives this woman to be married, but in this instance, we all give you to each other, as your lives have been intertwined since before they even began. This we do with our love, and by the authority vested in me by the State of Indiana, I pronounce you husband and wife."

I felt my eyes brimming and when I ventured a glance at Andie, she was mopping her cheeks. She caught my eye and we both began to laugh, albeit damply, then turned to hug our children.

We settled Jake to sleep and went into the kitchen. Jean and David were on their way out the door, moving covertly and wrapped in raincoats like two suburban Columbos. They waved. Jean ran back to kiss Sarah and Lo, then they were gone before we could stop them.

The kitchen counter was set up like a buffet, with platters of turkey and ham along with all the accompaniments. A lace-covered card table sat in the corner holding a miniature wedding cake and several bottles of chilled champagne. Two wicker laundry baskets, decorated with ribbons and lace, were full of envelopes and wrapped gifts.

I sniffled, and Andie said, "Leave it to Jean. She never fails."

Miranda laughed. "Those laundry baskets have made the rounds. I think they've been present at every bridal shower, wedding, and baby shower since I got married."

"Just like Jean's friendship," said Andie, "only it's far too big to fit into two baskets."

Her voice was wobbly when she went on. "I've found it so difficult to be thankful. It's like losing Jake is bigger than all the good things that have happened, and I just couldn't be grateful. But today, with one marriage and two fussied-up baskets, I've figured out that you can hurt and be grateful at the same time."

Phil opened the first bottle of champagne, pouring it into the glasses that waited beside the cake. "Andie," he said quietly, "would you like to make the first toast in Jake's stead?"

"I don't think I can," she said, shaking her head. "Suzanne?"

Good heavens, no one ever asked me anything like that. Phil should—no, he shouldn't. I raised my glass.

"To all of our sons and daughters, from all of us. May you know as much happiness as we have known, and have fewer troubles. To the bride and groom in particular, may your friendship and your marriage be long and prosperous. To Jake, because we are all so glad he could be here for this day. And to…" I stopped, looking at Andie.

Her glass touched mine. "And to the republic, for which it stands."

Vin

I had Thanksgiving dinner with my mother in the big dining room of her assisted living facility. We sat alone at a table, which I regretted because we had so little to say to each other, but the people she considered her friends were out for the day.

When I got there this morning, standing in her small living room with my raincoat drizzling on the carpet, I'd offered, "We could go out if you'd rather."

"I like it here," she said. "Hang that coat over the tub, Vin. You're dripping."

There was nothing wrong with my mother. She was in the assisted living portion of the upscale apartment complex because she'd never taken care of herself in her life, and didn't want to start.

At seventy, she looked no older than her late fifties. I kept her supplied with the kind of makeup Suzanne used to represent, and she had a healthy allowance in addition to her Social Security. She shopped a lot, getting on the facility's bus and spending days on end at the mall.

She liked being able to flash her credit card at the big department stores that had been laughably beyond the means of any of my stepfathers. I used to cringe when her bills came in, but Mark only laughed. "Just pay them, darling. It keeps her happy and out of your hair."

Her greatest concern when he died was that her allowance would stop, that her credit card would be cut off. "Will you marry again soon to someone who can take care of things?" she'd asked. "Will I have to move?"

"My friends and I will shop tomorrow," she said now, as we sat at our table for two. "It's such a fun day. What will you do?"

"Sit with Jake. And Jean and I will watch Carrie's and Miranda's children so their mothers can go shopping."

She frowned. "Why don't you hire nurses to sit with Jake? For that matter, why didn't Andie just put him in a home? It's not safe, having someone in the house with *That Disease*."

I noticed that a lot of people called AIDS That Disease. Did it make them feel immune, as though refusing to give it its name put them above such things?

"We're very careful," I said. "Andie didn't want nurses, and she didn't want him to die without family around him."

She sniffed. "It would surprise me if Andie doesn't have it. All those men that aunt of hers had in and out of that trailer, and then she died of that mysterious thing in her head. How could some of that wickedness not have passed down to Andie?"

Rage made the turkey stick in my throat. I picked up my glass of ice water and drank half of it. "Rosie took care of all of us. She kept us safe. How can you talk that way about her?"

"Kept you safe?" Mother said scornfully. "By giving you girls a place to run to every time things didn't go your way?"

For the first time in a very long time, I remembered the night my stepfather raped me. I could usually swing my mind away from it, but this time it caught me unaware, like someone opening the bathroom door when your hair's full of shampoo.

It was as it had been during the years of reliving it every single day; I could recall every second of an event that seemed to go on for hours. I could smell the mildew that climbed the paneled walls of the trailer, feel the gritty sheets beneath me, see the place I forced my mind to take me to in order to survive. I remembered my mother's voice—"Don't fight him, Vin. What will we do if he leaves us? How will we live?"

Rosie had taken me to a doctor she knew the next morning. She'd sat with me and held my hand and chain-smoked unfiltered cigarettes. "Just make sure she's not hurt, Fred." Her eyes had met Fred's over the table where I lay with my feet in stirrups.

I had been too numb to be humiliated or frightened. Too numb to understand her next words. "Make sure she doesn't have any little reminders of that asshole."

To this day, I don't know who Fred was, only that he was kind and that he didn't hurt me. And that there hadn't been any "little reminders."

On the way home, Rosie bought me a chocolate malt and told me quietly and succinctly what to do with my knee, where her gun was kept, and that there was nothing wrong with running like hell.

The day my stepfather's car was pulled out of the lake, Rosie went to the sheriff's office. We rode along with her, but she made us wait in the car. It seemed as though she was gone a long time, but when she came out, her bright smile was in place.

Afterward, we sat at the ice cream shop, with vanilla shakes this time, and Rosie said, "This part of you girls' life is over. You don't have to look back on it, remember it, or worry about it. You are safe and you're all together and I'll do my damnedest to keep you that way."

If there was any further investigation of my stepfather's death, I never knew about it, and there were no charges filed. Rosie's gun was never found and none of us ever talked to her about that day again. I don't know if I ever even thanked her.

I drank the rest of my water and refilled the glass from the crystal pitcher that sat on the table. "Yes," I said, "she always gave us a place to go."

Mother sniffed delicately. I propped my chin in my hand and looked at her. She was a remarkably pretty woman, beautifully made up and elegantly coiffed. Her nails were perfect, her clothes tasteful and expensive. I thought of Suzanne, with her fear that there was no depth of character behind her beauty, and realized my mother didn't even have enough substance to have that concern.

Then I thought of Jake, who had more grace dying of That Disease than the woman across from me had ever had. I thought of Mark, of Andie, of Jean and David. Of the wedding surprise I'd been unable to help with because I'd come here instead. I thought of Archie, puttering happily in the house on the island. And of Lucas, whom I loved.

What in the hell was I doing here?

I reached into my purse, pulled out all the cash I had with me, and laid it beside Mother's plate. "For Christmas," I said. "I have to go now."

I was all the way outside before the frigid air reminded me that my raincoat was hanging over the tub in Mother's apartment. I looked back at the front of the

building. Then I got into my rental car and drove away.
I didn't look back again.

Chapter Sixteen

Andie

I came awake suddenly, my eyes popping open in the darkness like those of the star of a made-for-television thriller. I had slept hard and dreamlessly, an unusual occurrence these days, and felt strangely rested even though I'd gone to bed only four hours ago.

"Mom?" Lo's voice came from the doorway. "Mom, wake up."

"I'm awake." I sat up, reaching for the robe on the end of the bed. "What is it?"

"I don't know," he said, "but something's changed. Dad's different. Sarah already called Miranda."

Jake was awake. He smiled when I sat beside him, and the expression eased the lines of pain from his skeletal face. "Close now," he said.

"I know." I took his hand, wanting to rub some warmth into it but knowing it was too late for that. Already his fingertips were turning blue.

"The kids know...how much...I love them?"

"They know. They love you, too." I touched his face. "And I do, Jake."

"You, too. Always...my best girl."

Although I could barely speak, I said what I knew he wanted to hear. "I better be your only girl, Logan."

The laugh was little more than a catch of his breath. "Keep on dancing."

"Just as fast as I can."

"You and the girls need to...go to Tonsil Lake."

"We'll go soon. Promise."

He moved his head, looking up. Miranda and Ben had come in, and they stood with Sarah and Lo around the bed as though if they guarded its perimeter they could stop him from leaving.

"Take care of your mom," he said, "but don't...let her...push you around." The laugh again, even weaker this time.

"We can handle her, Dad," said Lo.

"I love..." The words faded away, and his dimming gaze moved back to me.

"Sleep tight, Jake," I whispered. "I'll go to the lake. We'll be all right."

And he died.

Jean

None of us wore black to Jake Logan's funeral. We wore bright colors and jewelry that made noise when we moved. "No ugly black dresses or sad dirges," he'd instructed us. "If I have to lie there all dignified, I at least want to hear clanking bracelets and see women's legs with high heels on the ends of them. And the music has to make people remember happy times, not dwell on the shitty business of dying."

The funeral director hadn't been at all thrilled about playing CDs by the Beatles, Elvis Presley, and Crosby, Stills, and Nash during the visitation, but he had done it.

It was far too soon after Tommy's funeral that we once again found ourselves cleaning up after the crowd who had gathered following Jake's services. The flowers and most of the plants had been taken to the nursing home and the hospital. The contributions had been turned over to the police department's teddy bear fund, a field trip fund at the school where Miranda and Ben taught, and the Humane Society. I had passed out the letters Jake had dictated.

"Our mothers used to like this," I said. "Not that they wanted anyone to die, I guess, but they enjoyed the social aspect of funerals."

"Especially when they were the bereaved ones." Vin poured coffee for all of us and brought it to the table. "My mother loved being widowed, when the man she married became a hero and she became 'oh, you poor little thing.' "

"People even said that to me," said Andie, "though Jake and I had been divorced for twenty years."

She got up, restless in her red dress, and went to the doorway that led into her dining room. She stopped abruptly, with her back to us. "I'm still looking for him, still checking on him. When we came back from the viewing yesterday, I hurried into the house because I wanted to tell him how many of the kids he coached had come to pay their respects. That Lucas had flown in. God, wouldn't he have laughed the other night, Suzanne?"

She looked back at Vin and me and explained, "I woke up and came rushing out here to check on him even though some semiconscious part of me knew he was gone. Suzanne was already up, half-awake, staring at the dining room table as though it didn't belong there."

"Everybody does that," said Vin. "I woke listening for Mark. Suzanne heard Tommy calling out to her. Jean, after all those weeks of caring for David's mother, would wake every night at the same time and go sit in the dining room."

"It's where I'd slept," I said. "It was hard to get used to being in a bed again." I met Andie's eyes when she came back to the table. *Are you okay?* I was doing it again, asking the question we always asked, expecting the slight nod, the even slighter smile that meant *I'm fine. Don't worry.*

She nodded, smiled, picked up her coffee cup.

"I wake up mad," said Suzanne. "Tommy slept through the night from the time he was a few weeks old. Why is he all of a sudden waking me?" She looked haunted, and I reached to squeeze her hand.

"I keep thinking, though," said Andie, "how we didn't do that after they hauled Chuck out of the lake. We should have had nightmares, but none of us did. We slept better than we had for months."

I felt my eyes widen. We never, ever talked about this. Even when Rosie died and we stood gaunt-eyed and grieving beside her open grave, we hadn't talked about Chuck Hardesty.

"Our nightmares came from his living, not his death," said Vin tersely and accurately. "Although I have to admit that sometimes I wonder…"

She stopped, looking down at the cup in front of her, picking up the paper napkin that lay beside it and shredding it. There was silence between us, then Suzanne's hand came to the middle of the table. I placed mine on top. Andie's and Vin's hands came to the stack of intertwined fingers at nearly the same time.

"That's funny," said Andie, "when we used to do that, no one had wrinkly knuckles or brown spots on their hands. What the hell happened?" She rolled her eyes at Suzanne. "You, of course, still don't have brown spots or wrinkly knuckles."

Vin never finished her sentence. She didn't have to, because we all wondered the same thing. Had these past two years of our lives—deaths, illnesses, and emotional traumas—been punishment for something that happened nearly forty years ago?

It was time to go to the lake.

Suzanne

I have to go somewhere. Although Andie's guest room is comfortable and I'm glad I've been able to be of some help to her through these last horrendous weeks, that time has passed.

"Come and stay with me," Trent invited the first time we woke up together in his big house in one of Indianapolis's most affluent suburbs. "Let's see if we can make it work." He tugged at the sheet that covered my breasts and leered at me. "We know one faction of it does."

It would have been so easy to do that. I was more than a little in love with this man who'd been my first husband—I had, as a matter of fact, felt less for him when I married him than I did now. Having—and losing—a child together creates a bond that mere hormones and an urge to play house do not.

Not that there was one little thing wrong with our hormones now. This is something I wish I'd known during all the years I spent trying to stay young. It would have been nice if someone had told me that sex at fifty-one was a hell of a lot more fun than it had been at twenty or even thirty.

"So?" said Jean when I mentioned this to her. "It was a nice surprise." Then she got this satisfied expression on her face and I saw her looking at David's butt as he walked across the yard. If it hadn't been so cute, it would have been disgusting.

Watching her, I wondered how she'd done it. I remembered when she'd discovered David's brief affair.

I'd started cleaning my guest room and Andie had laid in a supply of white zinfandel in preparation for the stormy separation that was bound to occur before she forgave him. Vin had been home at the time, and the three of us had gone to Jean's house *en masse* to be supportive. She'd looked at us with hot, dry eyes, and said, "Let's go to the lake."

That's what we'd done. We'd driven up there in the dark and gotten drunk and talked about everything in our lives except husbands either present or past. David had come to pick us up, and somewhere between the Tonsil Lake Tavern and his car, Jean had forgiven him.

I guessed that's how they'd done it. They'd forgiven each other everything and never forgotten the love, and I was pretty sure they had great sex.

If I could have based my decision on sex and emotion alone, I'd be settled in Trent's house instead of living out of a suitcase in Andie's.

"You can always build a house on our property," said Sarah. She blushed endearingly and a slow smile crossed Lo's face. "You're so good at taking care of little kids, it would be nice to have you here in a year or two when we decide to produce a couple of little cops or veterinarians."

The idea of grandchildren turned me into an instant puddle, but I didn't need to be a puddle right in their back yard.

"I'll always be here," I promised, "no matter where I am."

That had been Jake's farewell in his letters to us. I don't think I'm particularly spiritual, but the words had made me feel better, just as Jean's had the night Vin arrived, when we sat on Andie's patio and looked at the stars. He'd told me to go back to being blonde, too, which had made me laugh.

"You should go to the lake, Suzy-Q." Lo looked up from where he was detaching Elmer's claws from his uniform pants. His gaze left me quickly, though, to settle on his wife. "The bed and breakfast is great, but the feel of the whole place is even better. Growing up hearing so much about it, we felt like we'd gone home. Maybe that's what you need to do."

Sarah nodded agreement, looking back at Lo with an expression that made me feel like an intruder. "It made the past few days more bearable," she said, scooping up Elmer and handing him to me. "Jake's letters said, 'Home's wherever you hang your heart.' You need to find that place, Mom."

I cuddled the cat. "I may go there for a weekend. It's been a while."

"Take your makeup," my daughter said. "I know you want to find the person inside you. Me, I just want my mom."

"Me, too. I want her mom, I mean." Lo looked at his watch and bent his head to kiss Sarah. "I have to go to work." He stopped beside me to kiss my cheek. "And lose the red hair."

Vin

"The islanders aren't going to know what to think

239

of you, taking off twice in one year." I lay on my side in the king-size bed in Lucas's hotel room, facing him across the crust of the pizza we'd just shared. "They'll be thinking that two years is up."

"I'm not so sure it's not."

"Oh, pooh." I pushed against his chest. "You're as attached to your practice and the people of Hope Island as Mark was to his boardroom. You'd never leave there."

He reached over, pushing aside the strand of hair that persisted in falling into my face; I hadn't yet found a stylist to replace Mr. Jacques, who was actually Jack Richards from the Bronx. "I would," Lucas said, "if my wife wanted to live here."

I stared at him. "Wife?"

"Would you consider it?" He moved the pizza box aside and pulled me into his arms. "Would you lie here in the dark with me and think about making it a permanent thing? Not permanently in the Lewis Point Inn, probably, but in a house that was ours."

"I don't have to think about it." I couldn't believe the words had come out of my cautious mouth, but once they started, they didn't stop. "I'd love to marry you."

He reared up in bed, pulling me with him. "You would?"

"You bet, but I'm only marrying you if you continue that two-year obligation until you're ready to end it."

He shook his head. "Be careful what you say. I love being a doctor. I especially love being a doctor on Hope Island. It could go on for a really long time."

"I'm counting on it." I hooked my hands around his neck. "But you're right about something, too. I want to be here part of the year. The Tonsil Lake girls and their families are important to me in a way that a week every summer no longer takes care of. I'd like it if you could be here with me, but if you can't, will it bother you if I come back here a lot?"

"It probably will if I can't come with you," he said. "There's another young doctor coming along in January who owes Hope Island two years. That should allow me to spend part of my year playing bad golf with David and Paul and talking shop with Trent."

We leaned back on the headboard, my head finding its comfortable place on his shoulder.

"So, when do you want to do this thing?" asked Lucas. "We need time to do a pre-nup and get some other ducks in a row." He slanted me an accusing look. "It would be easier if you weren't rich."

"Ah," I said, "but some things will be easier because I am. Are you willing to move into my house on the island?"

"Yes, ma'am."

"And are you willing to sell me your house to give to Archie?"

"No, ma'am. I figure *we* can give my house to Archie and she'll be so appreciative she'll keep on cooking for us." He shuddered. "I love you for a thousand reasons, Lavinia, but your cooking ain't one of them."

I couldn't argue that one. The cookbooks I took to the island this summer had been a success—with Jean, who was already a good cook, and with Archie, who was an inspired one.

"I'd like to get married in the spring," I said. "That'll give us plenty of time to do everything we need to beforehand."

"Works for me."

"And now I'd like for you to go home."

"Alone?"

"Uh-huh. I'll be there by Christmas."

"Okay." He nodded agreeably. "Any specific reason you don't want to come with me now?"

"Just one." I sat up straight to meet his eyes. "I have to go back to Tonsil Lake."

Part Five

"How could they return to this place that had deferred their dreams, broken their hearts, and made sinners of them all?

How could they not? It was home."

Jean O'Toole
Dancing in Moonlight
Gunderson Publishing, 2013

Liz Flaherty

Chapter Seventeen

Andie

"You're fine." Carolyn reached over and gave my hand a squeeze. "What made you think you weren't?"

I got to my feet, feeling embarrassed by the fear that had kept me in a state of suffocating wakefulness since Jake's death. "I don't know. Just a feeling."

She walked with me to the door of her office. "Life's kicked you in the ass the last couple of years, Andie. Take a break from it. Go back to that lake that's never far from your heart. Breathe."

But could I breathe at Tonsil Lake? We had been talking about going in the daylight, about spending a night or two at the Hendersons' bed and breakfast. This wasn't the usual memory lane drunk-fest in the safe cocoon of darkness that was the Tonsil Lake Tavern.

"We just rented the whole house," Vin had said. "It's only got four guest rooms anyway and it's wintertime so hardly anyone goes there. We may as well be comfortable." She grinned. "You won't even have to share a bathroom with Suzanne."

"I don't know," I told Carolyn. "The present's been pretty rough to live in, only God knows if we have a future. The idea of delving into the past is kinda scary."

Carolyn laughed loud enough that everyone in the waiting room looked up to see what was going on. "You're fearless, Andie. Go. Enjoy. Feel. I repeat,

245

breathe."

Outside, I turned toward home, wondering what had possessed me to walk to Carolyn's office in the first place. The sun had been out, I remembered, and the wind at my back, and I'd been fooled once again by Indiana's fickle weather. An hour-and-a-half later, the sun had disappeared behind the dirty gray marshmallows of winter clouds, and the wind was shredding the skin on my face.

It would be freezing on the lake.

"Hey, woman, what are you doing out here?"

I turned toward the shout and waved at David where he stood outside the driver's door of his car. "Going home," I called back.

"Let me give you a ride."

Before I could protest, he'd dropped back into his car and swung a beautifully illegal U-turn, coming up beside me.

"So," he said, when I'd sunk into the delicious heat of his passenger seat, "are you going to the lake?"

"I don't know." I looked over at him. "Jean is, isn't she?"

He frowned. "Yeah."

"You don't look very happy about it."

"Sometimes I think the past should just be left alone. I'm afraid she'll dwell on things that happened when you were kids. You know Jean; before it's over, she'll be taking the blame for everything and wondering what she should have done differently."

I couldn't argue that, since it was exactly what Jean would do, but I wondered if David's objections went a little deeper than he was telling. "Why don't you take me to your house instead of mine?" I suggested brightly. "It's just as close and your wife will feed me."

He dropped me off, waving to Jean when she came to the door to see who was in the driveway. She waved back to him, but she wasn't smiling.

"Okay, what gives?" I asked, tossing my coat on her couch in a way calculated to mess up the perfectly arranged pillows. "David looks grim and you look grimmer. I can't exactly go poking my nose into his business, but it doesn't bother me at all poking it into yours. What do you have to eat?"

She led the way to the kitchen. "We had a fight," she said, pouring coffee for both of us and setting it on the table with an entire cheesecake.

I snorted. "You and David don't have fights. He gets mad, you sulk, and the next day you're nice to him and he forgives you."

She stopped the knife halfway through the cheesecake. "You take that back."

"I will not. It's the truth."

My slice of cheesecake narrowed.

She sat across from me, scraping the tines of her fork over the surface of the dessert. "How did you feel when you found out Jake was cheating? I mean, I know it was different, but how would you have felt if it had been a woman you caught him with?"

"I don't know," I said. "I don't think I ever expected fidelity to go on forever. He traveled too much, loved women too much. I'd have been pissed, I'm sure, but not shocked."

I waited a minute, sorting through the levels of pain in search of an honest answer. "But we're different, Jean. I know you expected to receive the same kind of loyalty you gave. It hurt you more than it would have me."

She didn't say anything, just kept dragging her fork over the cheesecake until it looked like lumpy pudding on her plate.

I wanted to yank the fork out of her hand. "Jean?"

She looked up.

"I also know it's been at least fifteen years since David's...indiscretion. What in the hell are you doing pulling that particular skeleton out of the closet now?" I couldn't enjoy my own cheesecake, sitting there watching her shred hers, so I pushed it away with a regretful sigh.

"It jumped out at me," she said defensively. "Before I had surgery, I was cleaning some stuff out, getting rid of old things I didn't want David and the kids to have to worry over if...if something happened. Right there in my bottom drawer was the letter she'd written him that was how I found out about it. With it was the letter she'd written me afterward and also the card from the flowers he sent when he was still feeling sorry. I didn't read them then, because I didn't think I could stand it on top of everything else, but yesterday I did."

"You kept them?" I stared at her in horror. "Jean, what were you thinking, that they'd be a nice little thing to hold over his head for the rest of your lives?"

"I don't know what I was thinking," she admitted, "but there they were, right where I left them when I abandoned the idea of cleaning out that drawer, and I got upset all over again. David asked what was wrong and when I told him, he got mad. Now, I ask you, what forny business does he have getting mad? He was the one who cheated, not me."

She sounded for all the world like a petulant child, and if she hadn't been so serious, I would have laughed.

The slam of the front door made us both look up. David came into the kitchen, his features a study in controlled fury. He hung his jacket over the back of a chair and said, "We're, by God, going to talk about this. I want to spend the rest of my life with you, Jean, but I'm goddamned if I'm going to walk on eggshells the entire damned time. Andie,"—he tossed me his keys—"go home. We'll pick up the car later."

"Glad to," I said, practically leaping out of my chair. I patted Jean's shoulder, gave David's arm a squeeze, and got the hell out of there.

I swear I saw fireworks through the front window of their house as I drove away. It was kind of nice. Overdue, but nice.

Jean

I tossed David a scathing look when I heard the door close behind Andie. At least I hoped it was scathing. That's not something I'm good at, unless I'm practicing on Andie. "What's the point in talking about it? It happened. Nothing we say can make it un-happen."

"You're right," he said. He went to the coffeepot, pouring a cup for himself and bringing the carafe over to refill my cup. "It did happen. I was stupid. I was wrong. I was a grade-A asshole. But it was half a marriage ago, Jean. We worked to make it succeed even after I almost blew the whole thing wide open, so why are we rehashing it now?"

Anger came over me so hard and fast I felt physical pain when I leapt to my feet, like the cheerleader I'd never been, and yelled, "What's this *we* shit? *I* worked to make it succeed. You just went on your merry way, like all you had to do was buy the stupid little woman some roses and all would be well. Do you know how I felt, David? Do you?"

"No, I don't," he said calmly, leaning against the counter with his arms crossed over his chest. "You were so into being noble and self-sacrificing that you didn't tell me how you felt. 'We'll make it,' you said, and thank God we did, even though you've been holding a part of yourself back for fifteen freakin' years."

"Oh, no, you don't." I crossed to where he stood and poked my index finger at the front of his flannel shirt. "You're not turning this on me, buster. You cheated. You destroyed my trust. You destroyed me, for Christ's sake. You made it like I'd never left Tonsil Lake. I was still in a space all by myself having to be strong because people were counting on me. Well, by God, I counted on you, too, and you let me down. How could you do that to me, David? How could you?"

His hands came to rest on my upper arms and his blue gaze was intense on mine. "What was it like?"

Bewildered by his response, I shook my head. "What?"

"Tell me what it was like for you. I know you suffered. I suppose I knew it then, but I was so glad you were so calm that I never tried to dig too deep. I was comfortable, so I assumed you were, too, like I always did. Now I'm asking. Digging."

I stepped away from him because I couldn't think when his hands were on me, when I could see his eyes. I stood at the sink, running water hard into a dollop of dishwashing liquid, and stared out the window. Remembering.

"I got a bottle of sleeping pills. Not from Carolyn, but from the kids' pediatrician. And I set it on the top shelf of the medicine cabinet, behind the rubbing alcohol, thinking that if it got too bad, I'd just take them all and it would be over. I never took any, but I did lift them down a hundred times. I didn't throw them away for years after the shelf life had expired."

The pain of talking about it was excruciating, and once I started, I couldn't stop. "I found myself going through your wallet, your drawers, even that little zippered compartment on your golf bag where you carry tees, looking for evidence that you were still seeing her or were seeing someone else. I looked at other men, thinking if I could go to bed with one of them, then you'd be sorry. I met Suzanne for a drink one night and she caught on because there I was in a bar with her and I was wearing a dress and red lipstick. 'Don't,' she said. That was all, just 'don't.' And I didn't."

"Why not?" His voice was soft.

I still couldn't look at him, so I went to the table, getting the plates with the uneaten cheesecake. "Because I still loved you. I didn't want you to feel the way I felt. And maybe I was afraid you *wouldn't* feel that way, wouldn't care like I did."

I scraped the sad-looking dessert into the sink and turned on the disposal. "I used to look around when we'd get together with people you worked with and wonder how many of them knew. Did they all think I was a schmuck? I knew you were embarrassed by me being a romance writer, and that hurt, too, so it got to where every party was a nightmare."

"I was never embarrassed."

"Yes, you were. You would never talk about what I did around those people. None of them even knew until I let it slip one time, having no idea in hell you hadn't told them."

"Because I was afraid they'd hurt your feelings. You know how people are about romance novels."

I had to give him that. I'd answered the question, "When are you going to write a real book?" often enough to understand the truth of it.

"So why did you stay with me?" he asked. "Was it the money?"

The question made me look at him. I could feel my anger leaving me, dripping away like the soapsuds off my fingers. I regretted its loss because I wasn't ready to let it go, but I couldn't seem to get it back. "Is that what you thought?"

"Sometimes. We both saw Andie and Suzanne struggle on their own. You knew a lot of poverty growing up. Even though you made money with your books and I would have paid child support, it would have been a rough way to go if we'd divorced. So yeah, I thought that sometimes."

He lifted his cup and drank, even though the coffee had to be cold. "We'd come home from those parties and you'd be all silent and withdrawn and I'd think oh, boy, here goes the punishment again. And I'd buy you something because I thought that would make you happy."

"It wasn't the money." But I knew what he was talking about—I remembered the unexpected, and often unwanted, presents. "It was never the money, David. I was always here because I loved you." I felt tears pushing at the backs of my eyes and tried to laugh to dispel them. "That's not to say I didn't hate you sometimes, too."

He laughed, too, his effort as pathetic as mine. "I don't blame you," he said, "but why now? After all these years—most of them damned good ones—why are you angry?"

I made more coffee, thinking. "Because I can be," I said finally. "Confrontation is still way down on my list of favorite things, but I can confront if I have to. If our marriage ends because I get mad, it wasn't much of a marriage in the first place."

I remembered saying almost those same words to Carrie early in the summer. I hadn't believed them then, but I'd wanted her to. Even when I couldn't be any other way but how I was, I'd wanted better for my daughters.

But I wasn't done. "If my twelve-year-old editor doesn't like the books I write, well, I'll find an editor who does. If Andie and Suzanne squabble, I don't have to be the peacemaker—I can jump in and squabble, too."

I met his eyes. "Life's too short to go around not knowing who you are because you're making yourself into what other people expect you to be. This summer on the island, I found out who I was. I found out I have all kinds of faults and weaknesses but on the whole I'm a pretty good person and a hell of a romance writer. I'm a good wife and a decent mother and a wonderful grandmother. If I get mad sometimes, or unreasonable, or snotty, I'm still those things."

He nodded. "I agree."

"You do?"

"Sure do."

I started past him to rinse our cups before pouring fresh coffee. He snagged my sleeve, and pulled me into his arms. "I think part of what you're saying is that you're going to face up to things so that you can really and truly put them behind you." His gaze caught and held mine. "Is that why you're going to the lake?"

"Probably." I leaned back in his hold, picking invisible pieces of lint from his shirt. "I think maybe we want to open new doors and we feel like we can't until the old ones are closed."

I looked down at my hands, at the pair of bands on the left one. He'd placed the wide one there when we got married, the narrow, etched one twenty-five years later when we'd renewed our vows at a loud and laughing party in our backyard. I wanted the rings to stay where they were.

He sighed, his chest muscles moving against my hands. "Okay," he said, "as long as you remember one thing."

"What's that?"

His arms tightened. "I'm not just some old hollow veneered door you can discard like yesterday's kindling. I'm a genuine mahogany six-panel job, guaranteed to last a lifetime."

Suzanne

The gun felt heavy, even clasped in both hands. My index finger, wet with the sweat from my palm, was slippery on the trigger. I couldn't see worth a damn, and I kept blinking in the pre-dawn darkness, trying to make my eyes focus on the man in front of me. Andie's arm was stiff under mine, keeping the pistol leveled. Jean and Vin were crowded in beside us, their hands with mine. My finger slipped from the trigger and was replaced by one of theirs. The gun wobbled.

My eyes cleared just as the loud report of the gun rang in my ears.

"Tommy!" I screamed. "Oh, no, Tommy!"

"Suzanne!"

Trent's voice penetrated the horrible fog of the nightmare. I came awake as he dragged me into his arms. "Oh, Suzy, the same dream?"

I nodded and burrowed closer to sob uncontrollably into his shoulder. "I'm being punished, Trent," I said. "I'm not sure what for, but it's a punishment."

He didn't answer, just held me until I could stop crying.

Long after he'd fallen back asleep, I roamed his big suburban house, seeking safety in wakefulness. At five o'clock, I made coffee and called Jean.

"I'm scared," I said. "I'm scared to go back to the lake and scared not to. I'm afraid to go to sleep because I dream, afraid to stay awake because what happens next may be even worse than what already has." I thought of Sarah and knew there could be only one thing that was worse. *Please, God, not that.*

"You've been so strong, Suzanne." Jean's voice was as soothing as I'd expected it to be. "I think you're having a form of a collapse now, but you'll come back from it. Just keep talking. Don't try to keep it inside and handle it yourself."

"I can't," I whispered. "Even if I want to, I can't. It's just too big. No one should lose their child, Jean."

"I know," she said. "I know."

"I keep thinking, you know, if I'd just been a better mother, he'd be all right. But we can't undo the past."

"No, we can't," she said, "but you were a good

mother, Suzanne. Look at Sarah. It's no accident that she's as wonderful as she is, and Phil Lindsey certainly didn't do it by himself." Her voice softened. "Share it with Trent. He's feeling the same thing you are."

"Okay." I took a deep breath. "Thanks, Jeannie. I'll be okay now."

"I know you will."

I hoped she was right.

Vin

"It's changed so much," said Suzanne, peering through the passenger side window of Jean's back seat. "Of course, I don't think I've seen it in the daytime since Rosie's funeral." She looked pale and had been extraordinarily quiet on the way to the lake.

I truly hoped we weren't making a mistake.

"I was here a couple of years ago," said Andie, glancing over her shoulder. "I came up to punish myself for something, thinking if I did that the biopsy would be benign as my reward. I couldn't believe how it looked." With a grin, she added, "Or that God didn't fall for my trick."

"Let's stop and see Rosie on the way in, shall we?" said Jean.

She pulled between the wrought iron gates of the tiny cemetery that sat at the edge of Hendersons' woods. We used to pass it going to Sunday school and we always made Andie walk on the inside because she was fearless.

It wasn't hard to remember where Rosie's grave was. Although the church membership hadn't denied her access to consecrated ground, they'd made sure she was at the back, close to the barrels where the mowing crew threw the old flower arrangements.

But we'd taken care of her as well as we could over the years. Her stone was large and shiny, both of which she would have appreciated, with a rose etched artfully in the center above the name Rose Hart Bennett. A small white picket fence surrounded the site, and even in Indiana's blustery winters, greenery filled the urn that sat on one end of the tombstone's base. It held a small Christmas tree now, bristling with little suet-and-birdseed bells tied on with red velvet bows.

We took turns taking care of it, and the kids said the grave always looked best during Suzanne's years. But over time, others had joined us in looking after Rosie. Flowers besides those we ordered often filled the urn; the fence was painted annually and at one point had been replaced without our knowledge; someone had built an enclosure around the barrels. It was nothing more than four panels of privacy fencing, but it was painted white and looked a hell of a lot better than other people's dead flowers.

"Who's doing it?" Andie had asked Scott Parrish, the minister who used to pick us up in his Plymouth for services if it was raining. He'd been young then, and Jean had had a terrible crush on him.

"I don't know," he answered Andie, and added carefully. "Your aunt had many...admirers."

We didn't speak when we reached the site, just stood with our arms wrapped around ourselves against the cold, and grieved again.

"Maybe a bench," said Suzanne finally. She breathed in and out, very deep.

So did the rest of us, in unison. None of us wanted to blubber over Rosie now. Enough time had passed that we should be laughing gently at the good memories she'd given us, not weeping over her loss.

"Good idea," said Andie. "I'd like to sit and talk to her sometimes." She raised her head as though startled. "Good God, did I just say that? I swear, Rosie, I've just been around Jean too long." Her voice was a thin and shaky sketch of pain.

Jean put one arm around Andie. "I've done my best, Rosie, but she still swears in inappropriate places and blames me for everything."

"And complains." Suzanne stepped to Andie's other side. "What was it you used to say to us, Rosie? Oh, yeah, 'you'd complain if you were hung with a new rope.' She's got that part down."

"Nah." I stood next to Suzanne. "You'd be proud of her, Rosie. You'd be proud of all of us. The last two years haven't been so great, but we're still here and we're doing all right." I laid my hand flat on the rose on the stone, feeling the indentation of the etching on my palm. "We miss you."

"We think so much about what we didn't have," said Suzanne. "My mother being crazy, my father only stopping in long enough to get a little, take the money, and move on. Your parents being like they were and Andie not having any. But we all had Rosie. We were better off than we knew."

"She saved our lives," said Jean.

"She definitely did that." Andie looked over at the lake, choppy and gray under the clouds, with ice starting around its edges. "I wonder if they ever found the gun."

Chapter Eighteen

Andie

We'd been sleeping outside because the trailers were like small, dirty ovens in summer. We'd done it enough that we'd established our own little campground under the willow and sycamore trees that kept anyone from putting trailers on the south end of the lake.

We had a ring of stones where we built fires and an old cooler we'd rescued from the junk pile that we used for food and drink. It didn't keep things cold, but it protected our Kool-Aid and bologna and cheese from animals and bugs. Our sleeping bags were ones Rosie had gotten us at the Salvation Army store. We kept them stuffed under my bed when we weren't using them.

On this particular night, Vin wasn't with us. The welfare caseworker had made her rounds today, leaving Vin's mother in a pissed-off mood. Even if Chuck Hardesty hadn't been around in several weeks, she was still married in their eyes, and they weren't going to increase her allotment. So she'd kept Vin home, packing up Hardesty's stuff and setting it in a pile at the end of the strip of mud that counted for a driveway beside their trailer.

Vin had complained. "What's the point, Mother? You're going to let him come back anyway."

That had earned her a crack across the face that left her cheek red and puffy.

We were just waking up when Hardesty's car pulled in. The sun was starting to creep up behind the woods, but it was still pretty dark. We stayed in our sleeping bags, giggling because he ran over his own clothes.

"Serves the drunk old bastard right," Suzanne muttered.

"That's for damned sure," I said.

We'd recently learned that swearing didn't send us to hell—at least not instantly—and we practiced it a lot. Except for Jean, who had the hots for the preacher.

"Let's move up closer," said Suzanne. "If Vin needs out of there in a hurry, one of us can grab her and another one can go for Rosie."

"Whoa, Rosie will love that. She's got company." But I followed Jean's shorty-pajama-clad butt toward the Hardesty trailer. "The mosquitoes are the size of hummingbirds," I mumbled, scratching. "I'd love to see them chomp down on Hardesty's ass."

"There are other parts I'd like to see them get," Jean said primly, and we giggled again.

Then Vin's scream split the darkness and there was a mighty crash from inside the trailer. "Get Rosie," Jean yelled, "and haul ass!"

Suzanne ran the fastest, which really irritated me in phys ed class, so she sprinted toward our trailer. Jean and I moved toward Vin's. We were almost there when the door flew open and Vin ran out. Her pajama shirt was in shreds, exposing the buds of her twelve-year-old breasts.

Jean called, "Here we are. Come on."

Vin started in our direction, but before she could get to us, Hardesty was on her.

"Let her go, you piece of shit," I yelled.

Jean jumped on his back and I grabbed his arm, but he swatted us away like we were a couple of flies. We went back like we were on rubber band bungees, beating him any way we could even though he was holding off all three of us with one arm.

Rosie's voice rang through the early morning quiet. "Let them go, Hardesty."

There she stood, an avenging angel in red satin. She adopted a pose, one hand on her hip, her bosom trying like anything to escape from her bodice. "They're babies, Chuck. Leave 'em be."

"All right. I'd rather have a piece of you anyway. You been putting me off ever since I came here. Reckon you're coming around now, huh?" He lurched toward her, releasing us so suddenly that we fell together like puppies in the dirt.

"No," I said, pushing myself to my feet. "You leave Rosie alone, too."

Suzanne was running from our trailer, something in her hand.

Hardesty grabbed Rosie's arm, pulling her to him. With his other hand, he ripped straight down the front of her gown.

"Let...her...go," panted Suzanne, reaching us.

"It's all right, kids," said Rosie, her voice shaky. "You go on back to your campground. It'll be okay."

"No, ma'am," said Jean politely. "Please let her go, Mr. Hardesty. We don't want to hurt you."

Hardesty laughed and twisted Rosie's arm. When she cried out, Suzanne raised the gun. Her arm wobbled so much that I braced it with my own. Jean and Vin crowded in, putting their hands with Suzanne's. "Let her go," said Vin, her voice strangely calm, "or we'll fix it so you never hurt anyone again."

He came toward us dragging Rosie in his wake.

And the gun went off.

****

Hendersons' bed and breakfast was as nice as Lo and Sarah had said. The bedrooms were big and light, with little bathrooms tucked into unobtrusive places. There was a hot tub in a Florida room that had been added on the back, a sauna in a shed near the closed swimming pool.

The whole thing, including the farm it sat on, was for sale.

"If it's successful," I said skeptically, as we sat down to Eggs Benedict, "why are they selling it?"

Jenny Henderson Arthur, who had married the oldest son of the man who'd been sheriff when we were kids, came through the swinging door from the kitchen with more coffee. "You left here. You've seen things," she pointed out. "I've lived on this farm since the day I was born. I raised my kids here. Now my husband has an iffy heart, I've had a hip replacement that makes climbing these stairs a little hell all its own, and I'm ready to live somewhere else once I've traveled around and seen everything I want to."

We invited her to join us, and she did. We caught up on mutual acquaintances, heard the staggering asking price of the property, and laughed a whole lot.

"Do you know," I asked, "who helps take care of Rosie's grave?"

"I do," she said, "because she came along one day

when Cindy Hathaway was beating the tar out of me. She told Cindy to leave me the hell alone or she'd be sorry. Since there was something mysterious and vaguely wicked about Rosie, Cindy was scared of her and left me and my sister alone after that."

"She never did that for me," I said, mildly offended. "She told me to keep trying until I had Cindy as scared of me as everyone else was."

"She knew you'd have to fight harder for what you wanted, I expect," said Jenny, "and that I wouldn't. I suppose I'm embarrassed by that, but we were as aware of the differences between the Tonsil Lake kids and the rest of us as you were."

I nodded. She was right.

"But I'm not the only one who cares for her grave. My husband does, for reasons of his own that I think have to do with his father. Reverend Parrish does. Your husbands, at least some of them, came one day in the past year and put the fence around the barrels."

After breakfast, we walked around the lake, bundled against the cold, and Vin told us she owned one end of it, the end that abutted the Henderson farm. "It was my safety net," she said, standing under a huge sycamore and staring up through its branches. "You and Rosie made this place safe for me, at least in my own mind, so as soon as lots went up for sale, I bought them. I want to build a house here—a jumbled-up Victorian like the one on the island. One that feels like home."

Suzanne looked thoughtful, and there was a spark of interest in her eyes that hadn't been there since Tommy's death. "You know, the bed and breakfast would be a great place for a spa. Not a rich-bitch one like they write up in magazines with slick pages, but one for women who are just tired. They'd like to have their hair done, someone to tell them what makeup to wear, dinner on the table without having to decide what to fix. They'd like to sit in a hot tub and dream, in a sauna and think sexy thoughts, on a back porch and read the latest Jean O'Toole book with a glass of wine and no kids interrupting them. And they'd like to do it without breaking the bank."

"There may not be another Jean O'Toole book for them to read," said Jean, though she didn't look upset about it.

"Yes, there will," said Vin.

Jean

We never knew who pulled the trigger. We were all standing together, all of us touching the gun. Chuck Hardesty got this ghastly look of surprise on his face and staggered to his car. Rosie hurried over to the four of us, and we watched in silent and stunned horror as Hardesty drove right over his possessions lying there and into the lake.

The screaming started then. Mrs. Hardesty came stumbling out of her trailer and other trailer doors flew open. Rosie stood in front of the four of us, holding her gown together. She half-turned, giving us a shooing motion, and we retreated to the campground to sit on the bank and watch.

Sheriff Arthur got there first, very quickly, followed in minutes by Reverend Parrish. Then we saw them talking to Rosie and Mrs. Hardesty, looking over at us occasionally. The ambulance came next, followed by a wrecker and another police car that held other guys, real divers with all kinds of equipment.

On the bank of the lake, we moved closer together,

sitting with our shoulders touching. We said little.

When they removed Hardesty's body from the car, I thought I was going to be sick. A sidewise look at the other girls showed me they didn't feel much better.

"I wonder," said Suzanne, "if we'll have to go to jail."

Andie gave her a withering look. "Rosie will take care of it."

Vin nodded. "She always has."

The back doors of the ambulance slammed and my mother and Suzanne's walked Mrs. Hardesty toward her trailer. Rosie looked over at us, then went to speak to the sheriff again.

I took a deep breath. Maybe I wouldn't throw up, after all. "I think we should make a pact."

****

The pact had worked out well, I thought. I parked myself on a tree root and watched the other three. I listened to Suzanne's trill of laughter, Andie's deep-throated guffaw, and the musical whoop that was Vin's, and wondered what joke I was missing.

"Question of the day," Suzanne called. "Andie just asked it and it wasn't even her turn."

I sat up straight. "What is it?"

"Where did we hide the time capsule?"

Suzanne

How could we have forgotten about the time capsule? Not just one but all of us. Now that Andie had said, right out of the blue, "Where in the hell did we put that time capsule?" I remembered the day we assembled it, sitting around the table in Rosie's tiny dining area before we left for college.

"What was it in?" Vin said. "Wasn't it one of the

cracker tins that you got if you paid a little extra."

Andie's brows knit as she frowned. "Couldn't have been. We used the really, really cheap crackers, the ones that tasted just like the cardboard box they came in only they weren't near as crisp."

"That's right," I said, and turned to Jean as she approached. "What *was* it in?"

"Oh, shoot." She stopped a few feet away. "The ammo box!"

"The what?"

"It was an army surplus ammo box. It belonged to Chuck Hardesty. It was just lying there after...after everything, and we took it. God knows why. You probably kept part of your makeup in it, Suzanne. But I'm sure it's what we used for the time capsule. We put...Lord, what did we put in it?"

"A BeeGees bubblegum card, a copy of one of your stories, Jean, a newspaper clipping from the hostage situation in Iran, four locks of hair, a few other things that would have mattered to adolescents in the late nineteen-seventies. There was a letter, too, identifying you all and telling the finder what you hoped to achieve with your lives." The voice came from behind a tree, and Reverend Scott Parrish followed it around. He smiled at us. "The hair, as I remember it, didn't exactly match the colors I see on you today."

We all murmured greetings, exchanging embarrassed looks.

"Was there anything else in the box?" asked Andie.

"Yes, there was."

"Do you know where it is?"

"I do." He nodded toward the farmhouse. "The Arthurs have left. Their daughter is in labor with her first child. Would you like me to meet you there and bring you the contents of the box?"

"Yes," said Vin quietly. "Thank you."

The Arthurs had left us a note urging us to make ourselves at home. If they were not back before we left on Sunday afternoon, they added, please lock the doors and feed the cat. They hoped we enjoyed our stay and would come back soon.

We made coffee and rustled cookies out of Jenny's well-stocked pantry. By the time we'd placed the refreshments on the table, the minister was at the door. We looked at each other.

"I'm scared," I said. "It took me so long to lose that girl from the lake. I don't want to find her again."

"Suzanne, try not to be such a ninny," said Andie. Her voice was as wilting as ever, but she didn't look too comfortable, either.

Vin stretched out her hand and we all laid ours on it for a moment. "There are things," Andie reminded us, "that we'll never tell anyone."

Jean opened the door to the waiting minister. One look at his face and the ammo box in his hands let us know we didn't have to worry about telling him anything.

Because he already knew.

Vin

I felt a sudden, unreasonable urge to bolt the back door and run out the front one, but Jean's car was parked in the back, so if we went out the front our only option for escape would be the lake. We could row out to the center in the bed and breakfast's rowboat and just stay there until the world opted to leave us alone, but it would be really cold out there. I opened the door.

"Reverend Parrish," I said. "Thank you for coming."

He stepped inside. "Call me Scott. We're all grownups now, I think."

Suzanne took his coat, Jean ushered him to a seat, and Andie poured the coffee. I stood with one hand on the doorknob, not at all sure we shouldn't have prepared for a quick escape. I regretted that we hadn't allowed the men in our lives along on this trip. They'd have taken care of us, would have kept the past from rising up to...

What was I thinking? We could take care of ourselves. I let go of the doorknob.

The ammo box sat on a newspaper in the middle of the table. "Didn't we bury it?" I said.

"No, we gave it to Rosie." Andie looked over at me. "We'd trusted her with everything else."

"It was wintertime, our senior year in high school," Jean recalled. "We couldn't bury it because the ground was frozen."

How was it that everyone could remember all these details so well now after we'd forgotten the damned time capsule's very existence for thirty-some years?

"How did you get it, Scott?" asked Suzanne.

"Rosie came to see me shortly after you all left for college." He looked over at Andie. "She hadn't been feeling well and she wanted to get right with the Lord as well as get everything in order."

Andie looked as startled as I felt. "You mean she knew?" she asked. "Rosie knew she was going to die?"

"I'm not sure she knew that," said Scott slowly, "but she was aware something was wrong. Her lifestyle changed drastically those last months. She even started attending church, though she sat at the back and left as soon as services were over.

"When she chose her burial plot, she asked for one in the back. She explained that the person who sat on the back of the bus was the one who opened the emergency door in case of an accident and she thought maybe if she wasn't good for anything else, she was good for that."

Oh, dear God, but she had been good for that. I felt a sharp niggle of shame, though, because I'd thought the church membership had consigned her to the remote gravesite.

"I blamed the people of the church for putting her back there, saving the good spots for the Hendersons and the Arthurs and folks like that." Andie gave mumbled voice to my thoughts.

Scott laughed. "I imagine a lot of people looked at it like that. But Sheriff Arthur and Mr. Henderson even offered to pay extra so she could have a more choice final location." He rolled his eyes heavenward. "I'm sorry. I shouldn't have repeated that." He cleared his throat. "Well, would you like to see what's in the box?"

We looked at each other. "You open it," said Suzanne, pushing it toward him.

"All right." He reached for the hasp on the end of the box, but Jean's voice stopped him.

"Wait," she said, and we all turned to look at her, our heads moving in unison as though we were spectators in a tennis match.

"Why are we doing this?" she asked, color creeping up her cheeks and making her look healthy and strong. "We're fifty-one years old and no one's telling us what to do. Why are we sitting here scared to death something from our past is going to hurt us when we have the power to prevent it? It's not as though we had this delightful childhood we want to revisit."

She rose from the table. "You can go ahead if it's what you want to do, but I want no part of it."

"You're right, Jean." Suzanne got up, too. "Good heavens, guys, when I see that lock of hair, I might want to slit my throat because I can't duplicate its color."

Andie and I exchanged glances. "We don't need to have it opened," I said, halting Jean and Suzanne's flight from the room. "We can heave it into the lake this afternoon."

"All right." Scott pushed the box aside. "But I'd like to talk to you anyway." He folded his hands on the table before him and looked around at us. "About Rosie. And about the night—or more accurately—the morning Chuck Hardesty died."

Chapter Nineteen

Andie

"You know about that night?" asked Vin. "All of it?" Her face was pale and set, and I don't know whether it was by accident or design, but we all scooted our chairs a little closer to hers, to the point that Scott Parrish faced all of us.

He nodded and took a deep breath. "I was there."

"There?" Jean echoed. "You got there when the sheriff did, right?"

Scott was silent for a moment, then he said, "Before I met and fell in love with my wife, I met and fell in love with Rosie Bennett. She was ten years older than I, practiced a profession people of my calling would like to put out of business, and never gave me the time of day. But"—his face creased into a boyish smile that made me remember why Jean had had such a crush on him—"I thought she hung the moon. I'm not yet convinced she didn't."

Rosie had been dead for over thirty years, but sometimes I still thought I heard her whiskey voice, smelled the too-sweet rose scent of her cologne, felt her hand light on my shoulder. She hadn't been much for physical affection, but that touch had always let us know she cared. Scott Parrish's words were about the Rosie we'd known. I felt a wave of longing.

"Unrequited love plays havoc with one's sleep," he

271

said. "I was going down to the lake to fish when I heard Vin scream, not that I knew it was her. By the time I got around there, the car was already in the lake and the sheriff was diving, trying to get him out. I dived, too, but neither of us could do anything."

"You and the sheriff dived?" said Vin. "I don't remember that."

We shook our heads. "I know he got there fast," I said, "but I didn't realize he'd gone into the water."

"He was with Rosie."

Suzanne frowned. "That can't be. We'd have seen his car."

"Not if he parked behind the trailer," said Jean.

Scott nodded. "Which is what he did."

"They all did," I remembered. "Even ones who didn't hold elected office didn't want it known that they were visiting Rosie."

"After it was all over, the sheriff was praised for arriving so quickly," said Scott. "His wife knew where he'd been, and eventually his family did, but they didn't find it out from Rosie. Mr. Arthur remained sheriff for many more years, a good and popular one."

That explained why the sheriff's son helped care for Rosie's grave.

Only one question remained unanswered. I reached for the ammo box. "I have to know," I said.

"It's not in there."

We all looked at Scott. "Where is it?"

"In Chuck Hardesty's car."

"But that went to the junkyard. It was compacted and crushed and...well, whatever they do with cars after they do that," said Vin.

The minister nodded. "Yes."

"So it was all illegal," said Jean, her voice subdued. "It was hushed up that one of us killed Chuck Hardesty so the sheriff's reputation would stay intact. Rosie did that for us."

Scott's face went so white I thought he was having a heart attack.

We exchanged looks of concern, and Jean got up to get him a glass of water.

"Are you all right?" said Vin.

"Yes," he said, "but I thought you knew."

"Knew what?" We looked at each other. Didn't we know enough, for God's sake? What little gem of horror did he have to hand down to us now?

"An autopsy was performed, as the law decrees in cases such as this was, but the results were never made public. It was reported that he was drunk and drove into the lake and drowned. As it turned out, that's exactly what happened. The gunshot was to his shoulder and only incidental. You girls didn't kill him any more than I did."

Vin frowned. "If that's true, why didn't we know?"

Scott looked uncomfortable. "Perhaps you should talk to your mother about this."

"She won't tell me anything. You probably remember her well enough to know that," Vin snapped. "If we're to know the truth, it's got to come from you or the sheriff."

"Mrs. Hardesty filed a wrongful death suit against Rosie. She dropped it on the advice of her lawyer when she found out the results of the autopsy."

I wasn't surprised that Mrs. Hardesty had never told her daughter about that particular incident. I knew she'd hated Rosie and hadn't been too fond of us girls, either. But if she had known, I realized, so had Rosie.

Why hadn't she told us?

Jean

We were relieved to know we hadn't committed murder after all. Yes, I know self-defense made it something less than murder anyway, but I also knew the shooting of Chuck Hardesty had bothered us all.

But why hadn't Rosie told us? I could see the question written clearly on Andie's face and in Suzanne's eyes. Only Vin seemed undisturbed by the betrayal of the one person we'd all trusted.

The ammo box still sat on the kitchen table two hours after Scott had left. One by one, we sat down. We looked at it, at each other, then Suzanne shrugged and drew it toward her. "We know the gun's not in here. That was the only thing I was afraid of."

We nodded agreement, and she lifted the hasp.

The contents of the box were the items Scott had listed and we had remembered. The dreams we'd spelled out on lined paper were the ones I'd written about in my new book. Wealth for Vin. Fame and beauty for Suzanne. Family and true love for me. Andie's dream for life was summed up in one word: Survival.

We laughed over the BeeGees trading card and the awful story I'd written, sighed over the locks of hair. We sniffed, grimacing, at the nearly empty bottle of dime store cologne and tried to remember whose plaid ribbon was tied around an envelope of snapshots taken with the point-and-shoot camera Andie'd gotten for Christmas one year.

"Why didn't she tell us?" Andie muttered as we neared the bottom of the box.

"The same reason she didn't make Cindy Hathaway leave you alone," said Vin. "She had no reason to think those dreams were going to come true"—she pointed at the notes on the table—"but she had every reason to think we'd have a hard way to go. She wanted us to always be strong and to always have each other. As long as we shared knowing we'd killed someone, we'd maintain a connection, and knowing we'd killed for survival meant we were strong."

"I don't know, Vin," said Andie. "That's a stretch."

"Is it?" Vin picked up the envelope of pictures. "Rosie bought you this camera when the rest of us were still counting on the Salvation Army for our Christmases. She saved your stories, Jean, when no one else gave them a second thought. Remember that binder full of them we found after she died? And you, Suzanne—who taught you to put on makeup and to make the best of what you had? Who took me to the doctor and convinced me life could go on after rape, when all I wanted to do was die?" She laughed as tears spurted from her eyes. "Who made sure we had care packages at college just like the other kids did? The last ones were waiting for us when we went back to school after her funeral.

"Are we really going to wonder whether that person loved us or not? Are we going to question her judgment when hers was the *only* judgment that ever put our needs first?" She looked around the table at us. "Well, are we?"

"No, we're not," said Suzanne.

At last the relief felt real. Vin was right, of course. For the first time since that night, the four of us were completely free. "It feels good," I said.

"Yeah," said Andie. "But, you know, there's a little part of me that's disappointed we didn't kill the forny bastard."

She looked so pseudo-wistful that I burst out laughing. Suzanne got to her feet. "Come on. Let's go to the pub. I think it's time the Tonsil Lake girls got drunk."

Suzanne

It was snowing as we walked to the tavern, and even as we complained about the cold, we enjoyed the beauty of it.

"Where will you build your house?" I asked Vin.

"In the middle there," she said, pointing, "backed up into the trees." She looked between the three of us. "There are enough lots for all of us, you know, if you'd like to build houses." She grinned. "Or park trailers. Of course, you'll be living in the B and B, Suzanne, so you won't want one."

"I can't afford it," I said regretfully, "but I could probably buy one of your lots and build a little house on it. I'd like that, I think."

"You could afford it if you had partners," said Andie. "Jake left me a whole bunch of money I didn't know was coming, over and above the bigger bunches he left the kids. I think he'd like it if I invested it in your spa."

"And I sold Mark's mother's jewelry. I offered it to his girls, but they didn't want it and didn't mind if I sold it. I'd like to invest that somewhere," said Vin.

"It might never make any money," I cautioned. "I want it to be an 'every woman' type of place."

"Works for me," said Vin with a shrug. "I'd just like knowing you were right up the road."

"I'd like to invest, too," said Jean.

We all stopped walking and looked at her. Jean never bought so much as a pair of earrings without consulting David.

"I spend my book advances," she said. "I put them into the family budget and feel proud of contributing. But when I started getting royalty checks, David told me to stuff them somewhere for a rainy day. We withdrew a few times when all three kids were in college at once, but for the most part, it hasn't rained yet."

We reached the pub with our hair full of snowflakes and waved to the bartender, who called, "The usual?"

"You bet," said Andie, "and could you bring us some paper?"

He brought us our drinks and a stenographer's notepad, and we scrambled for pens.

An hour later, we had drawn up a workable partnership, contingent on the Arthurs dropping the price of the house a few thousand, on David not going ballistic, and on the results of a home inspection.

Two hours later, I was crying into my Margarita, Andie was telling me to stop being a ninny, and Jean and Vin were playing darts really badly.

So why was I surprised when the door to the pub opened and David walked in, followed by Paul and Trent?

Vin

I tossed Jean an accusing look. "You called David because you were losing, you big whine-ass."

"I did not, though I thought about it when you wanted the drunk at the bar to play William Tell with

277

us." She shook her head seriously. "It could have gotten ugly if you'd missed, since all the bartender had was those pickled eggs in the big jar, which are even smaller than apples."

She smiled brightly at David, though her eyes weren't focusing too well, so the smile kind of slipped past him. "Hi, honey."

"Hi, babe." He gave her a hug. "Got to missing you."

"That's sweet."

I wished Lucas were there. This reminded me too much of high school days when part of us had boyfriends and part of us didn't.

"I talked to Lucas," said David. "He sent you this."

He draped me over his arm and gave me a kiss, which would have worked out better if we hadn't both been laughing so hard. "I hope he does better than that in real life," David complained. "That could hurt a guy's back."

"Hey, O'Toole, you weren't supposed to do that," called Paul, "because he's...umph." Trent's elbow gouged his ribs.

"He's what?" I headed back toward the table, a dart still in my hand.

"Leaving our stuff up at the B and B," said Paul, keeping a watchful eye on my weaponry. "He said he'd walk down but we weren't supposed to tell you."

"You mean he's here?" I was already reaching for my coat. "He just went back to the island." The dart wouldn't go through my sleeve and I drew my hand back, looking down at it in consternation.

Perhaps darts aren't a good idea after several rounds of "the usual."

"Nope," said David. "He went to the airport." He looked wise. "I know that on account of I took him. Then he said, 'What the hell am I doing this for when I haven't taken a vacation in twenty goddamned years?' And we came back to Lewis Point. He's staying in Kelly's room, Jean, but he's not real messy."

"Unless you count his handwriting," said Paul. "We were playing Pinochle and whenever he or Trent wrote down the score, no one could read what they wrote."

"So we started playing poker," said Trent. He looked dolefully at Suzanne. "You know my house? I hope you weren't real attached to it. I think I lost it to Paul."

Lucas came in then, and draped me over his arm much more convincingly than David had.

We sat around the table in the tavern until after the bartender made last call. Then he sat down and had a drink with us before coaxing us out the door.

We walked back to the B and B, our feet crunching and squeaking on the snow that had obliterated the path.

" 'Night, Rosie," we called as we passed the cemetery, then "See you in the morning," as we passed the church.

A glob of snow fell out of a tree and went straight down the back of Andie's coat. We all stopped to brush her off, and turned back toward the lake.

"Oh, it's beautiful," said Suzanne.

It was. The sky had cleared when the snow stopped, and the moon turned the ripples of the lake to silver and cast a shade of blue over the snow. Stars shone overhead, and I picked out the ones we had allotted to those we'd loved and lost.

"There's Rosie's," said Jean, pointing, "and it's no forny airplane."

We started walking again, our laughter falling soft against the snow rather than ringing out as it had earlier. We girls walked with our partners of choice, our arms linked with theirs, but close enough that we could reach out and grab each other. "Hey, wait," we would say. "Remember this?"

"Home," Jake Logan had written to all of us, "is wherever you hang your heart."

We were home.

Epilogue

Archie

I never come to Indiana when Vin and Lucas do. My new husband, who is a fisherman, doesn't really like leaving the island, but he did this time. "It's a family reunion," Vin said firmly, "and you're family."

It has been fun, putting faces with the names I've known all these many years. For sure, I would have known Jean and David in a heartbeat because even though they're two separate entities, they're near to being joined at the hip. Jean's new book, which Vin edited and her employer published, is a hit. It's way down on those bestseller lists writers set so much store by, but it's there.

Andie's book was monstrous successful, but she doesn't care for the notoriety that's gone with it. She calls it "that book" and swears she won't be writing another one. She says she's not interested in getting married, either. She and Paul are together nearly all the time, and they seem content with that. I wouldn't be, for sure, but I spent twenty-some years loving a married man, so what do I know?

Suzanne runs the Lady of the Lake Spa, which is greatly successful. I don't go in for such things, but I certainly did enjoy the day she gave me as a gift. I felt wonderful afterward and my husband said, "You look younger somehow," which led to all kinds of private celebration.

She's married to Trent. They are apart a great deal of the time, but they like it that way. She's so lovely it near hurts to look at her, but you can see the pain in her eyes that never quite goes away. She's loved much and lost much, and it shows.

Vin and Lucas live on the island and on the lake, going from one place to the other at the drop of a hat. Although she wouldn't like admitting it, she's happier in love with Lucas than she was with Mr. Stillson. She still has a veneer of sophistication that serves her well in the business world, but she's quite at home in her bare feet or in oilskins on Lucas's brother's boat.

All of everyone's family is here this weekend in June for the reunion. The lake rings with the shouts of young parents corralling their children and the laughter of those children. Even Vin's stepdaughters are here, traveling alone and taking advantage of Suzanne's spa.

It's amazing, it is, how the families meld. Everyone watches everyone else's children. There's even a nursery of sorts under the trees with shaded playpens for babies belonging to Josh and Laurie, Lo and Sarah, and Brian and Kelly.

"God," says Suzanne, looking wide-eyed at the three of them and beyond at Carrie's and Miranda's children, "it's like when ours were little."

"Nah." Andie stood beside her. "We get to send all these home."

Jean and Andie have houses on either side of Vin's, far enough apart for privacy but close enough to meet for coffee whenever the mood strikes them, and it seems to strike them often. They all have little guesthouses, too, so there's usually room for everyone.

This weekend is an exception to that, of course, so Suzanne has closed down her spa to outside clientele to accommodate the overflow.

An early riser by nature, I woke this morning in time to see the sun peeping up over the woods. I stepped out on the porch of Vin's house in my bathrobe, something that's entirely acceptable here, and looked down toward the lake.

A huge boulder sat in the grass above the beach that had been created by bringing in sand. The men had rented a large yellow machine and hauled in the rock from a rear corner of what even I refer to as the Henderson farm although the Hendersons are gone from here.

This morning, the Girls—as everyone from their husbands to the minister to the bartender at the pub calls them—all sat on the rock, though Jean looked near to falling off. As I watched, they leaned in toward each other as though sharing a confidence, then their laughter rose and spiraled so that the morning had an extra glow about it.

Then Jean fell off the rock.

Or else Andie pushed her.

A word about the author...

Liz Flaherty has spent the past few years reinventing herself. The career postal worker who wrote on weekends and sewed whenever someone lost a button now writes whenever she feels like it and sews the rest of the time. She's not necessarily more productive these days, but she certainly does have a lot of fun.

She lives with her husband, Duane, in the farmhouse they bought in 1977 and intended to stay in until the kids grew up, at which time they planned to move to a small house that cleaned itself and cooked their meals while he played golf and she...didn't. This has not happened. Even though they occasionally discuss downsizing, neither of them is willing to go through a 36-year accumulation of stuff.

THE GIRLS OF TONSIL LAKE is her eighth book.

~*~

Thank you for purchasing
this publication of The Wild Rose Press, Inc.
For other wonderful stories of romance,
please visit our on-line bookstore at
www.thewildrosepress.com.

For questions or more information
contact us at
info@thewildrosepress.com.

The Wild Rose Press, Inc.
www.thewildrosepress.com

To visit with authors of
The Wild Rose Press, Inc.
join our yahoo loop at
http://groups.yahoo.com/group/thewildrosepress/

9107098R00166

Made in the USA
San Bernardino, CA
04 March 2014